Praise for The Performance

Esquire

"I must say it: it's a stunning novel. Claudia Petrucci, born in 1990—how can she be so good?"
PULP

"This is a manifestation of talent. *The Performance* is a miracle of perfection."
VERONICA RAIMO, author of *The Girl at the Door*

"Solid architecture, elegant prose, an uncanny story that subtly unsettles the reader. Claudia Petrucci has crafted a wonderful debut novel."
NADIA TERRANOVA, author of *Farewell, Ghosts*

"What's left of an actor when she leaves the stage? Who is she when she takes off her mask and is no longer just a character? These are some of the questions running through Claudia Petrucci's debut novel, *The Performance*, and they make for a very intense and original story."
La Repubblica

"An assertive incipit for Claudia Petrucci's surprising debut novel, the story of a love triangle revolving around the theme of mutual manipulation. Petrucci is skilled at challenging the notion of self-knowledge, as well as the notion that we know others, by showing the extent to which people's presumed transparency is as deceitful as their opacity. Petrucci transforms mental illness into something literary, an extremely sophisticated and intelligent psychological-thriller device. Thanks to the high-quality narration, the point is no longer credibility or scientific accuracy, but, rightfully, the intimate fictional truths of the characters."

Tuttolibri

"Despite the high meta-literary risk it takes, the novel performs well, thanks to the simple and swift prose. A brilliant and enjoyable exploration of identity, of the projections we have of others, the sky full of imaginings that characterizes every romance. These are some of the many themes Petrucci skillfully incorporates into the rhythm of the story. *The Performance* is the debut of a talented writer."

Corriere della Sera

"With dazzling narrative flair, an intricate and vibrant plot, and writing of rare elegance, *The Performance* stages the lives of Giorgia, Filippo, and Mauro, three characters who stick to the page yet are also separate from it. They lead their own lives, which are so sharp and three-dimensional that they end up overwhelming the reader."

Il Messaggero

"In these pages, in Petrucci's intense and sharp writing, throbs a deep question: from theater to everyday life, what is existence but a staging, a performance, the interpretation of a role, a practice of identity that risks intertwining with madness, a mask that becomes a face, a play that is in fact reality?"

Il Mattino

"Claudia Petrucci's novel captures the reader immediately and makes some very good choices. The first is setting the events in the world of theater. Then there is the story that unfolds inside Filippo's head. And, above all else, there's Petrucci's pure talent, which is the art of story-telling."
Il Piccolo

"This novel prods us to admit that effort in relationships is not limited to the productive, charitable effort we put into accepting each other, day after day, year after year; it is also the work of recognizing ourselves in the faithful and incorruptible mirror found in the ones we have chosen."
Il Tascabile

"A powerful, intense, and authentic debut novel that tackles complex themes with reverence and thorough-ness, in astonishing prose."
Satisfaction

"The witty plot, the sharp, subtle and suspenseful writing, and the emotions triggered by the main characters, especially Giorgia and Filippo, make *The Performance* a literary page-turner. It is like reading a perfect thriller, resonating with deep psychological nuances. A stunning novel on manipulation."
Philippe Rey, French publisher

"*The Performance* is an outstanding novel on how we build our identity and elaborate the reality that surrounds us. Claudia Petrucci's debut belongs to a rare category of books: high-quality literary novels that can become great commercial successes."
Wagenbach, German publisher

The PERFORMANCE

CLAUDIA PETRUCCI

The PERFORMANCE

Translated from the Italian
by Anne Milano Appel

WORLD EDITIONS
New York, London, Amsterdam

Published in the USA in 2022 by World Editions LLC, New York
Published in the UK in 2022 by World Editions Ltd., London

World Editions
New York / London / Amsterdam

Printed by Lake Book, USA

World Editions is committed to a sustainable future. Papers used by World
Editions meet the FSC/ PEFC standards of certification.

Library of Congress Cataloging in Publication Data is available / *British
Library Cataloguing-in-Publication Data*. A catalogue record for this book is
available on request from the British Library.

USA ISBN 978-1-64286-110-5 / UK ISBN 978-1-64286-110-5

First published as *L'esercizio* in 2020 by La nave di Teseo

Questo libro è stato tradotto anche grazie a un contributo del Ministero
degli Affari Esteri e della Cooperazione Internazionale italiano
This book was translated with the help of a grant from the Italian Ministry
of Foreign Affairs and International Cooperation

Twitter: @WorldEdBooks
Facebook: @WorldEditionsInternationalPublishing
Instagram: @WorldEdBooks
YouTube: World Editions
www.worldeditions.org / www.worldeditions.co.uk

Book Club Discussion Guides are available on our website.

And if the light in you is darkness,
how great will the darkness be!
—Matthew 6:23

PRELUDE

There is no distinction between what we think we know and what we know: what we think we know is all we know. Mauro says it's a matter of simplification, reduction to the bare bones, a strategy that we apply without being aware of it. We are unable to tolerate the weight of infinite possibilities—*we simplify, we reduce*—we choose a possibility that we sense is right for us—*simplify, reduce*—the only arbitrary choice we believe in out of all the infinite possibilities. We believe in it to the point of denying the evidence, constructing industriously on that single one, and the more capable among us go on fabricating for twenty or thirty years. Some even manage to build on arbitrary choices that have long since died along with those who made them; fortunate arbitrary choices can reproduce and flourish and become cities, empires, financial giants.

My arbitrary choice was Giorgia. Giorgia was the story I told myself, in a continuous, oblivious narrative. Around her I had constructed a dimension complete with physical laws, an itinerant world that followed her everywhere—spilling over into the past, lengthening into the future. If what happened hadn't happened she would still be there, I could go back to kidding myself about what I thought I knew, which was all I knew: the same given moment, eternally. Unrepeatable. Unreproducible.

I can't go back, my creation was taken from me. As Mauro says, from now on, for me, Giorgia will forever be an exercise.

I went quite far with my exercise, so far that I feel as though I can reconstruct everything from the beginning.

* * *

The beginning takes place in the midsize outlet of a huge retail chain, on Via Pitteri, not far from the apartment where Giorgia and I live. In these big-box chain stores everything is organized in the same way, the maps of the aisles, the arrangement of food and non-food items; the products are always the same too, and stocked in incomprehensibly excessive quantities. In these kinds of places, no matter where, everything is identical—the floor plans, the merchandise, the consumers—and a series of confusions arises from those diabolical similarities: you have no idea where you are, and just when you think you know, the map makes a slight deviation that shifts the fresh-baked bread from the corner on the left, as in Certosa, to that on the right, as on Via Rubattino—because that's where we are, right?—and everything is turned upside down, causing you to experience a baffling sense of disorientation.

Giorgia hates supermarkets, and she knows I hate them too. She hated them even before she started working there, me only since they hired her. Yet we longed for that supermarket the way you would a baby; we kept an eye on it for a long time during the troubling months of her unemployment, wondering where the three-step interviews would take us.

Giorgia now knows what it's like to work in a place that she always tried to avoid as a customer: she loathes the supermarket. The fact that everything pretends to be the same in all supermarkets makes people unhappy; for the first ninety-one days, Giorgia looked directly at each one of them, hundreds of faces flowing past the checkout, along with the conveyor belt, hundreds and hundreds of them, all yellowish under the yellowish neon lights. No one is happy to be doing the shopping, she's sure of it, not even the couples with ice cream and warming lubricant; they too start to brighten up a little only when they get out of there.

Giorgia describes her psychosis as *my empathetic problem with people.*

"Honey, please keep your hands away from there."

The customer is a woman in her mid-forties, graciously facing the trials of a Monday afternoon and harsh lighting. The little girl, about five years old, with two dark braids, does not take her hands off the conveyor belt: she stares at Giorgia who slides the items over the electronic eye. The girl's fingers, the nails cut straight by someone else, show smears of green marker. Giorgia visualizes in those marks a school, and in the school, the little girl who is wearing all the right clothes in the right places and blends in among her peers, something that hadn't often happened to Georgia, because of her weight. She thinks fat children stand out like bumps on a log. The little girl looks a lot like her mother, who is now loading the bags rather hurriedly, glancing anxiously at the next customer, worried about dawdling, about being told to hurry up. Giorgia adds the child and her mother together like interdependent factors, and her mind automatically processes, collects details as data, and those accumulate. The woman's leather handbag has a designer signature but is at least two seasons old; her arms are toned, and the tinted hair is a professional job. The abrupt movements reveal an excessive nervousness; the child is unhappy.

"I don't want to go to dance class," she says in a low voice.

The mother pays—the credit card has a man's name on it—and glances again at the next customer.

"I don't want to go," the little girl repeats, looking once more at Giorgia.

"Well, move, you'll be late for dancing."

"I don't want to go," the girl keeps repeating as they walk away, "I don't want to go."

Giorgia would like everything to stop at this stage. Instead, the details begin to arrange themselves into structures. There is the little girl, the braids, the mother, and now a father as well, there is the family and the only child who arrived just in time, motherhood then nothing more. There is a house in a well-kept but outlying neighborhood, an apartment building identical to those throughout the district, railroad rooms with a corridor that is a train and rooms that are its compartments. The life of this family therefore takes place in segments, in transit from the kitchen to the living room and from the living room to the bathroom, which is the antechamber to the night, to games, and additional bodily routines. Today it's raining and so Giorgia imagines a father who could be like any other, the kind who begin to gain weight and turn gray as they commute to and from work. This father is thinking about a briefing and very little about anything else, he feels bushed; starting with the child, the weekend has become an exhausting obligation to be fulfilled in accordance with the rules—so that the weekends are just like the weekdays but without a shirt and tie. Giorgia thinks of her father and the sense of suffocation that he all but covered up and rarely spewed out, for example Mondays on the road in the rain, or Sundays, the day for a movie and silent copulation. Giorgia can understand him, every now and again she also feels like that, unable to remember what she felt only three years earlier when, without me, everything was different. She keeps an eye on the mother from a distance, watches her pat the wrinkles around her mouth in front of a mirror, then the next customer enters the flow with her identity to be defined, her details.

Giorgia is unable to hold back her thoughts, it's always been like that. She knows that normal people don't function the same way. For her the surrounding reality streams by at a greater intensity, it's more vivid, like certain dreams before waking up in the morning. In her mind, numerous imaginary versions about the lives of these people whom she will never see again proliferate, images of their activities that take over her private life. Watching people helps her combat a certain sense of discomfort that plagues her—thinking of them as they straighten the sheets in rooms smelling of sleep, finding them loading the washing machine, getting grease stains on themselves in some garage, yawning in an office; then thinking of them again as they cook, shop, eat lunch, go pick up the kids at school, standing on the bus, all jammed in, because only eccentrics sit in back; when they return, someone opens the door and hugs them.

The supermarket exacerbates the phenomenon. Giorgia has never worked in a place where so many people flow past so quickly: it's impossible to resist. At the end of the shift she feels exhausted and just wants to sleep.

In the locker room, her coworkers are always talking, with or without her participation; sweaty, they jam their smocks into their bags or touch up their makeup before dashing out.

"God, I can't believe it's already Monday," says a woman who is almost always on the floor, restocking the shelves.

"Really, what a drag. But today is over, right?" Giorgia smiles at her, as she knows she should do, even though she is still thinking about the little girl as they walk out the door.

This is another of her specialties: functioning on more than one level. Giorgia is with her coworker and they're gossiping about the supervisor—he dyed his hair, *can you imagine, at sixty?!*—while at the same time, in some deeper part of herself, she is the unknown child and she feels sad. Her body withstands the dissociation: she smiles, scratches a forearm, kisses the woman goodbye; beneath the surface the little girl can't explain her unhappiness. When she's alone, Giorgia would like to tell her that it's not her fault, that sooner or later she will learn to not be just a go-between.

Giorgia takes the same route every day, she never deviates from the course. Between our house and the supermarket there is a little park, an oversize flower-bed with a slide, a swing, and a fence around it. It always reminds her of the fenced-in pens where dogs are allowed to run free. The boundary of Caserma Mercanti, the barracks right in the middle of Lambrate with its insurmountable walls and barbed wire, begins beyond the park; it is huge. Our apartment is on the mezzanine floor, building three, of a condominium complex. The air has a unique smell in Lambrate, different from that of the other Milan neighborhoods where Giorgia has lived. The same smell, denser, exists inside our house—she can't decide if it's the outside air drifting through our things or vice versa.

Most days, at the time when Giorgia gets home, I am preparing something to eat. Today she catches me in the middle of a phone call.

"No, we can't do this thing."

Giorgia can tell that I'm talking to my mother from the way I'm gripping the phone. In her eyes I am a soothing sight: after three years together there is really nothing new to interpret, no identity to construct. I am Filippo. I'm always here, present in the spaces where I should be. This too enables Giorgia to relax, the fact that each of us has our place, the space we share and those that are exclusive, we have the sound of our steps that are the same, invariable from day to day, we move like toy trains on their tracks. The repetitive patterns are comforting for Giorgia, because they relieve her of the obligation of processing them.

"Well, we agree that the money must be found somewhere, and we'll find it. But you can't get worked up like that."

Giorgia knows this has been a bad day for both of us. She can't get the little girl out of her head, and even thinks about her as she lifts the cover of the pot and sniffs, then kisses my shoulder and goes to change her clothes in the bedroom. The problem is the stream of thoughts. Starting with the little girl, a direct channel with her past was opened, a leak in a pipeline. From there, troublesome reflections flow incoherently.

"No, I'm not saying we won't make it. Really, everything is okay. Besides, now that Giorgia is working at the supermarket—yes, yes, I told you, full-time."

Every so often, especially when she gets into her pajamas, Giorgia would like to tell me. She would really like to tell me how she feels and why it's all so hard for her. Only she can't, she's paying for having put it off. Certain confessions, she knows, have to be revealed at the beginning of a relationship, when everything is still uncommitted. It's not fair to wait for stability to be established, for the relationship to settle in, and then unleash pandemonium. And time passes so quickly that she missed all the opportunities, now she's stuck. It was manageable, up until the supermarket. The supermarket has complicated things.

"I'll tell her you said hello. I'm going now, okay? Tell Pop that the business about the old tax returns is all taken care of, now we'll solve this problem and everything will be fine, okay?"

It's really a question of quantity, Giorgia is sure of it. There are too many people.

"Hey, here you are," I tell her, putting the cell phone in a pocket. "That woman drains me."

Giorgia smiles at me. A reassuring smile, that doesn't show her teeth, she's stable.

"How did it go at the café?" she asks me, from her chair.

She knows I like to talk. She knows that I am one of

those people who need to be questioned in order to feel permitted to express themselves. She always asks a lot of questions. It's a kindly deception: on one level, she lets me talk, while on another level, she develops strategies. At the same time she thinks about me and the debts I can't cover, as well as herself and the solution to her problem—how to avoid people.

"So many people today, I called Nico to help out. Only then he wants to be paid right away, in cash. I don't know if I'll call him again."

During supper I go on telling her about my surreal conversations with the customers, about the order of coffee I forgot to make, about the rolling shutter that doesn't close right. Giorgia really listens to me, and thinks that all this is very fragile. The apartment, me, our suppers together, our problems: it could all crumble at any moment and the fault would be hers alone.

"You, anything new?" I ask her, when we're done with our meal.

"They renewed my contract," she says.

She sees my relief, the wave of unwarranted optimism that washes over me, she knows that the news makes everything seem solvable to me, because that's how I am. She watches me open a bottle of wine—every now and then you have to celebrate—and takes a sip with me.

Why shouldn't I lose all this? she wonders, when I pull her over to sit on my lap. I tell her again, as I've often done in recent times, that everything will be fine.

One of my books, lying open on the cabinet beside the table, catches Giorgia's eye. She should tell me about the overload, about how she feels.

"Listen, could you lend me one of your books to read?"

"What? I mean, sure, of course." I follow her gaze and reach out. "You mean this one?"

Giorgia nods. "Why not?"

"I didn't know you liked science fiction."

"I need to relax a little, during the break."

Giorgia knows she has to be careful with her reading. She has her own method, as with everything else: she reads very slowly, no more than two or three pages a day. To some degree she follows the plot and to some extent she destroys it. At the checkout now, she tries to work while keeping her head lowered, to isolate herself.

People's voices keep beating against the glass, but Giorgia covers them with the story. The book is about a very distant planet, which does not exist, and this makes the process easier. Giorgia thinks about the planet, about what happens on the planet, about the spaceships, the zero-gravity skies, and right afterwards tells herself that none of this is real, she dismantles the imaginary constructions until they are reduced to what they are, namely, letters printed on paper. It's tiring.

One day, during a break, the usual coworker is telling her about a problem with her boyfriend, while smoking a cigarette in the parking lot. It's cold, their words condense in the midst of maneuvering cars, precarious parking.

"So he told me he doesn't give a damn, you know?"

Giorgia knows. She resists the temptation to think about the coworker's boyfriend, his reasons, how these two strangers appear to one another. She thinks about the planet Solaris, that's what they call it in the book.

Then it happens.

A hallucination is something where earlier there was nothing. It does not take shape, it does not follow the rules of objects that come closer from afar, you don't see it coming. This hallucination is enormous. It occupies one whole side of the parking lot and soars to the sky.

"I'm approaching a certain age, it's not like I want to wait that long. Everything okay, Giò?"

Giorgia nods but steps back. The hallucination has a colloidal consistency, she only knows the word because it comes from the book.

"I don't feel so good," she says, huddling in her jacket.

"Yeah, I can tell by your face."

"Maybe I'd better go home."

Giorgia hurries back in, leaves her coworker a little bewildered, doesn't look back. She talks to the supervisor and feels terror rising in her throat, her mouth is dry. The supervisor has no problem giving her permission to leave, he tells her she's so pale she looks like she's about to vomit.

In the locker room, she quickly unbuttons her smock; she knows she mustn't stop moving or she'll end up paralyzed. To herself, she starts reciting the emergency rhyme. *As I was walking by the clear spring ...* Once outside the supermarket, she deviates from the usual route, heads to the bus stop. *I found the deep pool so lovely I stopped to bathe ...* As she waits for the bus, along with an elderly lady, terror ties knots in her stomach. *I've loved you for so long, never will I forget you.* It's a sunny day, Giorgia chooses a vacant seat near the driver, where she can see little else except the street. *Under the oak's leaves, I lay and dried ...* She closes her eyes. *On the highest bough, a nightingale was singing. I've loved you for so long, never will I forget you.*

From the supermarket to the café it's fifteen minutes. Giorgia gets off at her stop and pulls up the hood of her jacket. *Sing, nightingale, sing, you with the joyous heart.* The street is busy, the metro stop is not far away; Giorgia blends in among the passersby, chooses the step of a closed restaurant, sits and waits. *Your heart is made for laughing ... mine can only cry.*

Through the café window, I am only visible when I stand behind the cash register. Giorgia watches and takes deep breaths, after a while her heartbeat slows. When she is calmer, she lets her mind travel through the fantasy that she never has the courage to actually realize. She imagines getting up, crossing the street, and entering the café, jingling the bell which has been hanging over the door, rusting, for thirty years.

She imagines me looking at her with some surprise, wondering why she's here and not at work; then telling me she only left early to avert my sinking feeling. If she were really able to, she'd wait for the end of my shift, watching me from inside the café, at the table in back, as I prepare espresso and smile at the few customers. Between one regular and another, we'd talk about neutral things. The right moment would arrive for us towards evening: she would tell me everything, every last thing. "Today I had a hallucination, Filippo. I hadn't had one in a long time. I think working at the supermarket is bad for me. I'm not well, Filippo, but I can do it, seriously, I can do it. I'm going to wall it all up, cement it inside, this thing, and the day will come when it won't emerge again. I don't want you to worry, okay? It's a long-standing problem, but I'm going to solve it. If you worry, however, the illness will begin to exist everywhere, even when it's not there. I'll stop being well, at least in part. I need to feel well in part. You make me feel well in part."

I've loved you for so long, never will I forget you.

The fantasy remains a fantasy and Giorgia has not moved from her step, but feels better just the same, as if she had told me the truth. She sits watching dusk fall around the window of the café: outside the streets get dark and inside everything lights up. Inside the aquarium, I'm reading; I jump up quickly when a customer comes in, and when no one can see me I wind my fingers into my hair and look like someone who is genuinely lost. Then Giorgia fantasizes about leaving me without any explanation. Not ever coming back, like her father did. No warning, no preparatory speech, with the power of a hallucination: something that is no longer there where it once was.

Giorgia keeps telling herself that this is just a bad time and that she is trembling for no important reason, because of the cold. Across the street, I struggle with the shutter until it rolls down and closes with a bang. She follows me from afar, at a distance from which she might mistake me for someone who looks like me.

I'm listening to music with earbuds, Giorgia is thinking she's sorry. She knows my dreams were entirely different—we talked about them before we lived together, often at her place, at her shared rental. Long before Lambrate and the supermarket, our many possibilities were our favorite topic. I told her that I would like to see her go back to her studies, see her graduate—"Right, Giò, we'll celebrate, laurels and all. What, don't you like the idea?" As we spun our castle in the air, reality was collapsing around us, embarking on an opposite course.

Giorgia remembers my father's second heart attack, she was there when I got the phone call one evening at a concert. The hurried drive to the emergency room, the staccato tapping of her heels like the hands of a clock, and the fear of being hopelessly too late have all remained fixed in her mind. She was also there when my mother persuaded my father to retire, leaving the café without anyone to run it.

We had spent six months desperately looking for a job that would enable me to get out of my responsibilities to my parents. In the end I wound up working in their café, despite all my efforts. From then on, our anxieties had begun to take shape one after another.

Giorgia knows that I'm not happy. We never talk about it. She sees the sadness in the contracted movements of my body: before, I was the kind of person who took up a lot of space with his arms, now I never reach out more than the bare minimum. It's not our fault. It's that possibilities all seem wonderful before you achieve them, they are the canvas you imagine painting, the song you imagine dancing to. Only when you get into things do you really know them.

I get on the #39, which will take me straight home, while Giorgia, who has been watching me from across the street, chooses another bus. She'd like to tell me that she appreciates my dedication, but she can't, because if she did, our entire fabrication would collapse. She knows we have a duty to keep telling ourselves that this is an unfortunate time, a momentary, adverse period even though we are unable to devise any other prospects: all our efforts to plan get mired in finances and fiscal obligations, monthly deadlines, expenses. Most of our time is spent thinking about money or pretending we aren't thinking about it. Like me, she is … immobilized in a curious situation: her salary allows us to breathe a little and at the same time terrifies us. In the days before each contract is due to expire, we both wish she would be fired, that something would force us to make a move towards an alternative, but then we welcome the renewal with relief. When we talk about it between us, we give our situation a fanciful slant, describing it as a parenthesis—*it can be fine, for now, it can work, for now*—but in fact, we know without having to say it that we aren't working on any solution, no medium-term plan. And we no longer know what became of the things we wanted, what they were—*for now*.

Giorgia's bus takes her a short distance from home; she has to go a little way on foot. As she walks, hands tucked in her pockets because of the cold, she's thinking she would like to quit. Wanting to and not being able to are the axes her life rotates around. She would like to overcome her illness or give in to it, and she can't do either. She would like to lie or tell the truth, stop or start over, explode or succumb. She's constrained to a middle ground. She still wonders, every now and then, if that's what her mother was thinking when she made up her mind. According to her calculations, at the time her mother must have been the same age as she is now. The significance of the age milestone has always weighed on her. It is at times like this that the world caves in around her—it is simply *too much*, the people, the hallucinations, her illness, our problems, her father, her mother. Is there any way out?

She waits in the hall for the usual time, sitting on the stairs: it's already late enough so that no one comes by. You can hear the fits and starts of the elevator under the load of tenants coming up from the garage, snippets of conversations between people behind the doors, people at supper, people and silent responses, people and televisions. People everywhere breathing and moving about, whom Giorgia listens to, and instead of being external it's as if they are inside her, and she isn't able to yank them out of her chest, and those people walk around and each of them has their own cumbersome body, their own pain, an aggregate of disconsolate suffering. Giorgia recites the nursery rhyme again, just to be cautious—because once more she is feeling short of breath.

As I was walking by the clear spring. She'd like me to come out for no reason, to surprise her on the stairs. *Would that the rose bush were still blooming ...* That's how decisive turning points in others' lives occur, right? An unforeseen occurrence that triggers a dramatic turn of events. *Sing, nightingale, sing, you with the joyous heart.* She feels like crying and wants me to surprise her and wishes she could tell me. Instead, she holds on to the tears, and with them the series of precarious constructions that we have built. She gets up and relegates this day to a second level of herself.

She will find another solution, she will try other ways.

"How did it go today?" she asks me when she comes in, after the usual greetings.

I tell her about the afternoon at the café that she has already seen, watching from outside; I make up customers who weren't there. Giorgia listens. The last thought to conceal is that, though we might not know it, we are drowning.

I've loved you for so long, never will I forget you.

Mauro's return to Giorgia's life edges into our delicate articulations, pries open a gap and widens it.

It happens when Giorgia has already worked out a new strategy. She abandoned books and devoted herself to lifestyle magazines. The magazines were joined by distraction techniques: she diverts the mind's attention from abnormal psychic events by redirecting it towards tangible elements, a trick she learned—a trick that she was taught. On Thursdays it's counting the shampoo bottles; on Fridays keeping an eye on the supply of biodegradable bags; how many packages of white meat in a day?

It happens on a Wednesday, the day when she's focused on the sound of barcodes read by the electronic eye. As she swipes a deodorant over the glassy eye of the checkout counter, a hand slips under her gaze, someone shakes her to get her attention. She recognizes him right away, before he says his name.

Mauro is wearing one of his shirts, just like in acting school. And just as in the days of acting school, it looks like he's worn it at least three times: there are wrinkles in the white cotton that tell of a night out, other wrinkles, on his face, that suggest a brief, fitful sleep. Then there are the distinctive traits, the persistent smile at the right corner of his mouth, the eyes that he uses like arms, to hold you close and push you away.

"Giò!" he exclaims. "What are you doing here?"

A prisoner in her white smock, Giorgia watches him apologize for asking a stupid question.

"How are you?" he recovers quickly.

Giorgia doesn't know what to think. Placing Mauro in the supermarket takes an immense effort. She fumbles with the deodorant, the electronic eye gets confused and reads it twice.

"Fine. And you? What are you doing here?"

Giorgia decides that he is too intense a stimulus and that she doesn't feel prepared. The line behind him begins to press forward.

"I came to see a friend, she lives right nearby."

"I live here too, right nearby," she says, grabbing his other purchases: a new toothbrush, a bag of chocolates, chewing gum.

Finally an appropriate smile spreads over his face.

"We haven't seen each other in ages," Mauro says, incredulous.

Giorgia hands him the receipt and he automatically holds out the fifty-euro bill that he had ready in his hand since who knows when, maybe even since before entering the supermarket, since before he ran into her; had he perhaps recognized her right away, had he chosen that aisle with the intention of saying hello?

"It's true, ages."

He stuffs everything into a bag.

"I see you're looking well. I feel like it's been years since I've seen you. We should meet for coffee," he runs the words together.

The next customer is a little annoyed about the slow-down; Giorgia nods an apology.

"Listen, leave me your number. I'll call you."

She already has a cling-wrapped roast chicken in her hands.

"Do you mind? Then I'll be on my way, I promise. One second."

Not waiting for the stranger's blessing, Mauro lays the receipt on the counter, leaning over the Plexiglas. Giorgia hands him a pen, dictates the number; now everyone is a little annoyed, the only one smiling is a girl at the end of the line.

"I'll call you, we'll catch up properly, okay?" Mauro slips the receipt into his pocket, looks at her, waiting for confirmation.

"Sure, okay."

He smiles again, walks away, and vanishes just as he appeared, swallowed up around the corner of the street that Giorgia can't see.

For the next hour she asks herself, what if it was a hallucination? She retraces the events, the moments, and before the break she checks the transactions: Mauro's bill is still there, with the deodorant, the toothbrush, the chocolates, the chewing gum.

In the afternoon, all the memories come rushing back with an energetic urgency. Giorgia finds herself reimmersed in prior winter months, in certain dark sweaters, in the numbered rooms of a building that still exists. Who knows if they are still the same, those rooms, and if Mauro still paces around their outer perimeters, never their centers, occupied by his talented students. Even now she feels as though she's a part of those rooms. No, she takes it back as she removes her smock at the end of her shift: it would be honest to say that the best of the worst of her has remained locked in those rooms, in those halls, in the walls of that building. It always gives her a bad feeling, to admit that a piece of herself is in exile, it reminds her of some distasteful pictures of her baby teeth that fell out in elementary school, the viscous presence of blood on her tongue. After she completed acting school, nothing grew back to replace that missing piece. There was nothing underneath, she found, only a slack hollow was left.

As Giorgia crosses the street, a surge of ferrous salmon swims up the rush-hour stream, and fog hangs suspended around the headlights and median strips, a white mist that creeps softly up the barbed-wire fencing of the barracks. She's thinking that she did what needed to be done. She's thinking that when she met me, she realized that it was time to choose: either this or that, there were no alternative options. It cost her a lot. She's thinking that, along with that one rotten fragment, she left her entire self behind.

When she gets home, Giorgia is already searching for a coherent version of the meeting with Mauro. Where to place it, what purpose to attribute to it? If Mauro had simply ignored her, she would not be having second thoughts about the theater now.

Before we go to bed, Giorgia and I linger in the bathroom. It's a time when our conversations languish, and we make vague plans for the following day, think about food supplies and bills.

"And then, I was thinking, we could pay the electric bill a few days late. You saw, last time. Nothing happens. You're always so nervous."

Giorgia watches me talk and foam the toothpaste.

"That's true."

"We'll wait for your paycheck, so we're not too strapped, what do you say?"

She looks at me from the toilet, sitting with her pants down around her knees. She feels exhausted. Her distraction techniques take a lot out of her.

"I met Mauro today."

I look at her, not understanding.

"My theater instructor. I told you I did theater, didn't I?"

"Oh. Yeah, sure. And where did you meet him?"

"At the supermarket," Giorgia says, getting up.

She flushes the toilet, pulls up her pants, and joins me at the sink to wash her hands.

"You know that feeling, when you're forced to remember something?" she asks me from the mirror.

I shrug and spit into the sink.

"How do you mean?"

"I mean that there are memories you go looking for. Like, when you look at photographs."

"Yeah, I think I know."

"And then there are memories that you're forced to remember. For example, with Mauro. I never imagined meeting him at the supermarket. But from there I was forced to think about the theater, about a whole series of things that maybe I wasn't even thinking about."

"Hmm."

"Isn't it strange?"

We go down the hall together without turning on the light—there's no room to get lost.

"I think we all do that," I tell her, when we get into bed.

She remains silent.

"Do you miss the theater?"

"Maybe, I don't know."

"I would have liked to see you once. You don't seem anything like someone who would go onstage."

Giorgia rolls onto her side and looks at me. *I don't seem anything like a lot of things*, she'd like to tell me, instead she smiles, reaches out a hand and runs her fingers through my hair.

"Maybe I do miss acting."

"Well, there's still time, right?"

"Sure, but it was nothing serious."

Giorgia sums up the enormity of what she is hiding from me in those words—*nothing serious*.

Mauro calls Giorgia ten days later. They arrange to meet for coffee. I walk her to the metro on a Saturday afternoon, before going to see my parents.

The place that Mauro chose is not unintentional,

Giorgia has been there before. It's a café in an area she frequented often, during the days of acting school—to her it seems that the people she knew and their conversations have remained stamped in shadowy outlines on the surfaces. He is sitting at a small table, waiting for her, talking on his cell phone. Giorgia already feels defeated, even though she's just walked through the door and their exchange hasn't even begun. It's the feeling of impending defeat on an uneven battlefield.

"Here you are!" Mauro hails her when he spots her. "Sorry, I have to go," he says into his phone. "Anyway, wait a few more days, then go ahead. Right, ciao, ciao."

When he brushes her cheek with a kiss, Giorgia remains rigid, arms hugging her chest.

"Did you miss the train like you did in the old days?" Mauro smiles as he sits down again, gestures to the waiter to order.

"No, Filippo took me. I'm just late."

"As usual, then."

He orders for her too and gets it all right, but lets the easy intimacy pass without a word. Giorgia feels a specific fear come over her, which she hasn't felt for a very long time, not since the last time she and Mauro saw each other: it's a fear associated with him, not panic, rather the resigned presentiment of a prey that is not quick enough.

"So, how are you? I mean, really, not like at the supermarket. How are you doing?"

Giorgia slides her hands under her legs and leans forward a little. She decides to try, and slips into a character.

"Fine," she replies. She measures the tone, the words. "Of course, it's a whole different life, more regular. But I'm happy. In fact, satisfied. That's it, I'm satisfied."

"Giò," he says, doling out the coffee cream with a teaspoon. "That was a very bad performance, let me tell you."

He stares at her with the intention of making her uncomfortable and Giorgia surrenders. She squirms in her chair and gives a frustrated sigh.

"You could at least pretend."

"Why?"

"Because we're friends. That's what friends do: they tell each other stories and pretend to believe them."

Mauro laughs and shakes his head. Giorgia feels sad all the same, even if freed from the pressure of having to act.

"Is it that obvious?"

"It's your expression, Giò, what do you think? I remember it well, your face, it's not this one. You look like you're holding your breath."

Giorgia fixes her gaze on the bottom of the empty cup.

"Anyway, thank you for asking, I'm all right."

Mauro changes the subject and starts talking about the school, the courses, how difficult it is to find someone who is able to follow him, about the important production for which he has secured funds.

"We have a year. It's not long, but it will be amazing, visionary."

"What is it about?"

"Oh no, if you think I'm going to tell you anything, you can forget it. I still haven't forgiven you."

"You're making such a big deal out of it!"

"You abandoned me in the middle of a season. Any other director would have burned you, you know."

Mauro has the same look as then, all the details are there, as if nothing has changed, but Giorgia knows that it is a deceptive impression. In three years the dimensions around them have changed, while the interiors, intact, have opposed change—but for how much longer?

"I'm glad," she tells him. "I'm glad you keep doing what you like, that you haven't stopped believing in it."

Mauro smiles again. He moves all the objects between them out of the way, one by one, pushing them towards the blind edge of the table until nothing is left, just an empty space that he fills with his voice.

"I have a part that only you can do."

The linear statement stretches out like a rope between their hands; Giorgia feels one end tighten around her wrist and is about to tug, to break the cord, but, in the end, she hesitates.

"You know I can't."

"Come on, Giò. We don't believe in coincidences. Finding you again there, in the last place in the world where you could have been. It happened because I don't have anyone like you, no one up to your level. I never found anyone like you again. I'm here to beg you."

"I haven't done anything in almost three years, it's not like it used to be."

"You know that's not it. I'd help you, I'd get you back in action in two weeks."

Giorgia feels her mouth forming a smile, she knows it's a mistake.

"I wasn't thinking of it. Then too, I have a job now, and Filippo, it's not like it used to be."

"Half of my actors have the same problems. We can make arrangements, you know that, tell me what I want to hear."

Giorgia realizes that she has slid too far forward in her chair. *We don't believe in coincidences.* Mauro is straining towards her, his body displays the same feverish anxiety that it did in the corridors of the acting school, when they wore out the linoleum together in search of the character—when Giorgia suddenly revealed to him that she had found it, pictured it. The memory of that excitement, incomprehensible to anyone else, overwhelms her.

"I can't give you an answer now."

She struggles to regain control. Mauro turns bland again.

"Let's do this," he says, mildly. "Think about it. Call me in a week."

"A week," Giorgia repeats, smoothing the wrinkles on her forehead with one hand.

"I don't have much time, I hope you understand," Mauro says. He slips his jacket off the back of the chair and puts it on. "Shall we go?"

They say goodbye outside the café, amid invisible shadows.

"Don't screw around with me, Giò," he says before walking away. "Three years ago you asked to take a break, and I let you do it. The break is over."

There are some forms of the past—thinks Giorgia, after the goodbyes with Mauro—some forms of the past that draw their breath from his breath, their resolve from his resolve, so escape is not practical.

On the way home, she feels guilty, mainly thinking about how I know nothing about all this, and she tells herself our story. She sees us meeting, we are a projection in the metro car's window, interrupted by numerous waves of unknown heads; swift waters of greenish concrete act as background, as we look at each other from opposite sides of a room. Around us a graduation party, alcohol in plastic cups, everyone is still upright and not on the floor. We share a condition of suspension, we have no intention of changing this state of affairs. I see Giorgia and I reflect that she has a gift of beauty that is out of place, a beauty that on the one hand composes her and on the other hand unravels her—the hair, the posture, the dress, everything is thrown off-balance in a constant flux. I see in Giorgia what I should see, namely, an individual on the edge of a precipice, and that is precisely why I feel attracted to her. Later, however, I decide to tell myself that I want her for her more acceptable qualities—she has a kindness from another time, she is empathetic, and she possesses the indispensable virtues of altruism and patience. Giorgia senses something harmless in me. Our images keep flowing past in the train window, there is us talking to each other, there's me lightly touching her hip and her perceiving me as a reassuring presence. The day she thought I could be the last outpost of a normal life passes before her eyes: it was three months after our first date, when I fell asleep with my head on her belly after sex. Bushy Afros wipe us off the surface, we end up scattered on the train's rubber floor, and everyone tramples us.

Giorgia's illness has a name that she doesn't want to say. She knows that, according to some doctors, she should be under constant drug therapy. She also knows that she can conquer it, she just has to focus on her tricks, do the exercises; after all, she isn't so different from any other human being of normal intelligence: everyone sees things that don't exist, only she sees them larger, more complex. No use denying it, during the last months at the acting school the situation nearly got out of hand; it was because of her disorderly life, an indolent negligence, living alone had been harmful, not having someone close had made her distracted. Now the situation is completely different, there's me, there is a house, a job, it's all organized. Now, maybe, she could do it.

She misses acting. She discovered theater among the offerings of the rehabilitation programs during her first hospitalization; she continued, afterwards, with private courses. Acting is the only structure in which the illness operates in a way that is functional and not dysfunctional to her body. Giorgia believes that everyone should have a designated place for losing control, a safe sanctuary like the one she had found, in which to feel allowed to let loose somewhat. Now she always feels pressured, her hands grip slippery reins. Instead, what was it like, in those rooms? *What was it like, what was it like?* she thinks as she slowly makes her way through the office workers' neurotic deviations. The reading of the script, the methodical construction of the characters, the moment when they would suddenly materialize and cross over the thresholds, when they acquired substance equal to or greater than the living. She has never spoken to me about this, nor about a certain countess of Illyria who had invaded her to the point of eclipsing her, about the hallucinations or mind alterations. Giorgia and I are fabricated around an omission.

Giorgia waits as long as possible. At the end of the week, she doesn't feel like she's made up her mind.

"I need to talk to you about something," she says.

Friday night is one of our favorite moments, because it's the start of the respite. Friday night is perhaps the only time of the week when for a while we go back to being what we were—the ghost of the university prelude to the weekend still exists in us, so it's not far off to say that we relax by virtue of a memory that has no connection to our current reality. On Friday nights we are lighthearted, even if drained by a fatigue that is not physical. All our energies are consumed in mental exertions, in attempts at self-persuasion and self-control, enormous structures that require constant tending.

Over the remains of Chinese takeout, we hold hands.

"Tell me everything," I say, drunk on sweet-and-sour sauce.

"Mauro made me a proposal, when we met. I didn't tell you right away because I needed some time to think about it."

"I hope it was something very indecent."

"Unrepeatable. He asked me to go back to acting."

Now Giorgia knows that she would like me to object, that, for some absurd reason, she'd like me to forbid her to accept. I have no reason to do that.

"Hey, that's great! Why are you still thinking it over? Wouldn't you like that?"

Of course, she'd like to. It could be a way out of the problem of overload, a way of managing the side effects of the supermarket. It's just that it's so hard for her to choose what's true.

"I don't know, it would be very demanding. I'd be busy with rehearsals a lot of evenings."

"So what's the problem?"

"We'd spend less time together."

"Maybe I could go with you sometimes."

"Yes, I think so."

I don't tell Giorgia, but I see her so resigned that it almost makes me angry. I think it's all wrong, all the opposite of how it should be.

"We don't do anything we like anymore, do we?"

I grab her by the wrist and pull her towards me, on my lap, because sometimes I like to talk to her at very close range, with my head resting on her shoulder. Giorgia doesn't know why, but my gesture moves her, so she raises her head and avoids my eyes. Again, she'd like me to intervene between her and the decision.

"Don't say that."

"But it's true. We have no hobbies, no diversions."

We're very close to telling ourselves that this life sucks, but I'm practiced at controlling myself.

"Okay. We can't complain in general. But you're stuck in there all day, it's not healthy. I think it would do you good. Don't you think so?"

Giorgia nods.

"I think it would."

"We lead an old fogies' life."

"No, no, come on," Giorgia says, kissing my forehead.

She keeps thinking about it, though. *An old fogies' life.* She doesn't stop thinking about it even when we go to bed and I reach for her. She's thinking about it as I touch her—*an old fogies' life.* There is something worse she would like to reveal to me, and instead she presses her fingers on my neck, caresses me. Something terrible.

The day of the first reading of the script is a Saturday afternoon.

"It's more like a picnic, you'll see," Giorgia says, holding my arm.

We decided to take public transportation to Mauro's house to avoid the hassle of parking. Today spring seems to be approaching, the sun glints off the pitted surface of the pavement, still damp from the overnight rain.

"A *picnic?*"

"Yes, something not very demanding, you'll see. Plus there will be loads of people."

"But what does it involve, essentially?"

"An unveiling. We give the script a quick reading, then usually we eat and drink. At least, that's what we used to do, back then."

Giorgia wavers between nervousness and excitement. She wonders how many members of the company she will be able to recognize—Mauro hadn't wanted to tell her anything, to date it's been fifteen days of total silence since their last phone call.

Mauro's house is located in a gated community, isolated from crossroads and traffic. The impression, once you pass through the gate, is that of being in a secluded parallel world, far removed from the city. Giorgia moves along the walkway with the confidence of someone familiar with the place, she almost feels like she's stepping into footprints left the last time. She knows there is an old path traced on the way out as well: it's from the day she told Mauro that she would stop, indeed, that she was stopping the very moment she said it—she would not come back again. She hides a capitulating smile and rings the doorbell. We hear strains of music in the background, a female laugh approaching.

A thin, blonde, somewhat petite girl opens the door. When she recognizes Giorgia, she clasps her in a hug.

"Oh my God, Giò, how beautiful you are."

She takes her face in her hands and kisses her on the nose.

"This is Amelia," Giorgia introduces her to me, smiling.

The girl releases her and holds out a hand.

"Amelia, Filippo."

Our reciprocal responses of "nice to meet you" over-lap as the girl pulls us inside and we're drawn into an exchange of pleasantries.

Giorgia finds many familiar faces, along with voices that have never completely dissolved, because she is unable to forget. Particular scents, the feel of certain fabrics, are like marks that others have embroidered on her. Giorgia has an extensive scar on her skin, which is sensitive to the touch. Though all I see is a reunion of old friends, she instead experiences the impacts, she's joyful, she's fearful, even if from the outside her greet-ings and hugs are like any others.

I am introduced to everyone; I never remember names. The last to present himself is Mauro, edgy and thin, with a tangle of dark, curly hair, wearing a white shirt. It's he who declares that we are ready for the reading, interrupting the conversations among the groups of participants. We are all invited to move downstairs, to the basement "pub."

Giorgia precedes me down the stairs, Amelia in front of her. "Like old times, Giò. How does it seem to you?"

"Nice," says Giorgia, in a low voice, and no one can hear her.

The pub is an emancipated space that exists outside of reality, like Mauro's entire house and like the studios of the acting school. A place that is real only for those who can see it. There is a long table of unfinished, solid wood, yet to be stained. Low windows at a point where wall and ceiling meet, which open onto the back gar-den—from there you can see the dark legs of the maples and the sharp fingers of blood-red leaves. The bookcase, which occupies much of the back wall, suffers under an explosive load of volumes—none of them look new, their spines are worn. The sofa, on the right, has been misshapen by invisible occupants.

Mauro hands out the scripts, and the guests, unprompted, arrange themselves between the sofa and the camp chairs scattered around the room. Giorgia's copy lands in her lap, it has already been opened and soiled by someone else, there are notes jotted in the margins on most of the pages. She leans over to me, sitting beside her, and shows me the cramped calligraphy.

"This means there's a lot of work to do."

"Don't start whining," Mauro scolds her, taking his seat. "So then, I'd say we can stop at the first act, for this afternoon. You all know the story, right?"

A few smile and roll their eyes, but most of the actors are already immersed, head down, in the script.

"Take five minutes for the parts and then we'll start."

Giorgia reads her name at the top of the list and bends even lower, hands and eyes fixed on the paper, to make it out. *Check the voice; ideal body weight: thin; moves swiftly but calmly; can hair be cut short?*

"Are you serious about the dog costume?" a man's voice rises from the back of the room.

"Very serious."

Mauro takes a cigarette out of the pack on the table, puts it between his lips without lighting it.

"But don't we go onstage in May? It's going to be hot. For sure ..."

"To be is to suffer. Any more enthusiastic remarks?"

No one replies. Mauro looks around, cigarette between his fingers, then crosses his legs and relaxes against the chair back.

"We will remain strictly faithful to the 1904 version. I don't want anything Spolinian, keep the Forsberg in you at bay. Any special effects will be left to the technical apparatus, we will remain pure and classic. Who found he has the opening line?"

A young man raises his hand.

"Please."

As soon as the reading begins, Mauro stands up, paces slowly between the chairs and around the table. Giorgia looks for her lines, prepares them, waits. When it's her turn she joins in, following the imposed rhythms: the lines bounce from one mouth to another with very little lag, describing rooms, clothing, imagined movements. In the reconstruction Mauro's voice slips in without breaking the flow, gliding just above the surface—"Here I'd like a lavish synchronization, to fill the stage"; "I really want to see this, but it shouldn't be more than a step. A resounding suggestion"; "Oh, everyone will love it, you'll see. Just everyone."

The conclusion of the first act comes sooner than Giorgia would like. She keeps leafing through the script, even when food and bottles appear, until I'm forced to draw her attention.

"Do you want something to drink?"

"Oh, sure. Thanks."

She holds the script folded to her chest, relegates her impatience elsewhere, picks up the threads of the conversations around her. Everyone wants to know the usual things—What has she been doing in recent years? What is she doing now? *Oh, in a supermarket?*— then the ritual of memories, of anecdotes, begins. There is a lot of talk about acting school and Giorgia feels an intense nostalgia for what she's missed. She discovers that time has passed in the classrooms, the school has had its new protagonists. And she, where was she, had she really been living? Is there really another life, outside acting school and the theater?

What do people who aren't here do? Do they exist or just think they exist?

The wine circulates abundantly in glasses and veins; Giorgia is glad that, after drinking a little, I too finally seem at ease. She watches me ask questions, observes the prodigious efforts of those who try to explain things me, to instruct me.

"Where's the bathroom?" I ask at one point.

"Upstairs, first floor," replies the girl who welcomed us when we arrived. "I'll go with you, so then you can help me bring down a few bottles."

Giorgia smiles at me, then watches me go up the stairs with Amelia, shoulders hunched as they usually are when I feel awkward and clumsy. When she turns around, Mauro's eyes are asking her a question that she refuses to answer.

"So where do you and Giò live?" Amelia asks as we walk upstairs. "Come, there's another flight."

"Lambrate," I tell her, following her to the first floor.

"Oh, near the university," she says. "Second door on the right, I'm going to get something from my room. I'll be back."

In the bathroom I look at myself in the mirror and see that I'm a little befuddled from the alcohol. It's a pleasant sensation, which I haven't felt in a long time. In the alcoholic haze, elementary thoughts tumble out—Mauro's house seems immense, a rich person's place, and only now that I'm not entirely lucid do I realize it. Even the bathroom, for example, I think after flushing. I run a finger over the shiny tiles lining the walls, wash my hands under the hot jet of the washbowl, sink my fingers into the fluffy towel. Someone knocks at the door, interrupting my study of the surroundings.

"Everything okay?"

Amelia is waiting outside, she studies me.

"I think I drank too much."

"Everything okay then. Come on."

Waiting in a guest room are two cardboard boxes. Amelia grabs one easily, leaves the other to me, and leads the way back downstairs, to a spot behind the kitchen peninsula, where we drop the weights on the floor.

"My father sent it all yesterday, we didn't have time to put it away," Amelia explains, opening one of the boxes. "It looks like good stuff, anyway."

She hands me a dusty bottle and tells me to set it on the marble countertop.

"I can't believe Giò is back, you know? When Mauro told me she'd agreed, well, wow. You know?"

Another bottle.

"Have you ever seen her perform?" she asks.

"No. By the time we met, she had already stopped."

Amelia's eyes widen as she crouches in the semidarkness of the dim kitchen light, another bottle in her hands.

"Oh, believe me, she's something to see. She's just the type of performer who keeps you from noticing the difference."

"What difference?"

"Between reality and fiction, between what's acting and what's not. With Giò it's real, you watch her and you have no doubts. She was a legend, at the school. She could do it all in half the time, we hated her."

"Oh."

"I mean, affectionately."

Amelia's face clouds over.

"It was very strange, to tell you the truth. Imagine: her name had begun circulating in the theater world, which is what everyone wants. Then Mauro, who was also starting to make his way during that same time, put on a small but noteworthy play, got some dates, was scheduled into the season. He and Giò were very young by all standards, they were the school's two modest phenomena."

Amelia stands up.

"They worked great, together. The opening night was a success, they got some excellent reviews, they ended up in the papers. Brief articles, small stuff, but still a nice win. Mauro obtained confirmation of other dates, everyone was excited about Giò. You know the feeling when everything falls into place, that things are about to take off? Well, that was the idea you got, looking at them."

She sets the bottle on the marble counter, seems to be lost in thought, then she crouches back down between the boxes. It takes me a few seconds to realize that I haven't missed a part of the story: she simply broke off.

"And then?"

Amelia looks up at me.

"Well, then Giò said she was stopping."

"Just like that, out of the blue?"

"That's right, mon ami. Out of the blue. Oh, it was a thunderbolt all right."

"But why?"

She gives me a sad smile.

"What do I know? I thought you'd know."

"She never told me about it."

She hands me another bottle, the last one, then gets up and starts wiping the dust off with a dishtowel.

"I don't know, Mauro would never tell me. Believe me, he was furious. Afterwards there were performances with the understudy, of course, but it wasn't the same thing. If you had seen Giò, you'd know what I'm talking about."

"How strange."

"Yeah. The worst thing, though, is that after that she disappeared. So we all realized that Giò is one of those people."

"What people?" I ask, defensively. Even though I'm a little tipsy, I don't want to hear Giorgia badmouthed.

"It's not a criticism, mon ami," she says, patting me on the back. "One of those people who disappear, who one moment are there and the next are gone. So that you never know when it might happen."

I'm thinking I really don't know what Amelia is talking about, that she's a stranger after all, and that Giorgia doesn't disappear, in three years she's never disappeared, not even for an afternoon. I'd like to tell her that, find the words.

"Hold these," she stops me, putting the bottles in my arms. "Now everything is back in place though, did you see? Giò is back."

She seems genuinely happy now.

"You tell her. No playing around this time, okay?" she winks, then starts back.

I follow her, wishing I were lucid enough to process, think. When we return to the pub, Giorgia is talking to the dog-costume man and I unwillingly get drawn into the conversation.

The afternoon comes slowly to an end, the guests leave a few at a time, Giorgia and I are among the last to go. Our clothes reek of tobacco—as soon as the room emptied, Mauro started smoking—and we have dark stains on our sweaters, splashes from a glass of wine that someone knocked over.

During the metro ride back, Giorgia falls asleep on

my shoulder. Back home, it all seems like a dream to her, as though none of what transpired in the last ten hours really happened: this morning's alarm clock, the preparations, Mauro's house, the reading. She looks for the wine stains on her sweater, the cigarette smell in her hair, looks at me and asks me what I thought of her friends, whether they made me feel comfortable.

"They're really very nice," I say.

I look tired but happy, she knows I don't lie. She joins me on the couch and we choose a film, something old that we've seen at least once. She stretches her legs over me, gives a contented sigh.

"How come you stopped?" I ask, at one point.

Giorgia doesn't know what I'm talking about, she looks at me, confused.

"What?"

"Why did you quit the theater?"

Giorgia figures she should have expected this question, that there's no danger. She feels prepared.

"I was too stressed," she says. "I was living alone, I was still undecided as to what to do about the university; they had suspended me. There was too much to think about and I had a breakdown."

I nod and go back to watching the film, although we've both lost track of the dialogue on the screen.

"And now, how do you feel?" I ask, without turning around.

Giorgia looks at me. I am a silhouette in the dim light, defined by a blue, artificial profile, the most concrete presence that has ever existed in her life.

"I feel good," she says. "I can do it now."

* * *

Six months later, at the end of rehearsals, Mauro walks Giorgia to the tram stop. He is just back from the summer holidays and pale skin can be seen in the webs between his tanned fingers. He doesn't look rested and Giorgia thinks it must be because of his obsessive concerns about the show. He called her almost every day in the last two weeks, even late in the evening, using her as a notepad for recording his ideas. I got annoyed and didn't say anything, but Giorgia felt compelled to apologize, justify it—he's like that, when it comes to his work, he has no discipline.

"What did you two do?" Mauro asks, lighting a cigarette.

"We stayed in the city," Giorgia says.

She thinks about the deserted wasteland, about us drifting through the streets like plastic bobbing aimlessly in the surf—our desultory conversations, the heat smelling of tar, the feeling of being in a place when everyone is somewhere else.

"I see. It's that one, isn't it?" Mauro studies the list of tram stops.

"That's it, yes."

"It just passed."

They sit on the bench under the bus shelter's canopy. The city is still only a half-full container and Giorgia thinks it's a shame, because September is a very lovely month in Milan, with the linden trees still green and the sun pouring onto the asphalt.

"It's going to be perfect," Mauro says, blowing out smoke. "The flying scenes will be amazing."

"I hope so," says Giorgia.

"Sure. And everything else too, Giò, you'll see. I'm so happy with what we're doing."

Mauro stares at a point on the empty street with the

ecstatic expression of someone enjoying an exclusive world. They remain silent until the tram comes, then he says goodbye with a hug.

Giorgia also feels happy: she inadvertently realizes it when she takes a deep breath that makes her ribs hurt. There is a special energy on this Tuesday that makes it all worthwhile—the rehearsals of the last months, the upended schedules, the increasingly less time spent with me. Going back to the theater after such a long time has given things a different perspective, it's all more justifiable now.

He materializes in the wake of this thought, two rows ahead of her. He has his back to her, beyond the passengers in cotton summer shirt sleeves, and his hair, reddish, with rebellious tufts, plays hide and seek behind the fake leather seatback. All she can see of his body is a pale neck, the edge of a childish cheek, and small shoulders covered with autumn leaves; a silver spiderweb extends between his shoulder blades, crushed by the metal seat frame.

Giorgia misses her stop. It's the first real illusion in three years, the last time it was Olivia, and she still remembers her perfume, the pace of her steps. When they show up, they do so by presenting themselves at a certain distance, as if to ask permission. They are delicate and discreet, they never meet her eyes before the appropriate moment, they gain ground by being polite. This time Giorgia would like to dissolve the space, make him turn towards her, but she resists and comes back to reality. She gets off at the next stop and leaves *Him* behind, wondering if he's looking at her the way she looked at Mauro only a few minutes earlier, if *He* sees in her eyes the same radiant thoughts.

Giorgia handles the hallucinations with lucidity, for her they are a physiological part of the creative process. There is, in this naturalness, a form of presumption that she decides to underestimate. Quelling the alarms of the body and also those of the mind, she convinces herself that she is managing the pathological insurrection. Even when He breaks loose from rehearsals, from the school's studios, and begins to conquer more distant territories, going so far as to intrude into our home, Giorgia keeps telling herself that she's the one who invited him in.

I am unaware of his presence. I accompany Giorgia to the rehearsals, sometimes I go back early to pick her up and listen from outside, barred from the studio. I'm not allowed to watch, Mauro made that clear to me right away. I don't know that He eats at our table, writes on our walls, sleeps at the foot of our bed. Giorgia, who knows, takes great care to manage her reactions—it's not always easy. He makes funny faces, he's a very likeable kid, his drawings blow you away; she also thinks he's growing up and would like to tell him so, but they don't talk to each other, not yet. He only communicates with his eyes. One night, when we're having sex, he stays instead of leaving. He and Giorgia exchange long looks, they confess secrets to one another as I make love to her.

Giorgia wakes up happy on May 14th, the last day we will spend as faithful versions of ourselves. I don't know that yet: today, at this moment, her awakening has no significance to me, I scarcely appreciate it. Yet as a result of the exercise, I will very soon be forced to look back at this morning and then everything will have to be reformulated, every element dissected and magnified. Revisiting it for the twentieth time, I will notice the hidden smile—or I will only imagine it, based on an arbitrary deduction.

While we have breakfast, Giorgia is thinking about a number of things and she condenses them into slow gestures. *He* is still here, sitting at the head of the table.

"It's going to be a very long day," she says, taking the last biscuit. "Opening days never seem to end. I was right to take two days off."

"What time do you have to be there?" I ask her.

"Mauro said 10:30, that means 10 o'clock."

He tugs at her pajama sleeve, trying to get her attention back. Giorgia feels an electric shock run through her body and just wishes it was already time to stop resisting.

"Oh, afterward we're all invited to Mauro's house."

"After the show?"

"Yes. It will be fun," Giorgia says, then takes a sip of coffee. "After a show, even if you're exhausted, you don't feel like going to sleep. You're still very tense."

She watches me raise my eyebrows and shake my head.

"I don't know how you do it," I say. "If I had to get on a stage, in front of an audience, I'd want to die. How can you be so calm?"

"No, no, once you're onstage you don't even think about it. It's all over so fast you don't have time to notice."

"I can't wait, you know?" I tell her. "I'm really curious."

A world unfolds behind me, in rooms where I am not present. While I'm in the bathroom, Giorgia stands in front of the living room window and breathes deeply, filling her belly like a vessel. From the deepest pit of the stomach, then up into the chest, and again, until the air flows from the nostrils. An open hand at the diaphragm, where the voice must find its place and from there project. In our bedroom, I slip into any old clothes for a Friday. The boundary of a wall, a door, a few steps divide us—if only I could close that distance, if I could catch her imagining she's caressing *Him*, there at the window, watching the 6 a.m. passersby; I'd find her with her fingers entwined in the little boy's hair, indulging her illusion.

Giorgia and I say goodbye to each other at the door and our last day branches off in separate directions. She lingers in the bathroom, and under the hot jet of the shower, stares at the little boy's silhouette that appears in shadow beyond the glass. *He* is unusually quiet but always close by, and doesn't leave her side; *He* clings to the sleeve of her bathrobe while she dries her hair. They go out together, there's no seat on the tram, *He* sits on her lap.

Empty theaters carry the promise of infinite space. When the lights are off and the seats unoccupied, the dark rear depths dissolve, creating the illusion that they continue on. Giorgia likes to think that, if she wanted to, she could explore the theater for eternity, settle among the orchestra seats awaiting no one. Only when vacant, deprived of its function, does the theater show itself for what it really is—an escape, an imaginary realm—and yet here, only here and nowhere else are they able to *exist*.

As soon as they set foot in the theater, *He* starts running around between the rows of seats.

"There you are," says Mauro, looking out from the stage, when he spots Giorgia. "Come on up, let's try the second flight right away."

Giorgia goes up, lets them harness her, by now the

movements are imprinted in her body's memory and they manage it without a hitch. Mauro is barely watching, yet she knows he sees. After the flight, it's time for the technical rehearsal, a sequence of the openings and closings of all the scenes, the ordeal of changing the light. Mauro observes from the center of the orchestra, moves up or down the aisle, verifies the result from different angles, insists on opening the second act. On her lunch break, Giorgia joins him with a coffee and they both sink into the threadbare cushions of a balcony row.

The scene opens on a series of superimposed painted backdrops: the first is a starry night sky, which ends with a lagoon that drops off into the leaves of a forest. The stage gradually empties, the backstage chatter fades, tangled cables remain on the edge of the proscenium, the scattered notes of the prompter are spread open on the forestage.

"It's near perfect," says Mauro, his eyes fixed on the stage. "We're almost sold out."

He is not talking to her but to himself, so Giorgia just nods and listens.

"I wish it were already time."

It's merely an automatic thought, Giorgia knows it. For him, this is actually the best moment: the wait preceding the creation. In the morning, just like all of them, he'll wake up with a part of him missing and feel like he's losing his mind. There will be the subsequent performances but it won't be the same, there is nothing that equals an opening.

"How do you feel?" he asks her.

Giorgia would like to tell him that maybe it was a mistake. *I'm scared*, she thinks.

"There's a moment, onstage," she says, not looking at

him. "When the identification starts and everything else stops. You know I'm only here for that, right?"

To finally be able to let go. Accept the illness in its fullest expression, allow it to dominate her. Accept the pathology's potential to make her something that she isn't, in a dimension that has no correlations—a condition that is in part identical to that which seems to have afflicted all of them. Very soon there will be no past to cling to, there will be no mothers, fathers, memories or people who will withstand the impact, and Giorgia will be free to no longer exist as herself.

"I know," Mauro says. "I'm here for the same reason."

Giorgia doesn't add anything further, because they've already talked about it, in a distant past when everything was about to begin—she knows that he remembers.

I don't feel the loss of myself as an individual, an abstract concept and summarily worthless. What am I? They force me to ask myself a question that has no answer. What should I be nostalgic for? A terrible childhood, the family I didn't have? I want what everyone wants: I want to dissolve.

The seated rehearsal goes smoothly, Mauro doesn't want them to get tired out and works solely on the fluidity of coordination, making almost no adjustments to the performance. At five o'clock the dressing rooms fill up, the actors begin to vanish into their costumes. Giorgia prefers to get dressed alone, going off to a corner in her dressing room. For her there is no stage makeup, just a wig and her costume; she puts them on and waits.

Giorgia is like me, she always turns her back on what is going on around her, she chooses a clear view and hides there. *He* is so close now, hugging her so tightly, his head against her breastbone, it's as though the tip of his nose were wedging its way between the cartilage. Giorgia looks out the only window: the twilight is sectioned into perfect squares by a metal grate; along the street the first spectators are hurrying to the theater, along with a few passersby chained to their cigarettes and groups of girls in a festive mood. There are a lot of lights, the orangey orbits of streetlamps and the white irises of cars stopped at the traffic light. You can feel summer approaching, like an electrical current in the air. It's May 14th.

I join Giorgia half an hour before the show. The smell backstage reminds me of confectioners' sugar. A thick white powder winds around the lightbulbs, drifts unpredictably over the lacquered heads of the Sirens, then slides down my throat, leaving a cloying taste on my tongue.

"Sorry."

Their pale blue tails sweep the wooden floor and, in an attempt to avoid them, I end up wedged in the arms of a large dog costume. A human face stares at me glumly, framed by synthetic fur: I recognize the unfortunate guy from the first reading.

"Sorry!"

He waves a paw and proceeds down the corridor, passing an oncoming wave of Lost Boys. Seen up close, the dark stubble of their beards pokes through the greasepaint. Excitement is visible in pupils that are at first dilated then tiny as pinheads, in words mumbled under the breath. Constantly pushed back against the wall, I manage to reach the last dressing room on the left, the one all to herself, isolated from the world. The door is closed, I'm about to tap it with my knuckles when a cold hand grabs my wrist. I recognize the blonde girl who was introduced to me at Mauro's house.

"Give her another minute."

Behind the door I hear Giorgia's voice reciting the lines like a prayer.

"I just wanted to ..."

"Later, mon ami."

My idea suddenly seems stupid. She shakes her head and a cloud of gold glitter rises from her wig, dusting every available surface.

"How annoying," she hisses, rolling her eyes. "Come with me, let's wait here."

There is a chair on the other side of the hallway, under a tiny window overlooking the street. The girl collapses on it, leaving behind a luminescent cloud, then lights a cigarette she pulled out from who knows where. To while away the time, I stand in front of the window.

"It's going to be a great show," says Amelia—now I remember her name. "Damn."

She wipes away the ashes that ended up on her dress, checking the damage: a burn hole appears on Tinker Bell's costume. She is about to add something when she is interrupted by the arrival of Mauro, who knocks on Giorgia's door and opens it without hesitation.

"Everything okay?" he asks us in passing.

I watch the door close behind him.

"Well, he's the boss," says Amelia, trying to hide the burn hole in the folds of her skirt.

Another minute of awkward silence, interrupted only by her sighs, then the door reopens. Mauro comes back out of the dressing room with a radiant expression, followed by Giorgia, who is pale and tense, arms crossed over her chest.

"Hey," he murmurs, when he recognizes me.

The boy's face is fused into her chest by now, the nape

of his neck appears between her breasts and the whole back of his body protrudes from Giorgia like a landmass. I don't see him, I hug her and our embrace presses him in more deeply. I've left the roses safely in my seat, I'm going to hold them on my lap the whole time, hoping they won't wilt.

Giorgia lets me stroke her. Her hands grip mine weakly, but I don't notice it. I'm thinking it's suffocating in the dressing rooms, I want to get out of there.

"Fifteen minutes to curtain time, I'm going to take a look at the lights," Mauro says as he leaves. "Oh, Amelia, if you croak onstage I'll personally kick your ass."

She bursts into laughter and blows a stream of gray smoke after him.

"How do you feel?" I ask Giorgia, trying to ignore everything around us.

She rests her forehead on my shoulder and sighs, her face hidden by the reddish wig. The green costume seems to swim on her a little, as if the last hour in the dressing room had drained her a little more. Amelia gently pinches her cheek, smiling tenderly at her.

"Don't worry, you're sensational. I'm going to get ready to go on too, okay?"

Giorgia nods slowly.

"I'm a little scared," she says, when Amelia has gone.

"Me too," I admit.

She straightens up and looks at me.

"Thank you for everything."

"I didn't do anything."

"Sure you did. You allowed me to be here."

Suddenly, I perceive a jarring edge. An anomaly that diverges from Giorgia's words and flares in her eyes.

"We can bolt, if you want," I instinctively joke.

Giorgia tilts her head. There, she's back again. Something inside me reacts to the false note and an inexplicable feeling of dread tightens my throat in a vicelike grip. She felt it, too.

"No, it'll be fine," she says.

I try to hug her a little tighter but Giorgia gently eases away.

"We'd better go join them too."

I comply, following her down the corridor that is now almost completely empty. The actors are crowded near the curtain. Giorgia is shaken by a tremor; I can feel it run through her, under my hand, and continue down to her legs. I feel spent, as if at any moment I myself would have to go onstage.

Giorgia turns her back on the curtain.

"You have to go."

"Okay," I say. "It'll go well, you'll see."

She squeezes my hand. A few of the actors move past the curtains that divide the stage from the wings and take their places in the little beds that occupy the set. Giorgia suddenly reaches towards me and hugs me again, so tight that for a moment I can feel her heart beating against my chest: a manic, driving rhythm. A whisper moves her lips, but I can't understand it.

"At least some gloss, Giorgia!"

A makeup artist wedges between us, I'm forced to move away and there's no time to even say goodbye.

This moment will not have any particular significance until 11:47 this evening—

I don't yet know that I should be wishing to be back in Giorgia's arms, back to this morning, under the blankets, and farther still, rewind the six months that led us here.

Beyond the thick curtain that separates us, beyond the riggings, beyond the joists and beams and bodies,

Giorgia begins to vanish. I could still grab her, but I'm distracted by elementary thoughts.

Giorgia vanishes, completing the process of identification, the result of an obsessive analysis of the subtext, of repetition and memorization, of monumental building on the character. Around her, the actors are crowded into the wings; a subdued murmuring binds them together. When the lights dim and finally go out, only the gleam of the aisle lighting remains visible. A stranger's breathing brushes her ear, a cold sweat crystallizes on her skin—the audience drowns in darkness and the stage is brightly illuminated.

Giorgia is barely thinking, all that remains of her volition is what's necessary to make her disappear. *He* breaks free altogether, it takes an instant. A moment before she enters the scene, she vanishes and I've lost her forever.

CHAPTER ONE

AN UNDERSTANDABLE COMPLEX

Details clutter our parting: the blue of the dark circles under Giorgia's eyes, the visible and invisible presences that besieged us, her scent—it lingers in the pillow-cases at home, and in the last clothes she wore, stub-bornly persistent, despite the four months that have passed since the tragedy. Now Giorgia smells different, maybe it's the medications, maybe the disinfectants that permeate the sheets at the clinic. I can't help but think about that, about her new smell, as I drive from Milan to the institute buried among the rice fields.

The Lomellina is a flat plain lying along the water; reflections of ash trees punctually ripple in the pud-dles and pale clouds swell on the horizon, threatening another storm. The Fiat Panda emits a few distressing groans, but I don't worry about it. I haven't been wor-ried about anything for about a month. Each week is marked by activities that are repeated in an inexorable sequence: work, home, clinic, home, work. It's a per-verse process, but it's better now than it was early on. I haven't forgotten the panic: in comparison, the recent numbness is healthy. It was the same for Giorgia as well. In the beginning, her psychotic breakdown completely crushed and destroyed her, leaving her shattered and badly reassembled in the hospital bed. When the therapy began to work, the clinical picture was confirmed as a catatonic state.

During the first phase I kept hoping that, with the right treatments, Giorgia would come back to life. I had to face reality after she was moved to the Anastasio Care Facility. Though the drugs quell the monster, they shut down all the rest with it, including Giorgia herself: they fail to discriminate between the abomination and what is precious. It's all gone, mowed down, she no longer remembers me, or who she is, or anything else.

There are rare moments of lucidity when I know I'm facing an untenable situation. My friends, my parents tell me this, but none of them comes home with me in the evening. None of them has to stare at Giorgia's finger-prints left on the bathroom cabinets, stained with the foundation she hated but always put on, and none of them can know what it means to find a strand of her hair coiled up like rings on a finger.

The clinic's parking lot is almost completely empty and the Panda hobbles along to a spot beside the hedge. I feel just like the car, we are reciprocal extensions, battered, beaten, and grimy. The walk from the courtyard to the clinic and then up the stairs to Giorgia's room is already written, and rather than happening, is fulfilled, like a prophecy. I have the usual feeling, namely, that I'm not myself but someone else, in a depersonalized, alien version of events. I watch myself push open the heavy glass door, and slow my steps as I pass the reception desk. In the large painting hanging on the wall, Saint Dymphna awaits her beheading with a doleful air. At the foot of the saint, the kind lady on the Sunday shift greets me with a smile, but today too she doesn't ask how I am.

To allow time to get acclimated, I prefer the stairs to the elevator. The first floor is always quite close, whereas the corridor is endless. At the end, overlooking the garden, is a window without cranks, just like the one in Giorgia's room. On her best days she stares at the sky the whole time.

I'm almost at the door, which is wide open and secured to the wall with a chain, when an unusual sound, a voice, surprises me. It doesn't belong to Giorgia—she no longer speaks—nor is it the nurse's. It's a male voice, but I have a hard time piecing the words together. For a moment I think it's the clinic's medical director, but the tone is different, lighter.

"But yet I cannot love him. He might have took his answer long ago."

Giorgia is curled up on her side, her back to the door, and there is someone sitting next to her with a book in his hand. He's not the doctor. I recognize Mauro. He immediately looks up and his face widens in a broad smile.

"Filippo!"

I watch him place the book on the windowsill and come towards me, gripping my arm in the perfect interpretation of an old friend who hasn't seen you in a long while. The last time we saw one another, Giorgia was still in the hospital. He'd turned up late for visiting hours and hadn't stayed long: just long enough to look in on her.

"How nice, you're here too." Mauro doesn't loosen his hold. "I was reading something with Giorgia, do you mind?"

"No, of course not."

"You take the chair, I'll stand."

"We can ask the nurse to …"

"No, no, look, I've been sitting for too long already."

I walk around Giorgia's bed just to do something, to ease the awkwardness of this unexpected encounter.

Her eyes are open and blank, her eyelids shiny, a little bruised, and her face is expressionless. The delicate groove between her eyebrows has smoothed out, her forehead is a placid white sheet, as if someone had applied a coat of whitewash to erase everything. Giorgia is Giorgia, but she isn't Giorgia. The dark hair, clean from her Saturday shower, is growing back—in the early days she used to tear it out, they had to cut it off. Her hands are tightly clasped under her cheek. Today is evidently a so-so day, not dangerous but not good either, a day as listless as she is.

I move closer and kiss her head; in her smell there is a bit of everything I already know, soap, medicines, slept-in pajamas. Then I sit down and look at her. I usually tell her about my day, something interesting that happened during the week, the customers' absurdities and, only occasionally, about how I feel. I'm very careful not to say anything that might upset her, because as I said I don't know what's behind that wall. Inside, Giorgia may be crying or she may be happy. Maybe it's just a matter of depth.

Mauro's look asks if he can continue, and I nod. He starts reading again and I don't get it. His presence here is unexpected, yet he acts as if everything were normal. Fragments of that night come back to me, his fingers gripping Giorgia's ankles to stop her from kicking, his eyes staring at her mouth, wide open in an endless scream. I clear my memory by focusing forcefully on his voice, which glides along slowly. I repeat his words, one by one, inside me, until everything dissolves and the muscles loosen. After a while the murmur becomes a comforting sound, drifting over everything, the sheets, my legs, spilling onto the floor like rain. Maybe it's exhaustion, maybe the feeling of not being alone, a kind of relaxation that sneaks up on me and plunges me into sleep.

In the dream Giorgia is sitting by the window, a summer sun illuminating her. She's talking but her voice is indistinguishable, I see her lips moving, as she gestures judiciously, a pale knee folded against her chest. Now I know she's talking about the script, that's why her eyes are lit up, sparkling with exceptional intensity. It's not a dream. It's a memory and it dissolves. I wake up with a start, dropping back into the clinic's dreary backdrop. Outside the light is leaden. Giorgia is also sleeping. I'm overcome by the mortification of having fallen asleep: the clock on the wall reads six o'clock and it's almost time to go. There's no sign of Mauro. I spend the last half hour watching Giorgia in silence, until the nurse finds me sitting on the bed, caressing her face without ever touching it.

"I'm sorry, but visiting hours are over."

I thank her and say goodbye to Giorgia in our new way, without uttering a word. Outside the room the day's purpose is concluded and there are only a few hours left to kill with survival chores, some quick shopping at the supermarket—which is never the one she worked in—and choosing a film in which to bury the evening. I'm thinking about this when, after nodding goodbye to the lady at the reception desk, I spot Mauro standing outside the glass door. He's smoking with his back turned; the white stream of smoke swirls upwards, against the current, as though his head were in spontaneous combustion. Contact is inevitable.

"Oh, there you are," he says as soon as I walk through the door. "I've been waiting for you."

He tucks the book under his arm and seems less cheerful. I look at him closely, he too is scruffy and tired: his shirt is wrinkled and the sleeves rolled up on his forearms look like they've been that way for a few days.

"Sorry if I showed up without notifying you."

"No problem, it's good you came."

Mauro's eyes quickly gauge me as he takes a drag on his cigarette.

"How do you find her? Do you think there's been any improvement?"

"She's been like that for a while now and for the time being there's no talk of reducing the dosages. They tried, but she's too unstable."

Mauro nods, shifting his gaze elsewhere. I wonder if he too is thinking of Giorgia trying to jump out the window at the end of the performance. It was the last time we spent more than thirty minutes together.

"I'm going, I'm beat," I tell him. "Come back whenever you want."

"Sure, thanks. We could get together some night, if you like."

"All right."

We don't even make an effort to exchange numbers. Mauro ends the conversation with a vague smile and a nod. He keeps watching me as I get in the car and turn the key, and continues watching when the engine refuses to start, in a fitting conclusion to the week. When I drop my head against the seat back, defeated, he comes over and speaks through the window.

"Do you want a ride?"

Mauro's Alfa is crammed with stacks of papers stapled together and scattered everywhere, some already yellowing between the windshield and the dashboard, others stuffed into the door pockets or rolled up and forced into the glove compartment. I catch a quick glimpse of the titles of plays typed in capital letters.

"Sorry about the mess," he says as soon as we leave the clinic behind. "I'm looking for a new script."

"No problem. Have you found anything interesting?"

"No, they all suck. We may have to wait until next season."

"Too bad."

"That's always the way, but maybe something will turn up at the last minute, who knows."

It starts to rain and for a few minutes the conversation languishes.

"Then too, I miss Giorgia." Mauro speaks softly, but her name explodes in the silence. "I don't have anyone as talented as she is."

His words make me shudder. Silence again, for a long time.

"You live in Lambrate, right?" Mauro tries again, after a while.

"Yeah, near the barracks. You?"

"Maciachini district. You came there with Giorgia, didn't you? For the first reading."

"Oh, that's right, I didn't remember."

Mauro smiles understandingly, without taking his eyes off the road.

"I'm not myself either. Would you like to stop and have a drink at my place? Then I'll take you home."

For a while the proposal floats in the air; I'm thinking I should say no, go home and enjoy a shower, but just thinking about it oppresses me. I wish I were in a position to bargain with myself.

"Okay, thanks."

Mauro nods, satisfied, then turns on the radio. Along the way, the conversation gets off the ground and we talk a bit about everything; we discover by chance two acquaintances we have in common, and plunge into a discussion about student movements that in a round-about way leads us to the Iraq War. I find that Mauro has a firm opinion on almost everything, that though diplomatic is nauseatingly certain, that he proceeds gingerly when speaking and asks a lot of questions. I find myself talking to him more than I've done with anyone else in recent times.

After sitting in city traffic for about twenty minutes, we reach his house. We don't linger long in the garden, it's raining, but I vaguely remember it now.

We enter through the main door, which opens into the living room and stairs leading to the upper floors.

"Don't mind the mess, I had some ill-mannered guests this weekend," Mauro says, preceding me.

Scattered around two sofas and a glass table are empty cartons, pizza crusts, soiled napkins, and wine bottles. There is a strong stale smell, and Mauro hastens to open a window with an embarrassed smile.

"Mauro, is that you?" a high-pitched voice calls down from the top of the stairs.

"Yeah, with a friend."

Mauro shouts up the stairs but there's no response, except for a distant chuckle, an echo. A shiver runs down my spine and it's certainly fear, but not of the present. I start thinking about when and if Giorgia may have climbed those steps, in a past I am unaware of, and even whether her shoes or T-shirts ever got wedged between the sofa cushions. In a white flash I picture her tickling a buttonhole of the shirt that Mauro is wearing. Then he smiles at me and Giorgia disappears.

"Let's have a drink," he says.

We drink; I barely have a chance to take in the word when I am swallowing sips of a red-hot substance along with it. It has a brown, muddy color; I've already forgotten the name. Mauro is telling me about the unseen difficulties of performing seemingly simple characters—"... it's like real life, you know? A simple character has endless pockets and it's impossible to guess what they contain. A demanding but feasible undertaking with a complex character becomes practically insurmountable with a simple character. Do you see what I mean?"

I can't manage to wrap my head around the subject, so I try to confine it by gulping down the liqueur as quickly as I can. I haven't had a drink in months. I avoided alcohol out of some kind of superstition. What if, in this glass, there were a little of the madness that has affected Giorgia? Since the day of the opening, the only thing that is quite certain to me is that madness is everywhere and that it's invisible.

Mauro lights a cigarette whose glow pulsates in the white light of the storm; everything becomes sharper and incandescent, as always, before obscuring completely—like his eyelashes and the visible part of his profile.

"It's like with you and Giorgia, you know, maybe that's clearer." And a corner of his mouth smiles sadly. "She was complex but understandable. You're simple but unfathomable. Right?"

I don't know how to answer that. The truth is that right now, at this moment when the alcohol has dulled the edges, all I can think about is her and that night. The memory that I have avoided and spews out like vomit.

"She thought she was Peter Pan," I grip my head in my hands, and the truth surges over me. It's horrible.

"The way she screamed ... That was the last time I heard her voice."

Mauro doesn't look at me.

"She said something to me that night, before she ... I've thought about it a lot. I've thought back, I've gone over it, and I heard it: she said 'Sorry.' You know? She apologized to me. She knew it."

He doesn't answer. The admission, as atrocious as it was inevitable, does not ruffle him. I watch him get up and walk slowly to the window, turn his back on me and my words.

"I'm too exhausted, I can't drive you home. You'll have to stay here," he says. "There's room. I'll take you back in the morning."

I tell him no. I'm thinking that our apartment, mine and Giorgia's, has become a refuge for ghosts. I pour another glass, then I repeat the ritual once, twice, five times, Giorgia, the ghosts, a glass, until Mauro returns from his exile and leads me up a mountain of stairs, and into a welcoming burrow.

The last thought unravels on the brink of consciousness: *Sorry.* Giorgia had said "Sorry."

I awake under the sloping ceiling of the mansard roof. I stare at it, I don't recognize it, I search for an answer and from there I reconstruct the previous day—the clinic, Mauro, the drinking. The autumn morning light that is at variance with me climbs along the wooden beams. Since Giorgia is no longer living with me, I can't get my bearings anymore; no matter where I find myself, it's the wrong place for the right memory. Now, in this unfamiliar house, which I first saw with her, the feeling of estrangement is oppressive.

When I drag myself up to a sitting position, I find that I'm wearing yesterday's clothes and that my shoes are waiting for me at the foot of the bed. The furnishings around me are the impersonal décor of guest rooms—an untrodden kilim rug on the parquet floor, an uncomfortable ottoman relegated to a corner on the left, round, bare nightstands, a built-in closet with a mirror. In its pale wood frame my reflection appears as a dark stain. I'm ratty-looking: I need a shave, my eyes are puffy, and I'm thinking that anyone looking at me could guess that I'm falling apart. I feel as if all that's holding me together are my sweater and pants, forcing the body into a shape and form that, if I were to undress, I would lose. I picture myself breaking into glass marbles on the floor and rolling down the stairs that I climbed last night—who knows how, with what strength? Maybe Mauro supported me?

"Awake or not, I'm coming up, okay?"

I realize that it's this call that roused me out of sleep. The female voice coming from the lower floor is faint and gets clearer as it approaches. It enters the room ahead of its owner, who follows right behind it.

"Ah, you're awake," the girl says, stopping at the door.

I recognize her, but I again find I don't know her name. She's blonde, petite.

"How do you feel?" she asks, hands on her hips. Then, not waiting for an answer: "Pretty shitty, it seems to me."

"Yeah," I say, getting up.

She's wearing a light jacket, as if she just got back or is about to go out.

"Mauro will be back in half an hour. I got you something for breakfast, you'll find it all downstairs. Wait for him, please, he doesn't have the keys."

"Okay."

She appraises me with her eyes, fiddles with a corner of her scarf.

"Okay then. Take care," she says. "See you."

She goes away quickly, the way she came, taking her heels and her voice with her.

"Be careful at the last step," she yells from below.

Right afterwards, a door slams—then the gate creaks, the girl is gone and I fixate on the embarrassment: a stranger's house, last night. If it weren't for her request, I'd like to slip away, as she did.

I put on my shoes, and orient myself in the hallway—three doors, two to my left, one to my right. I find the bathroom with the same fluffy towels as the other time; I avoid a second encounter with the mirror. The temperature in the house is warm, as are the colors, there's wood everywhere, paintings hanging on the walls that lead up the stairs. When I get to the ground floor, I notice the last step: it's got a gaping hole, the wooden laths are shattered and you can see the dark opening beneath. The dining table has been cleared of last night's traces—the glasses are gone, the bottle back in the cabinet, the chairs straightened. Only a turned-up corner of the carpet gives us away, hinting at the turmoil that preceded the night—I can still feel it, inside me there's an implosion, like a building demolition.

There are four high stools around the peninsula that divides the kitchen; I choose one and climb up. From a white paper bag comes the buttery smell of croissants, probably the breakfast the girl mentioned, but I can't make it there: I watch the greasy stains widening, my arms motionless. The clock hanging on the wall by the window tells me it's already too late for everything. I think of the café, the customers who will come looking for their coffee; they'll think we've gone under and won't ever come back. I think about the café, then that I want to leave and I can't, that I smell of alcoholic sweat and filthy clothes—that I want to leave and I can't. I think about Giorgia who can't even recognize her own skin, how is that possible?

Appearing through the kitchen window are leaves that have begun to turn yellow, and beyond the leaves an indistinct evergreen; the city does not exist. I focus on the silence now, which is deep, like being in the country. The metro is a few steps away, the Monday traffic—here, instead, a hyperbaric stillness.

I'm afraid to move about, I'd rather just swivel on the stool and look around. The sound of the key in the door catches me like that, contemplating the photos hanging on the far walls.

"Good morning," Mauro says as he walks in.

I watch him toss a newspaper on the sofa and take off his jacket, which ends up crumpled on the stool next to mine.

"Your girlfriend said to wait for you because you didn't have the keys," I say.

He looks at me and smiles knowingly. "Who? Amelia?"

"Yeah, the blonde girl."

"She's my sister. I'm sorry, but it was the only way to make sure you would still be here."

He grabs one of the croissants from the bag and bites into it, then goes to the oversize American fridge and pulls out a carton of milk.

"Listen, don't make that face. Last night too you couldn't wait to get out of here, I had to talk you into going to bed," he adds. "Want some coffee?"

"Sorry, I don't remember," I say. "I'd love some."

"What, don't you like croissants?" He stops midway through a movement and stares at me.

"No no, I like them."

"So eat then."

I obey and put a hand in the bag to take one.

"Did you get some rest?" he asks, tinkering with the coffee machine.

"Yeah."

I didn't dream, something that hadn't happened to me in a long time. Ever since Giorgia was hospitalized I've been dreaming of something. There's one dream in particular, a kind of recurring nightmare: Giorgia and I are spreading clean sheets on the bed, then from her eyes I realize that it's not really her, I understand that the real Giorgia is locked in the closet: when I go to let her out, I find she's dead.

I quash the memory of the dream, and accept the espresso that Mauro offers me. He's shaken off the grubby air of the day before—he's wearing a clean shirt, and he's in a great mood. I reappraise the striking nose, the olive complexion; I notice that we are almost the same height.

"You and your sister don't look alike," I say.

He sits on the other side of the peninsula, nods.

"I took after my mother and Amelia hers," he says. "Do you have brothers or sisters?"

"No, an only child."

"I was an only child myself, too, for a while. Amelia and I met when she was a teenager." He gulps his coffee in one sip. "Now eat though."

Again I obey. I'm not hungry. I am reminded of some of Giorgia's observations about Mauro's peremptory ways: I think she was right, he doesn't seem like someone who leaves room for options. I do what he says so as not to be rude: if he wants me to eat, I'll eat. Even with his eyes lowered, I know he's watching me. Every so often I take a look around, a couple of times I meet his gaze and find him friendly, like yesterday at the clinic. The silence makes me nervous, all the more so when broken by the sound of my chewing.

"I may have found a script," Mauro says, abruptly getting up. "A promising adaptation."

He takes a pot from the cabinet, fills it with water. He turns on the stove, then goes to look for something behind another cabinet door.

"It was last night, you'd been sleeping for a while. I went to look for a text down in the pub and spotted it. It's been here for years and I'd forgotten it."

He waves a package of penne in my direction.

"It was because you were here."

He says it as if it were obvious. Then he offers me a paper napkin to wipe my greasy fingers.

"I'm going to propose it to the company today, I've already made up my mind," he continues, leaning on the marble sink. "I don't believe in coincidences. Giorgia may have told you that I'm somewhat superstitious."

I shake my head, take a few sips of the coffee, now cold.

"We all are, in the theater world," he says. "You though, how are you?"

The conversation's sudden swerve finds me unprepared.

"Fine ..." I reply.

Mauro studies me, arms crossed at his chest—I can see the judgment he is holding back.

"Considering the situation," I add.

"I'm not good at dancing around, you have to excuse me. May I be direct?"

I can tell that his asking me that is really costing him some effort.

"Sure," I say.

I'm thinking about the conversation we had last night. I didn't drink enough to forget—Mauro walking away to the window, looking out at the dark.

"It's clear you're not fine," he says. "Is there anyone helping you? Someone you talk to?"

The water starts to boil. In the time I have, I search for an answer and I know that, since Giorgia was hospitalized, I haven't wanted to think about it. With my parents I had to deal with the subject tersely: a phone call to my father from the hospital—short of breath, the discussion with the nurse: I was not authorized to follow Giorgia into the ward, for them I was nobody. *Pop, Giorgia is ill.* I'd had to explain that illness before I understood it.

Like me, my parents also thought that drugs would cure Giorgia in a reasonable time. Since she was moved to the clinic we've started talking less and less about it—now Giorgia and her illness exist only in reports of my movements, accounts of my days. After the hospital, I no longer wanted them to visit with me at the clinic: I'm terrified of seeing their faces, of hearing them beseech me to move on. I gave my friends vague explanations: severe exhaustion, something acceptable. I minimized contacts to avoid going into painful details. Now it's just me and Giorgia.

Just me and Giorgia, I think, and I realize that Mauro is staring at me: he's waiting.

"It's complicated," I say. "It's a hard thing to understand, I mean, for those who haven't been through it."

"Do you go to some self-help group?"

"No."

"You should consider it. I went to one, when my mother had cancer. It was helpful."

Mauro pulls a plastic container out of the freezer, drops a cube of sauce in a pan, and for a few minutes we watch it melt over the flame.

"What diagnosis did they give her?" he asks then, without looking up.

I recall my first conversations with the medical director. He's the one who monitors Giorgia's condition at the clinic. He visits her twice a week, on Tuesdays and Fridays. When Giorgia was first transferred, the checks were more frequent, the doctor often monitored her reactions during visiting hours. I told him that I was the person who took care of her, that I needed to know.

"Paranoid schizophrenia," I tell Mauro. "But the doctor always says that every diagnosis is reductive. It only serves to give a name to something you don't really know."

"Meaning? The diagnosis is more complex?"

"Yes."

At that moment we both realize that I don't want to continue.

Mauro drains the pasta in the sink, I focus on observing his automatic actions—water drained from the colander, spoon taken from a drawer, penne mixed with the sauce. All without ever raising his head, with the same calm expression on his face. He's not worried, there's no sign of yesterday's nervousness at the door of the clinic—no cigarette, no urgent tone in his voice. He fills a plate, sticks a clean fork in it. The kitchen clock reads half past nine. He comes over and slides the plate towards me on the marble countertop.

"Eat."

I should rebel. Mauro looks at me, not just me but my wrists, the clothes falling off of me. For the last three weeks I've skipped dinners with my parents, replacing Sundays spent at their house with phone calls—I fabricated special open hours at the café on weekends and they didn't probe. At home I'm never hungry, I eat tuna and canned meat chunks out of an instinct for survival. I feel exposed. Mauro doesn't give up.

I eat.

He goes back to telling me about the script, stays until I swallow the last mouthful—"I'm going down to get my stuff and I'll take you home, okay?" he says when I'm done. Alone again, I'm thinking I could use someone to tell me what to do. I'll do it. Anything, I swear. I implore the furnishings, the beam of autumn light.

It takes us an hour to get to my house. I tried to persuade Mauro to drop me off at the nearest metro stop, but he was adamant. When we arrive, he insists on parking in front of the gate.

"It's a nice area," he says, studying the surroundings through the windshield.

"Yeah, it's not bad."

I see him looking down towards the end of the street, where you can see the supermarket sign.

"So, your number?" he says, taking his cell phone out of his pocket.

I give it to him.

"Do you have someone who can help you with the car?"

I'd forgotten all about it. "I think so," I reply, already starting to estimate the unexpected expense.

"I know someone, if you want. He's a friend, he can

take it where it needs to go."

Before I have a chance to say anything, Mauro has already texted me his friend's number. "If you don't find anyone else, call him. Tell him I sent you."

"Thanks for everything," I say.

"Don't mention it."

I don't know what else to add, saying goodbye to Mauro is strange again, like running into him in Giorgia's room. I've already opened the car door when he grabs my arm.

"What time tomorrow?" he says.

I don't understand, I'm a little slow from the hangover.

"Visiting hours. I'll drive you to see Giorgia if you like."

"From five to seven ... But you don't have to, I can take the bus."

"I'll come pick you up at half past four, okay? I can't make it any earlier, I have a class."

"All right ..."

"Perfect, see you tomorrow."

He releases his hold, lets me go. Before he drives off, he waves out the window. I watch the Alfa until it disappears around the corner.

The house is cold. Once inside, the darkness bothers me. Not taking off my shoes, I raise the shutters in all the rooms and measure the dust accumulated on the surfaces, on the crumpled sheets. I undress in the bathroom, and gather up my clothes and bed linens in a heap. Before showering, I brush my teeth. I can't avoid being ambushed by my reflection. I see myself pale and skinny; shadowy hollows mark my chest, the muscles have lost their tone. My beard has grown into a scruffy reddish patch extending down to my throat. The scar on my cheekbone has deepened, the edges sunk in a dark recess. This is the man Mauro met, the same man who collapsed, drunk, in his bed: now his altruistic impulse is the response to a cry for help. For the first time in months, I see myself through a stranger's eyes and worry about my condition.

Giorgia had also lost weight before the performance. Under the hot water, in the shower, I think of her body. Sensations return to my fingertips, especially after the visits: they lie just below the recent tactile memory, hidden in the deep epidermal layers; not touching her through a sheet, but the ghost of her warm skin as my hands run up her ribcage. Giorgia's thin body is here with me—and the next moment it's been washed away, sucked back down the drain.

Now clean, I'm thinking I should fumigate this place, instead I collapse, still damp, on the bed. I don't even have the energy to jack off, and I'd want to: I fall asleep imagining Giorgia.

CHAPTER TWO

PHANTOM LIMB

Giorgia liked the café. Before it became my parents' café, it had been a small, abandoned slaughterhouse. My parents had invested in the business during the expansion period of the Città Studi district. My father had wanted to keep the shiny white tiles, so they had only bought furniture and equipment and installed a tiny bathroom in back, which soon became noncompliant: now customers who come in just to piss have to make a pilgrimage to the door of the neighboring condo.

I grew up in here.

My earliest memories are of sounds: the splutter of the steam wand that froths the milk, the metallic clatter of the portafilters in the dispenser units, the voices at a very high volume, swelling and incomprehensible.

Around the age of five, the visual catalogue takes over—my mother who, before closing, wipes the customers' fingerprints off every surface, flattening herself against the wall like a gecko and studying the reflections of light on the tiles; my father who holds me by the hand as he secures the shutter: *Just think, at one time they butchered animals here.*

Until middle school, when I was allowed a copy of the house keys, the last table at the back was my room, my play area, and my homework desk. When she came to see me, Giorgia would sit at that same table: once she said that the view from there is complete, you can see the orchestra, the stage, and the wings—that's just what she said, *orchestra, stage, wings,* at a time when those words had no other meaning but an indifferent, innocuous one.

I sent Mauro a message with the café's address, telling him that he would not find me at home. It's been almost six hours: he hasn't answered. Since then there was a breakfast eaten on the bus, only a few customers, a question about yesterday's closure—I made up a story about an unexpected plumbing repair. The tenant of the building across the way, who is my only regular, kept me company until two o'clock. We ate two packaged sandwiches together, him sitting at his table, me standing behind the counter. The conversation I had with him was the most relaxing moment of the day: a sporadic exchange of mechanical responses, his comments on something in the paper, my replies. We always say the same things, except for special events in the Cup calendar. At three o'clock my mother called, worried about yesterday's silence. Since my father had the heart attack, she's been trying to have me fill in and cover his primary functions: now it is my responsibility to comfort her, reassure her about the debts, credibly deny her dire predictions—when she says something negative about the receipts and I don't offer her a more rosy perspective, she brings up the subject of my pointless studies again, as if to say that if I can't make her feel good, we'll feel bad together.

The bell over the door tinkles and catches me checking the hourly bus schedule. The customer is one of the bathroom crowd, I can tell from the way he scans around: when he spots the door at the back his eyes light up. "An espresso, thanks," he says, wiping his sweaty forehead with his shirt sleeve. He doesn't have the nerve to ask right away and fidgets in place, drumming his fingers on the countertop, squinting at the neon-lit sandwiches in the fridge.

The bell jingles again as I'm grinding the coffee. A dark head of hair appears behind the man: with surprise I recognize Mauro and say hello as he approaches. The customer barely notices. His impatience irritates me.

"Listen," I say, handing him the keys. "I'll make the coffee afterward. The bathroom is at number 27: outside, first door on the right, second door to the left under the staircase."

The man doesn't turn a hair: he grabs the keys, thanks me, and dashes to the door.

"You don't clean the bathroom, do you?" says Mauro.

He has an odd, asymmetrical smile: he grins with the corners of his mouth turned down.

"No, thank God," I say. "I thought you hadn't gotten my message."

"Yeah, I'm sorry, I had a hellish morning."

"No problem. Coffee?"

"Yeah, thanks."

Mauro looks around, observes the surroundings as if he were taking notes.

"Is it yours?" he asks, as I fill his cup.

"For now it's in my parents' names," I reply. "Have a seat."

He thanks me with a nod. I watch him choose a table and for a moment I'm afraid he'll go and sit at the last one in back; I feel a foolish relief when he sits at one in front of me. He's exhausted again, like he was two days ago at the clinic; unshaven, wearing the same shirt as yesterday. I look at myself in the chrome surface of the espresso machine: I'm glad to find my face clean-shaven.

"And do you like it?"

"It's not bad" I say, and I don't know if we're talking about the work or the place. "Where do you work?"

"Here and there," he says. "I teach acting classes at the Civic Schools, at a few institutions, and occasionally I do public-speaking workshops for inept Brianza executives. I get by."

The bathroom customer returns, his face dry and relaxed. He hands back my keys, then keeps his promise of an espresso. The whole time he's talking to me—a quick chat about the construction of the new metro—Mauro scrutinizes him. When we're alone again, Mauro comes over to the counter and returns the empty cup.

"How long before we can go?" he asks, glancing at the clock hanging behind me.

"A quarter of an hour to closing."

He nods and sits down again.

"You see a lot of people," he says. "You don't get bored."

"Yeah, it's pretty busy."

That's not true, but I don't want to appear pathetic. I don't want to reinforce the idea he might have formed of me.

"Have you always worked here?"

"No. I started here a couple of years ago."

"And before?"

I know his questions are innocent. The only reason I

feel cornered is that these kinds of conversations are always stressful for me. I haven't yet resigned myself to the idea of this job. There hasn't been a day, these past two years, when I haven't wanted to say the hell with it all. If I didn't quit, it was only because of Giorgia, to allow us a chance to build the bare minimum of a life together. I'm still only doing it for her.

"I worked at a press office, wrote for a local newspaper … Then my father got sick, my parents couldn't make it here alone anymore."

Mauro's cell phone rings. He apologizes, takes it from his pocket and stares at the screen interminably, so long that I think it will stop ringing before he answers it—instead, when he takes the call, he finds the caller still waiting.

"I thought I told you not to call me again"—the tone is calm, but I feel embarrassed. I start emptying the dishwasher. "Yes, Lara, I'm sure. And you said it was fine. It's the new rule, remember?" I burn my fingers on a hot cup and suppress a groan. "Yes, it's the new rule: you don't call me and we don't see each other more than once a week. I just don't understand what's not clear to you." I start drying the glasses, pretending to study the calendar: it's still turned to last May. The fourteenth is a dark day like the others, a Friday identical to the rest. "Lara, let's not start this again." I hear Mauro get up from his chair abruptly, then I see him go outside. He takes a cigarette out of the packet, pats his pants a while with no results. I watch him stop two passersby, the phone still at his ear. When a girl gives him a light, he accords her a completely different smile than the one he offers me: canonical, not lopsided. He's not upset about the conversation, he stands there and doesn't talk much. Then he turns without warning and catches me staring at him through the window. I lower my head immediately, and busy myself closing the cash-box.

Mauro comes back a few minutes later, as if nothing had happened. He helps me lower the faulty shutter. On the way to the street where he parked, he tells me about the acting classes for beginners that will start this week, and asks if I'd like to attend one. I think of Giorgia, and tell him that these things aren't for me: I don't like having people's eyes on me, being the center of attention.

"It's a common belief and, as such, shallow," says Mauro, when we get into the car. He tosses two scripts and a thin book at me, and sticks another cigarette in his mouth without lighting it. "This conviction that the actor is some kind of brash egomaniac is so sim-plistic it gives me a headache."

"I didn't mean ..."

"*An actor. Someone who wants to be applauded,*" he per-sists. "Sorry, it's just that, for me, defending this pro-fession is a mission. I work at it all day, with actors, with aspiring performers. Don't get me wrong: proba-bly some of them start out with a kind of self-delusion, telling themselves they want to be admired. That's be-cause preconceptions about the figure of the actor are widespread and stubbornly promoted by the media."

"I don't mean that all actors are egocentrics," I man-age to reply, while we're stopped at the traffic light. "I only said I don't like being the center of attention."

Mauro looks at me: he has a friendly expression, he's not really bothered by my judgment. Maybe he's teas-ing me.

"Let me finish what I was saying," he says, shifting into first again. "It's very important that you understand, because of Giorgia as well: I think it's funda-mental."

Mentioning her name, Mauro upends the meaning of the conversation.

"Think of her: has she ever given you the impression that she is someone who likes to be the center of atten-tion?"

"No."

"I agree. Of anyone I've ever known, Giorgia is one of those least interested in attracting others' attention. You never saw her fishing for a look or a compliment, wanting someone's admiration. She's always been atypical that way. After all, we all want someone to look at us and say 'bravo,' don't we? We all give in to that temptation, sooner or later."

"She wasn't like that," I confirm.

"No. She *isn't* like that," Mauro repeats. "And she's the most promising performer I've worked with. The most talented, in my opinion, and not only in my opinion. That's not the point. Like Giorgia, an actor worthy of the name wants to be applauded, we agree, but not as himself. An authentic performer wants the audience to recognize his ability to efface his identity. He wants everyone to remind him how good he is at being some-one else and offer him flowers in return. This makes him one of the most unfortunate creatures on earth. Have you ever pretended to be something you're not?"

I try to absorb his words; I haven't had such an in-tense conversation in months. Since I've been alone, I've become used to silence: I feel slow and empty tak-ing part in the discussion.

"How do you mean?" I ask.

"We all do it: say we like one thing instead of another, pretend to be happy when we're crushed, and so on.

Haven't you ever done it?"

"Sure. I think it must be … natural?"

"You're right. It's natural. It's a matter of survival: appropriate smiles, mediated reactions, and other more subtle forms of acting assure us a place in the world, at all levels. We instinctively enact this unstructured performance—mind you I'm not referring to lying with intent: I'm talking about automatic mimesis, the little necessary deceptions."

"I follow you."

"Good," says Mauro, taking the cigarette out of his mouth and wedging it behind his ear. "So then, we instinctively act. The actor, on the other hand, when he assumes another identity, is aware of it and keeps at it until he disappears. Here's the hitch: who in his right mind would efface himself? We all do it constantly, of course, but providing we aren't aware of it. Someone more clever than me said that the actor is an actor if he likes himself when he's acting. I say the actor is an actor if he likes himself *only* when he's acting. *Only* when he is someone else."

We turn onto the ring road at the hour when the sun goes down and reflects treacherously on the glass. Fiddling with the corners of the scripts on my lap, I have a question on the tip of my tongue but I can't manage to get it out. Mauro turns on the radio, a neutral background.

"What about directors?"

I don't know if I'm trying to provoke him: after all, he hasn't said anything irritating. But those are the only words that come out of my mouth.

He laughs briefly.

"Come on, it's obvious," he says. "Directors want to be God."

Then he turns up the volume of the music and puts an end to the conversation.

Giorgia is waiting for us at the clinic, crystallized in the usual position. They changed her pajamas: plump purplish chicks scamper along her arms, tucking their beaks under the bedspread that circles her waist. Mauro brought the book with him. Now he's leaning against the windowsill, reading. On the way up he asked me what I know about Shakespeare and I rattled off a couple of things I'd learned in an English lit class, a lifetime ago. I admitted however that I don't remember anything about *Twelfth Night*, the play he's reading to Giorgia. He summarized the plot for me, the theme of mistaken identity, and again I felt that question crash over me.

I look at Giorgia but she doesn't look at me, or at Mauro. I wonder if or how I could not have seen it. Giorgia didn't want to be someone else. Giorgia was happy with me. Not an electrifying happiness, not a fleeting spark: hers was the kind of happiness that I respect more, even and steady, constant. I never had the impression that she wanted to escape from an enclosure, that she felt penned in.

Mauro reads: "*Olivia*: Stay: I prithee, tell me what thou thinkest of me. *Viola*: That you do think you are not what you are. *Olivia*: If I think so, I think the same of you. *Viola*: Then think you right: I am not what I am." The sound of a page being turned. "*Olivia*: I would you were as I would have you be! *Viola*: Would it be better, madam, than I am?"

The difference in the tone of his voice is minimal but sufficient to distinguish the two characters. I wish he weren't here with me. His presence bothers me, I feel guilty sitting here watching Giorgia motionless as time passes by in a recovery that stretches on and on. For four months we've been relieved of the responsibility of living. In the clinic everything is temporary, the stay here an interim condition on its way to being resolved; even during the first month, every day it seemed that Giorgia would be discharged the following week. Now Mauro's involvement gives substance to the time that has passed, which suddenly seems infinite and incomprehensible, forcing me to face myself in a mirror and relive the disastrous slope of events. It all happened, it's all real, and if the course does not deviate, it will continue to be real forever. I can accept what I've seen—that she has lost her sanity, that a horrific illness has emerged in the vessel I love—but only within the limits of a transition. I need to know that we are moving towards a partial restoration of normality, and no one can assure me of it. No one.

Mauro goes on reading. My gaze slowly inches up Giorgia's wrist that swims in the wide mouth of her sleeve; I continue resolutely to her shoulder, along the childish pajamas. I cross the barrier of the neck, and move past the cartilage of an ear lobe: I remember her folding it over with two fingers, telling me that she felt made of rubber. I'm almost certain it was during one of the unfiltered conversations from the early days, the phase when we didn't talk to understand each other but to accumulate data: the intensity of the voice, its pitch, the sound compatibility. I'm afraid to find signs of what's happening on her skin, the blind alley of a new wrinkle or the first gray hair. I search deeply into her eyes; it's agonizing to think of them when they were still alive and find them now dead. I feel like reaching out and messing up her hair, tugging at it until it grows as long as it used to be, but I can't overdo the touching, they instructed me: best not provoke a reaction. So I contemplate her intact, unchanged on the outside and uprooted from the inside; I imagine her growing old in this bed.

"I'll leave you alone."

Mauro's voice doesn't completely rouse me. I feel him touching my shoulder, then walking away down the corridor.

Once silence has returned, I wish he hadn't left. I get up from my chair, and put a few steps between me and Giorgia. In the garden in back are two patients accompanied by nurses; a third one in a wheelchair is parked near the fountain. Their eyes are all fixed on inanimate objects: the concrete step of the fountain's basin, the acrylic collar of a robe, the base of a linden tree. They move slowly, taking small steps, as if gravity were suspended. I'd like to open the window, let in some fresh air, but the glass is thick, the unbreakable kind, and there are no cranks.

All of a sudden it's impossible for me to stay here, yet I can't move. I am a prisoner in the corner of the room, like Giorgia in her bed. I can hear her breathing, I see her chest rising and falling, smoothing out the folds in the sheets. She is organically alive, I acknowledge that: my phantom limb that keeps on moving. We had built our own version of reality together and the two of us kept it standing, with enormous effort. Now that we have an audience, it's all starting to collapse.

I think of tearing the bed apart, grabbing Giorgia, and taking her away from here. And even if she screams, even if she bites my hands and wants to scratch out my eyes, I'll tie her up in a safe place until the storm is over. A place far away from this limbo. As I fantasize about our violent escape, Giorgia keeps breathing in and out, and I hear her but I can't find her; I go looking for her outside the room, I very carefully search the deserted visitors' bathroom, and my hunt ends in the third desperate crying jag this month.

I don't wait long enough for the signs of congestion to clear. When I join Mauro in the car my eyes still look peculiar, swollen. He pretends not to notice and doesn't say a single word; instead he immediately starts the car and screeches out of the driveway in reverse as if we were in pursuit. When I think he's going to slow down, I see him exceed the speed limit. Five minutes later he races onto the highway doing over 80 mph. I try to make eye contact but he ignores me, driving stone-faced. I am still debilitated by my crisis in the bathroom and I can't manage to formulate a coherent protest, so I give up and brace myself in the seat. I'm about to reason that I don't care if we die, then he passes two cars not to miss our exit. I cling to my seatbelt and close my eyes at the horn blast from a truck we're cutting off. In response to my swearing, Mauro turns the radio on at full volume.

As we approach the first stoplight, I'm no longer so sure he'll slow down. He does, but we still finish our wild race dangerously close to the bumper of a Fiat Multipla. He turns to look at me, remarkably calm, and for a few seconds we stare at one another.

"How do you feel?" he asks.

"Do you mind telling me what got into you?"

Mauro relaxes his shoulders against the seat as we start up again.

"We needed it," he replies. "How do you feel?"

The adrenaline has swept it all away, but I don't tell

him that. He lowers the music and smiles, satisfied. "We needed it," he repeats.

We remain silent the rest of the way and I'm too drained to consider the possibility of a precarious state of mind—it would be an endless nightmare, a dimension governed by madness. He drives us to our destination with complete composure.

"We have to talk," he says, when we're in front of my house. "Do you mind if we take a little walk?"

Not waiting for my answer, he gets out of the car before me, and starts walking down the sidewalk without me. When I follow him, he triggers the car's locking mechanism.

The days are getting shorter, a subtle chill can be felt, but all the same the setting sun—suspended in a low ceiling crossed by a jet's vapor trail—is as red as on a summer evening. As far as the first corner of the barracks Mauro doesn't speak. I wait for him to light a cigarette, but he doesn't meet my expectation. We continue walking beside the yellow wall. Across the street the huge neon sign of the supermarket where Giorgia used to work casts its ugly light on us.

"This situation is not healthy," Mauro says finally.

The opening does not come as a surprise. As though it's all I've been expecting since Sunday: that he would pull out; that I would be left alone again.

"I realize that, you're not obligated. Thank you for being with me these last couple of days," I tell him.

He stops in the middle of the sidewalk, near the bus stop. We're overrun by a flood of passengers exiting the #54.

"Hey, no, Filippo!" he says, spreading his arms. "That's too much!"

We attract curious looks from some passersby.

"Excuse me?"

The meaning of his outburst escapes me, I'm bushed. I'm thinking of turning around and walking away, but Mauro takes a step towards me, grabs me under the arm, and drags me with him. It's almost worse than the car ride.

"There's a limit to everything," he says. "I didn't have the courage to come and see Giorgia in the hospital, I show up after four months. You shouldn't tell me everything's fine and thank me. You should be furious at me! Nail me to the wall, kick me!"

He stares at me, eyes blazing, like a madman. He waits for some reaction from me, but before I can respond, the air goes out of him with a sigh, and he shakes his head. He searches for a cigarette in his pockets and asks a passerby for a light.

"I'm her friend and her mentor," he says, after the first drag. "Being a mentor as I was to Giorgia, for so long ... my negligence is unforgivable."

He trails off. I focus on what he said, looking for some rage, but no matter how hard I try, I can't even find a vague hint of irritation in me. Since the day of the opening, I haven't had intense feelings about anything other than Giorgia. I feel as if I've been soaking in a tub: under the surface everything is blurry, muted.

"I think it's difficult," I say, and Mauro raises his head. "You don't know what to say, what to do ... And besides, you came to the hospital, didn't you? I was there too, remember?"

He rubs a hand over his face, and when he looks at me again, his eyebrows are wild. It's the first time I've found him ridiculous.

"I couldn't even look at her. I walked into the room and all I saw were her feet," he says. "I've spent this time wondering how I could not have noticed anything. Then I decide to come back; I find her in that bed, and you, falling apart. You should despise me."

"I'm not falling apart," I try to say, but the words die in my mouth.

"Don't you have any friends who can be with you?"

"It's complicated." I force myself to go further. "They didn't know Giorgia well, before."

"But you can't deal with this situation on your own either," Mauro says. "Did I mention self-help groups?"

"Yeah. But I'm not going there only to hear about other people's vegetable cases. Just the thought ..."

This is how the dike collapses, I think: Mauro breaks through the protective wall telling me about Giorgia's feet in the hospital, and I keep picturing him entering the room, I keep hearing his voice telling me he can't look at her. I understand what he's talking about, he understands what I'm talking about. The confession unfolds in an incoherent account of the nightmare. I tell him about the first rounds of treatment, when they tried to reduce the dosages of her medication and that "thing" in her emerged in violent outbreaks, glass stuck in the palms of her hands, blood smeared on her face and on the walls; I tell him about the screams from the hallucinations, and when she tried to burrow into the nurses' bodies to seek refuge. I tell him that to keep the beast dormant it is necessary to subject Giorgia as well, to nearly complete sedation, very close to a deep sleep.

I tell him about my hopes, my ignorance, my despair, I tell him that from some point on I stopped feeling anything, as if my sensitive surface had been scarred. Deep inside I go on suffering—I would like to let myself go completely, of course; I'm still trying, of course.

Mauro listens like someone whose diagnosis is being confirmed: he encourages me to continue when I get mired in the details, and follows the account of the four most devastating months of my life. When I'm done I have no answers, Giorgia is still there in her bed, but I feel released from the burden of lying: there is no need to apply any filters, dilute the truth. He knows what Giorgia was before, he remembers her, like me. I'm not afraid he might try to erase her.

"I just want to get her out of there", I say, realizing that we have almost completed the rounds of the barracks' perimeter.

"It's a private clinic, right? Who's paying?" Mauro asks.

"Yes, it's private. Giorgia's aunt is paying, but she's never been seen there. She sent her lawyer to the hospital, and then to the clinic to make sure everything was in order."

The only hint of contempt I feel is for this stranger. Giorgia had told me very little about her, only that she had been placed in her aunt's care, and that later there had been a parting of ways due to personal differences. The fact that someone could decide to abandon an orphaned girl had struck me at the time. I had formed a terrible impression of her aunt, then I'd completely forgotten her: after those brief mentions, Giorgia had not returned to the subject.

"Who chose the clinic?"

Mauro winds a strand of hair, continues on the track. "Her aunt. She's Giorgia's legal guardian. The lawyer showed up with the signed papers, I was only informed because he took pity on me."

The lawyer had introduced himself as a representative of Mariella Brentani as I was straightening out

Giorgia's bedlinens in her hospital room. Right after she was hospitalized I had searched through her things for a trace of a phone number or an address for her aunt, to tell her what was happening. My search had turned up nothing.

"How did the aunt know that Giorgia was hospitalized?"

Mauro and I slow up when we're in sight of his car.

"I have no idea. I think the police must have reported something because of TSO requirements. It didn't take the lawyer long to get there, though."

The man, gray haired and in his fifties, had been informed of the nature of my relationship with Giorgia. He told me that Ms. Brentani would handle the matter from a distance. He showed me the papers signed by the judge, one after the other; I read them, trying to understand. As her legal guardian, Giorgia's aunt had the right to decide on any measures concerning her niece: in less than forty-eight hours ownership of the person I love had been transferred to someone I had never set eyes on.

The second time the lawyer returned, he informed me that Giorgia would be transferred to a private facility. He asked to see my documents, collected my data, then said I had been granted permission to visit her as and when I wanted.

"We should talk to her," Mauro says.

"I've tried. I've looked everywhere for her aunt's name: there's not a scrap of an address anywhere. I also tried to call the lawyer's office, no one ever answered."

"But I know where she lives."

For a moment I think I heard wrong.

"What?"

"I know where Giorgia's aunt lives."

Mauro is as confused by my reaction as I am by his words.

"When I met Giorgia, she was still living at her aunt's."

"I didn't know that."

"We could give it a try, show up there and see what happens."

Mauro takes the car keys out of his pocket.

"But what's the point?" I ask.

"To understand things a little better, make sure all avenues have been considered: other medical opinions, facilities that are more recovery-oriented."

I'm of two minds. Mauro's suggestion offers me the first real hope in months, however tenuous. At the same time, the fact that he's the one proposing it irritates me. I feel jealous, then immediately ashamed.

"Great idea," I say.

"Let me think of a good time," he says, opening the car door. "I only caught a glimpse of her aunt a few times. I want to avoid the possibility of her sending us away."

"You think she might?"

"Oh, yeah. I think she might," Mauro smiles knowingly. "Okay, I'm going."

He gets in the car, with one leg still on the sidewalk.

"Oh, listen, I noticed your car still at the clinic and I called my friend. He'll bring it back to you here tomorrow afternoon."

"Yeah, I didn't have time ... Thanks. Thanks for everything."

"No problem. I'll call you tomorrow to keep you posted."

He shuts the door, and I watch him through the window a moment, before stepping away: in his profile I see the same exhaustion that overlays my reflection. I walk off and don't see him leave, but I sense when he's gone. I head back to my isolation cell, yet I move as if I weren't alone, as if a piece of my phantom limb has been restored.

Mauro decides on Sunday morning. We meet early, at the Cadorna metro station. I spot him in the unusually silent tunnel connecting the metro lines: he's studying a huge billboard very closely, as if to assess the grain of the poster. Today he's wearing a blue cotton scarf around his neck, and during the train trip he keeps tossing the ends over his shoulders. He's dressed more meticulously than usual, the shirt doesn't have a single wrinkle. I too tried to make myself more presentable compared to the standard of the recent period—"These are well-to-do people," Mauro had said on the phone when we arranged to meet. "Let's try to make a good impression."

Well-to-do people. I realized that I hadn't considered the possibility that Giorgia came from a monied family. She never mentioned any wealth: when I met her, she was juggling expenses, tuition fees, and temporary jobs—serving at tables Friday through Sunday nights, cleaning stairs on Mondays and Thursdays, plus putting in a few hours as an intern in a downtown office. I remember her hurriedly changing clothes between one activity and another, skipping classes to pay bills: in the end she had given up on a degree.

Giorgia's aunt lives in the heart of the Brera district, on a side street off Via Pontaccio. We pass an antique market that's being set up, go halfway down the walkway paralleling it.

"It should be nearby ..." Mauro says, checking the numbers on the doors.

He stops in front of a double-doored archway of dark-green wood and studies the brass intercom panel: "It's here." He buzzes, straightens his hair, considers his reflection in the brass plate. I copy him, check my belt, stare at my shoes: seeing them with the eyes of a stranger, I find them scruffy.

"Who is it?" a youthful voice says, coming from the speaker with a background sputter.

"Good morning, I'm Mauro Franzese, a friend of Giorgia. I don't know if Ms. Mariella remembers me. I'd like to speak to her, if possible."

A sequence of crackles in response.

"Just a moment."

The communication breaks off. Mauro looks at me and nods soberly, rubs his palms together slowly, then stands there contemplating the door. He's assessing our chances or maybe revisiting a memory that I'm not part of. Ever since he told me he'd met Giorgia's aunt, I can't help but picture the moment of that encounter. I see him introducing himself with a symmetrical smile, I see Giorgia radiant as she has never been; then, in my fabrication, they remain alone in an indistinct space and Mauro caresses Giorgia, slowly stroking her cheek. The image has come back to me intermittently in the last few days, threatening to go further, and I've checked it, blocking it and setting it aside. I zoomed in on the most important thing, which is to get Giorgia out of that clinic.

"Please come up."

The voice cuts as abruptly as it appeared, the door opens with a click.

Mauro makes his way up the flight of stairs. In the silence, the sound of a reinforced door turning on its hinges can be heard. We reach the dimly lit third floor without breaking the stillness. I wipe my sweaty palms on my pants, discreetly, and the dark-skinned girl in the doorway doesn't notice as she welcomes us with a courteous smile. She's wearing a white shirt and black pants, a different uniform than I expected. She doesn't look like a housekeeper.

"Good morning," she says.

"Good morning, I'm Mauro, this is Filippo. Is the lady at home?"

"She's awaiting you." The tone of voice is low but the language is unmarked, with no inflections. "This way."

The girl steps aside as we go past her and stop to wait on the soft carpet. The entry hall is poorly illuminated and there's no time to study the surroundings. "Mariella is in the conservatory." We let her lead us into the living area where the natural light filtering in from the balconies is reflected on the pale parquet. The lines of the furniture cast square shadows on the surfaces—a long blue sofa with a low back, the angled slash of a sharp-edged dining table, four empty chairs, a bookcase lining the back wall; there's a painting where there should be a TV: a black square on a white background.

The conservatory occupies the side of the south-facing apartment; the sun's blades slant through the glass and disintegrate in the watery vapor of an atomizer. A woman is bent over the profile of an orchid. The girl steps back, motions for us to go in. When we walk through the door, Giorgia's aunt turns around unhurriedly. She looks a lot like Giorgia, the same dark hair gathered in a long braid, the same sad tilt to the eyes, and something similar about the proportions of the thin body. It's Giorgia as she might look around the age of sixty, and for a moment my courage fails, I avert my eyes.

"Good morning" she says, in a soft, flat voice. "How are you?"

I turn back to them, as Mauro responds with a measured smile.

"Very well," he says. "This is Filippo, Giorgia's boyfriend."

I go through an automatic procedure: I take two steps, hold out my hand and she shakes it briefly. "Pleased to meet you." She studies me a moment, the next instant she's looking elsewhere. She sets the atomizer on the wooden shelf that runs along the conservatory's entire perimeter, filled with small plants, orange flowers with pointy tips, the rounded heads of cacti.

"Would you like to sit down?" she asks politely, pointing to a wicker sofa to her left, wedged between the pots of two large ficuses.

We both thank her and take a seat.

"Excuse me, I'll go have Ambica make us some coffee."

We watch her walk away, closing the glass door behind her. From here it's impossible to see inside: the reflected light blinds us to the interior of the house. I sit sedately amid the cushions, and start to feel hot. I think about the courteous welcome, then about Giorgia who preferred to clean stairs rather than ask this woman for financial help, and again the questions overwhelm me. I feel like I'm swimming against the current, always stuck in the same place, at a point where I can't explain any of what's happening to me.

Mauro studies the surroundings and, to distract myself, I study him. He keeps changing his perspective, moving his head, leaning forward slightly to examine the wicker armchair in front of us; he stretches his legs out in front of him until his knees bump the wooden table between our seats and that of the invisible guest. He's sizing things up. When he realizes I'm staring at him, he gives me a questioning look. We're interrupted by the return of Giorgia's aunt. The girl who showed us in follows her with a tray.

She sets the tray on the coffee table and withdraws without making a sound.

"Please, serve yourselves," Giorgia's aunt says when we are alone again.

I'm about to decline the offer, but Mauro precedes me and fills two small cups with espresso from the Moka.

"Thank you for letting us come up," he says, offering me a porcelain handle. "I would have liked to notify you of the visit, but I wasn't able to find your number."

The woman does not respond, she simply smooths the folds of the dark vestment she's wearing, a kind of long, loose garment in raw cotton that gives her a monastic air.

"Are you still directing?" she asks then, chin resting on her hand.

"Yes, between glitches and disasters of various kinds," Mauro replies.

"When was the last time you were here?"

"Five years ago I think, before Giorgia moved."

"I remember, you know? That day you were studying your part in the living room. Giorgia was furious."

The two deep creases on either side of her mouth give way as she smiles.

"Yes, my fault, as usual."

Mauro takes a sip of coffee, the attention moves to me.

"And you? How long have you been together, you and Giorgia?"

"Three years," I say.

She's not smiling anymore now, she looks at me coldly.

"How is she?" she asks.

I lower my eyes, then I meet her gaze again in a surge of courage.

"Better," I say.

"Don't worry, I know what we're talking about," she says, suddenly drained. "I've read the hospital reports, the breakdown was very severe."

"The first two months were difficult."

"Did you know that Giorgia was ill?" Giorgia's aunt turns to look at Mauro, "And you? Did you know?"

We've come to the fated moment and I panic at the idea of the truth that awaits me here. I think of Giorgia apologizing before going onstage, of all the justifications I came up with to put that memory behind me, the many times I told myself that I had imagined it. I think about the shadow that had come over Mauro as soon as I'd confessed those words to him; the fear, in him too, of something that we could have foreseen or prevented, something that, had we known ...

"No," Mauro says.

"No," I repeat after him.

The woman nods, leans back in the armchair.

"And what version of the truth did she tell you?" she asks. "What do you know about her past?"

I shuffle back quickly. Giorgia had told me about a car accident her parents had had returning from a vacation in Liguria: both had been killed instantly. She, having stayed home with her aunt, had survived them. We talked about it in the early days of getting to know each other, when any and all topics were safe. I reacted awkwardly, but as I was thinking about what to say, Giorgia in fact smiled serenely, saying that almost thirty years had passed, and that hers had been an atypical but happy childhood: she had been cared for, had grown up protected, whereas the world was full of orphans who were less fortunate. Over time, the fact that she had been orphaned no longer fazed me. I had searched for signs of grief in her and I hadn't found any. So the bereavement had lost its magnitude, slowly fading into the background. Now I think about the absence of details, about the photos that Giorgia said she'd left at her aunt's house ... I still don't know the truth and I wonder how I could have believed her, why I hadn't persisted and pressured her. But to find out what? What information?

"May I help you out?" asks Giorgia's aunt. "Is it the story about the accident?"

Inside me everything goes still. I nod.

"I'm sorry, I've always urged her to be transparent, I've always believed it was the safest way," she says. "Giorgia's parents did not die in an accident."

I'd like to put a stop to this conversation, but I'm turned to stone. I want to ask this strange woman to leave my reality intact and I can't, I'm a captive.

"My sister committed suicide when Giorgia was five years old. Her father abandoned her when she was seven, and I've been taking care of her ever since. For as long as she let me, that is."

* * *

Mauro and I have a tacit rule: during our visits, he only stays for the first thirty minutes. He reads the whole time, and he never approaches Giorgia's bed, sometimes he doesn't even look at her. I see him walk in with his eyes fixed on the pages, looking for the place he already knows. I think it's his way of protecting his recollection of her.

Since the day we met with Giorgia's aunt, whenever Mauro leaves the room, I adopt the opposite technique. I stare at Giorgia persistently, I subject her body to exhausting interrogations and I keep telling myself the truth, breaking it up into small doses. I return to the house where she grew up, to the stranger who looked after her, I listen to her tell me about Giorgia's life, which I know nothing about.

I imagine Giorgia's mother the way she looked in the photograph I was shown, her hair a dark cascade down her back: it is 1982 and her name is Milena. Milena's illness has ups and downs. Milena refuses ongoing therapies because they slow her down and she, instead, needs to be quick: she wants to graduate in architecture before Giorgia is born. The belly and the father are not visible in the photo: "He studied philosophy, they were members of the same collective. He wasn't a bad man, but he was utterly unprepared. He really thought he could make it, with Milena. We thought so too." After Giorgia's birth, Milena's illness worsened; the family managed to persuade her to start a new course of treatment.

For the first two years Milena was unable to look after the child: "She suffered a great deal from the fact that she was unable to raise her as she would have liked." When Milena's condition improved, she decided to go and live with Giorgia's father: "We consented only on condition that they find a place to live near my parents' house. We tried to be there as much as possible." When Milena had a serious relapse, Giorgia's father opposed hospitalization. "We should have tried an interdiction. We didn't have the courage. We always thought that respecting Milena was more important than anything else. The mere idea of having to appeal to a court to gain control of her life terrified my parents."

What do you remember? I'd like to ask Giorgia. Her aunt said that when it happened, Giorgia and her mother were alone in the house: "He should have been there, home with them; we had shifts." They found the girl sitting in front of the bathroom door. It was already too late for Milena.

There should be signs somewhere on Giorgia's body: a scar like the one I have on my cheekbone, some indication of a door that closed forever, of her father who disappeared and never returned. Yesterday I succumbed to temptation. The irrational instinct to examine her came over me. I waited for it to become quiet, for the nurses' change of shift. I turned down the quilt, undid her buttons one by one while she went on staring out the window, as if to tell me *hurry up, quick, I'll pretend I don't see.* I found no wounds, the skin on her chest, around her breasts, and on her belly is unmarked. There is no sign of the tragedy between her legs, along her thighs. I persisted, down to the soles of her feet. Afterwards I dressed her again slowly, one bit at a time.

Giorgia is damaged on the inside. She hid the truth deep within, and the illness as well. Her aunt said that the first diagnosis came around the age of fifteen: her heredity had exposed her, perhaps doomed her. Over time, Giorgia learned to conceal it, she discovered drugs, the doses, the effects. Like Milena, she began to oppose ongoing therapies.

"She pretended to follow the regimen, then she put the pills in her pockets. She had her own personal reserve: she took what she needed to get through the worst moments. She said the drugs didn't allow her to function properly. Until she turned eighteen, it was a battle." After telling us about the grueling struggles she'd faced to enable Giorgia to live a normal life, her aunt sagged in her armchair.

Once she was no longer a minor, Giorgia had claimed her right to decide for herself. Her aunt was excluded from her medical life: "She threatened to leave home if I tried to interfere." The balance was precarious, however, the resistance difficult. "I attempted the impossible. She left anyway." In the years away from home Giorgia kept the promise of a phone call a month, to report the state of her condition. Other than that, no other concession.

And so Giorgia had constructed her second world, in which she pretended to be well. She had drawn me into that world without hesitation, so strong was her conviction that she could exercise control. She'd spent six years playing hide-and-seek with the illness, then it had returned—or more simply, it had never left.

The report of Giorgia's hospitalization in May had come from the admissions office: they called the last number of a family member recorded in the medical file. Having certified the gravity of the situation, the aunt had filed for interdiction.

Mariella Brentani accompanied us to the door personally. She did not apologize for her absence the last few months: she said she wasn't ready, that for her it would be like going back twenty-five years, entering the bathroom where she'd found her sister dead. She reiterated that she would consider the prospect of releasing Giorgia from the clinic only in the event of significant improvement. She didn't invite us to come back, didn't mention the possibility of us seeing one other again. She dismissed us with an enigmatic phrase, saying that the fears we don't know are the most terrible, because they all come true. Or perhaps she didn't speak, perhaps I said those words to myself as I went down the stairs in the dark.

CHAPTER THREE

REAWAKENING

The car is beyond repair. A piston is shot, the cost is higher than I can possibly afford and in any case it's at the bottom of the list of things I can deal with. I try to keep it clean, even if it's not being driven: when I have a moment I go down with a bucket and rags, wipe off the dust. I'm afraid it will become like one of those abandoned cars parked for months in the same spot, the tires flat.

Getting around is not a problem. I use public transportation, just like I did before to save on gasoline. Mauro takes me to see Giorgia every other day. He finished the book, started reading it over again. The bleak November winter has begun.

For the entire past month Mauro and I have been talking about the revelations made by Giorgia's aunt. Giorgia lied to both of us. It's hard to accept that someone as kind as her decided to tell such a huge lie—or conceal herself to such a degree.

I feel an even stronger desire to talk to her, to ask her why, to hear her answer me in her own voice.

Yesterday Mauro said that maybe the truth doesn't surprise him: he always thought there was a shadow in Giorgia's past. He said, *There was something.* I searched and couldn't find it; the idea kept me up all night. A shadow, such a long shadow, and all I saw of that shadow was the body it belonged to.

I don't remember when the last time I came to pick Giorgia up at the school was. Today I'm walking back there, on a sun-drenched Saturday afternoon. Mauro insisted that I attend rehearsals for the new show, he says I need to get out of the house, deviate from the pattern of work and visits to the clinic. I only agreed because he seemed to care a lot about my being there.

In the lobby, beyond the main entrance, are some white tables and chairs, a few occupied by young people chatting together. The long reception desk is unattended, so I ask the nearest group for directions. They point me to the right wing of the building, on the ground floor, room twelve. At the end of the corridor, I immediately spot Mauro. He's talking with a girl; she winds a strand of hair around her finger a few times, he shifts the unlit cigarette from one side of his mouth to the other, gives a restrained smile. The corridor is empty and their voices are clearly audible.

"Elsa, it's very important, it allows you to enter a certain type of world. You're almost perfect, I told you," Mauro is saying.

The girl agrees several times, with brief, firm nods.

"Why are you preparing Stefania for this part too, then?" she asks.

She can't completely contain her anger, the strand of hair is stretched taut between her fingers, she doesn't soften until Mauro lays a hand on her shoulder.

"I just want to see how you both work. I need to figure out which of you is best suited to the kind of performance I'm picturing. You have physical traits in your favor, but it's not enough. You know how I feel, it's still all yet to be decided."

She doesn't have time to reply, Mauro notices me and leaves her—"Excuse me, I have to say hello to someone." When he turns away from her and moves towards me, I catch the girl's furious look as she marches back to the classroom.

"You came!" Mauro says, spreading his arms.

"Sure."

"Of course. I knew it. It's just that Amelia and I made a little bet. Come on, it's almost time."

I follow him into the room. A long window overlooks the inner courtyard, the silhouettes of about thirty people are moving about on the parquet. Some move slowly, in a gentle warm-up. In the center of the room, a man and a woman are repeating the lines of a vocal exercise face-to-face—"We speak hoarsely or clearly from the throat or we search for other resonances in the nose as well ..."—their voices following the timbres in a rising variation. From a corner across the room, Mauro's sister greets us with a smile.

"All right, let's get started. Everyone take a seat please," Mauro says loud enough to be heard over the buzz of voices.

Everyone gathers unhurriedly along the side wall and Amelia joins us.

"What to my wondrous eyes ..." she says, looking me up and down. "Welcome."

"You'll pay up tonight," Mauro tells her. "I leave him to you."

With a wave he motions for me to follow her and I too

end up in the group of actors sitting on the floor, backs against the wall.

"How are you?" Amelia asks, pulling her hair back in a ponytail.

"Good."

"So then." Mauro draws everyone's attention again, pacing in the center of the room. "Today we don't have much time—as you know, rehearsals have begun for the junior group's Christmas recital and we have to vacate the classroom earlier than usual, so I ask for your maximum concentration: let's try to push ourselves to at least the third scene without stumbling. Has anyone seen my script? Luca, did I leave it with you?"

A young man slides the text across the parquet floor, to Mauro's feet. He picks it up and thumbs quickly through the first pages.

"Luca, as I told you just before: at this stage, let's not stress Moritz's melancholy too much. We know he's going to commit suicide, but the audience doesn't, or they'd like to pretend they don't know until the time comes. Let's indulge them."

The boy nods vigorously. I look around: they're all staring at Mauro like nocturnal animals hypnotized by a car's headlights. The only one bent over her script is Amelia.

"Fabio, just the opposite: we emphasize Melchior's vitality. More emphasis in the movement, don't hold back. Sara and Amelia"—she raises her head at the mention of her name—"there's something about your interaction that still doesn't convince me. Let's follow the guidelines established Wednesday night, we'll see how it goes. Are there any questions?"

A devout silence follows.

"Very good. Let's begin."

Amelia is the first to get up, followed by a rather tall girl. Mauro closes the classroom door and positions himself in a corner, the script tucked under his arm, one hand supporting his chin. Amelia and the other performer look at each other for a long moment, without speaking, just the two of them filling the stage— the empty room with its audience all crammed over on one side. The rehearsal suddenly explodes in Amelia's fingers pretending to touch the skirt of a dress, then in her voice. The transition from real to fictional is abrupt: by the time I manage to follow the lines it's already time to switch. Amelia sits down again, the actors of the next scene take their places according to a prearranged pattern.

From a certain point on, the movements capture my full attention. I think about how the bodies go along with the mise-en-scène, arranging themselves without apparent effort in accordance with the code of deception: the mouth, mind, legs, arms, and eyes deceive along with the staging. There's one actor, the best I think, in whom the two dimensions never diverge—"Why didn't they let me sleep peacefully until all was still again," he says. "My dear parents might have had a hundred better children. I came here, I don't know how, and must be responsible because I didn't stay away."

As Mauro had hoped, the first rehearsal flows smoothly to the third scene without any interruptions. At the end, he makes some adjustments—he stresses gestural expressiveness, he has a precise design in mind and moves the actors as though he were following a tracing. They do not rebel, they adapt to his vision and follow his instructions looking for alignment.

They go over the scenes for an hour, sometimes only performing a small part of an action or the tone of a sentence. Watching them, the same relaxation comes over me that I feel when Mauro reads at the clinic, in Giorgia's room. I follow the few clues of the plot and try to reconstruct the characters: a soft blanket comes between me and reality; there is a moment, before the conclusion, when I am completely gone, when Giorgia and everything around me vanishes. When I vanish.

"Coming?" Mauro asks when rehearsals are over.

I'm still sitting on the floor. Around us, the actors are heading towards the door in small groups.

"Amelia and I are going to eat something with some friends," he adds when we're in the corridor.

A horde of kids around ten years old, dressed in black, almost knock us over as they march firmly towards the classroom. Mauro ruffles a couple of heads, greets the breathless colleague who accompanies them.

"Will you join us or do you have other plans?" he says then, but you can tell he doesn't really consider the possibility.

"No," I reply, as the last child in the pack stumbles over me. "I have no other plans."

In the car Amelia insists on sitting in back, and on the way she wedges forward between our two seats: when she's not giving Mauro directions about the route, she's asking me questions. She inquires about my state of health, the location of my café, she asks me what I think of the rehearsals, but before I can answer we've parked and are headed towards a door in the Corso San Gottardo district. Mauro and Amelia begin discussing the performance of one of the main actors, the young man I thought was good, and they demolish him: I listen to them tear him apart, bit by bit, dismantling the exaggeration, the posing—"He's actually very good," Mauro tells me, under his breath, when it's time to buzz the intercom. "It's our duty not to be too indulgent." Amelia nods knowingly, hopping up and down from the cold.

Our hosts, I discover, live on the third floor of an apartment building built around a central courtyard. I am introduced as a friend, Giorgia is not mentioned, but I feel nervous just the same because I know I wouldn't be able to recognize any of those who were present at the events of the opening. For a while I expect a compassionate glance or pitying look, but nothing happens, instead I get recruited into the dinner preparations and assigned to slicing tomatoes. The accents are varied—that of the Calabrian pair, the very slight Tuscan of a thin young man, Amelia's Veneto. When the meal is ready we sit around the table; there is no tablecloth and none of the dishes match. The conversation quickly becomes exclusionary. The main topic centers on the last performances, and Mauro, sitting next to me, acts as intermediary, enthusiastically filling in the gaps for me. Despite being unprepared, I am drawn in: thanks to him everyone wants to explain the theater to me and from the theater the discussion branches out, I learn that the Tuscan boy is about to complete his studies with one of the professors from my course, we bring up names and anecdotes that I never thought I would remember again.

By the end of dinner, the air inside is hot and unbreathable. The wine is gone, someone is sitting sideways on the couch strumming a guitar. Mauro has stepped outside and is watching us through the crack of the semi-open window. I join him on the balcony and we look out over the railing. I hadn't seen one of these housing complexes—one of these evenings—since my university days.

"Humanities," Mauro says, standing beside me. "I didn't realize you'd studied humanities."

"Yeah," I say. "Graduated with honors."

He smiles at my glum tone.

"And you?" I ask.

"Me, nothing. I mean, nothing that led me to a degree, much to my mother's disappointment. She wanted me to be an e-commerce entrepreneur or a CEO."

I watch him blow smoke down from the balcony, his hair out of control and his shirt crisscrossed by slanting wrinkles. Picturing him employed in finance is an effort of imagination that is beyond my reach.

My mother had something like that in mind too, I think," I tell him. "That or the manager of an elegant café, maybe in the center: I could have climbed to success at the Cova Montenapoleone or the Camparino in Galleria."

"You missed your chance." Mauro grins and snuffs out the butt on the wrought iron. "A tricky business, mothers. My mother wanted me to be the custodian of the family estate and the result is that I have absolutely no interest in it. She says I came into the world to defy her hopes."

"When you put it that way, it sounds awful."

"No, it's not that bad. Maybe one day I'll let you meet her. She's just a beautiful woman with a taste for melodrama. And she's rich."

"Rich?"

"Filthy rich. So rich that she's never had to work. The house I live in is hers."

I think about maintaining the place, the upkeep of the grounds, and I realize that it could not be otherwise.

"Now you'll think I'm some kind of radical chic dilettante with a capricious fancy for theater," Mauro says, studying me.

My opinion doesn't really matter to him. I have the impression that he enjoys cornering me, as if to provoke an unpredictable reaction.

"Not at all," I say.

"I know, no worries. You never think badly of anyone, right?" He doesn't wait for my reply. "I have an annuity, of course, but I only touch that money for Amelia: I'm paying for her college. If my mother knew, she'd be furious. She didn't speak to me for six months when Amelia came to live with me."

He turns around, leans his elbows on the railing. I imitate him and our view is reversed. The window panes are screened by a thin veil of curtains, and from the balcony, the interior of the apartment is clearly visible. The young Tuscan man picks out a classic by Claudio Lolli on the guitar strings, the chorus around him is subdued, interrupted by a few laughs. Amelia is sitting on the arm of the sofa, toying with the hair of a girl curled up at her feet. The physical differences between her and Mauro are startling: whereas he is olive-skinned, she has a rosy complexion and straight blonde hair smoothed behind her ears.

"She took it as a betrayal. My father broke up their marriage for Amelia's mother: for her it is inconceivable that I should consider Amelia part of the family. But my father is a disaster, always on the verge of bankruptcy, and Amelia's mother is a primary school teacher. What was I supposed to do? Keep it all for myself? She's my sister."

We remain silent for a few minutes. He keeps looking at Amelia, then abruptly makes a sweeping gesture in the air that takes in the perimeter of the window.

"How did you like the rehearsals? What do you think of the script?" he says, changing his tone.

"It's very good. And dark. What work is it?"

"*The Awakening of Spring*, by Wedekind. Do you know it?"

"No," I admit.

"A great classic. Late-nineteenth-century Germany: a group of fourteen-year-olds collide with adolescence in the most brutal way possible. The discovery of sexuality, suicide, abortion. The background of events is an obtuse, cruel adult world that's arid and greedy."

Mauro smiles joylessly now.

"Challenging," I say.

"It is. It's a huge risk, with a sacred cow like Wedekind, but I think it will be a success. I'm going to make them perform as though they were already old, I'm having them put on gray makeup. If I could, I'd force them all to dye their hair white."

I think he's joking, then I take a closer look at him and see he's dead serious, practically irritated.

"Shall we go?" Amelia calls out to us.

She looks at us through the crack of the open window. Mauro's face relaxes, he agrees, then invites me to have a drink at his place. Amelia's friend joins us.

The trip back is a very long drive. In the Navigli area, Saturday-night groups crowd the sidewalks. Through the car windows, we watch them stream by as we advance slowly: the cold paralyzes the shimmering bodies and the fog from the outlying fields slithers on its belly all the way into the canals.

At Mauro's we droop languidly around the table. With the second glass of poitín, heat envelops my fingers and from there spreads through my body; around me, the voices of Mauro, Amelia, and the unknown girl. They smile at me wearily and I no longer feel alone. By two in the morning I fall asleep on the sofa. Just before dropping off I see the unfamiliar girl sitting on Mauro's lap as he disappears into the embrace of her hair; Amelia is a white hand on the back of a chair.

In the dream I'm home again. Giorgia appears when the sheet we are spreading on the bed sags. For the first time I recognize it: the dissimilarity is in her eyes. She looks at me as if she's about to tell me the truth, her face hard and cold, and I'm terrified. I open a door of the closet, where I already know I'll find my Giorgia, the real Giorgia—and there she is. She's dead, yet her eyes are open, they're tender, her original eyes, but the fear doesn't go away; no, the fear doesn't go away.

In the weeks that follow I am included in Mauro and Amelia's social activities. The heterogeneous circle of acquaintances and close friends takes me in, and I begin to recognize people by name, to distinguish them at the rehearsals that I attend more and more frequently. My routine is revamped: there's the café, the visits to Giorgia, then the rehearsals, and dinners at this or that student's house. Mauro has a hyperkinetic social life, he knows a lot more people than I've known in my entire life. With the start of the theatrical season I am drawn into a whirlwind of performances and related events.

My parents are thrilled that I have to decline a couple of their Sunday dinner invitations. One day, on the phone, my mother bursts into tears and tells me that she had lost hope, she's so happy that I'm back to living again. I think of Giorgia, how my mother loved her right away, and I wonder what she tells herself when she thinks about her, so intense is the effort she makes to pretend she has forgotten her.

* * *

Mauro lets me go first at the entrance and I push open the glass door. He follows me into the lobby of the clinic, lowering his voice: he's been talking on the phone all the way here and I had to drive instead of him. These days he's negotiating dates for the season. Amelia says it's a very difficult moment but Mauro isn't worried, he calmly maneuvers between sponsors and directors and plays a different role with each of them. I heard him change his arguments, approach, tone of voice, often three or four times in the same quarter of an hour. As if he'd read my mind, he himself told me: people are more inclined to be persuaded by those like them, or by those who they think are like them; it's a survival technique.

I greet the woman at the reception desk, and she responds with a smile. On the way up the stairs, Mauro ends his conversation.

"I'd like to bury this phone in a hole."

Wandering around the hallway on the floor is the occupant of room three, a tiny old woman in a blue robe and slippers, walking silently, hugging the walls: our presence provokes no reaction. As we near Giorgia's room, Mauro reminds me that we're invited to an exhibition tonight. We both go in thinking about something else—I tell him that I might not feel like going, he says it will be fun. We notice the empty bed when we are already at our posts, me sitting in the chair, him leaning against the windowsill, the book ready in his hands.

Giorgia is gone. The sheets are folded open to where the body left its mark. We stand there staring and for a long time neither of us moves. The first to speak is Mauro.

"They must have taken her somewhere, maybe to have a bath ..."

Right away I think of a breakdown but I pull myself together.

"No," I say. "They never do it at this hour." I stand up.

Mauro follows me back into the corridor, then down the stairs. At the desk, the receptionist smiles again.

"My girlfriend is not in her room," I say.

The clerk recognizes me, she knows who I'm talking about.

"Odd," she says. "Are you sure she's not out with Olga? I know she's the one on duty on the floor."

"That's not possible, Giorgia never leaves her room." I feel like saying she barely moves, but I restrain myself.

"Don't worry, let me check." She picks up the phone, enters a number, and waits; she hangs up, tries another number. "Celeste? Yes, listen, the girl in number five is not in her room. I tried to call Olga on the floor but she's not answering."

She listens, then gives me a reassuring smile. "All right, thank you very much." She comes around the desk, the bunch of keys she carries attached to her belt jingling.

"Come with me."

We follow her down the corridor that goes off to the left, at the fork we turn right. When we reach the fire exit, the woman energetically pushes the crash bar, opening the door. We cross the gravel driveway that surrounds the building and come to the garden in back. She stops and looks over at the fountain.

"There she is," she says, pointing to two figures. "Celeste said it's the third time she's been out this week."

Giorgia is walking and the nurse is following her closely. I hadn't seen her on her feet in the last eight months.

I hear Mauro thank our guide, and meanwhile I am already halfway across the distance separating me from Giorgia. She moves uncertainly, swaying at one point, and the nurse grabs her by the arm, then quickly lets go. She's wearing a big quilted men's jacket that covers her down to her thighs and from there the hem of her robe peeks out, along with her pajamas and the only pair of shoes she entered the clinic with.

The nurse stops me with a look. Mauro is beside me and we both stand there motionless. Giorgia doesn't notice our presence, it's still as though we didn't exist, she goes on walking in the December afternoon: she makes wide concentric circles in the grass, moving away and returning in waves, following the rules of her personal tide.

The chief doctor's long legs are crammed into the opening under the desk; at any moment it seems the knees will pierce through the laminate. You can see the tension triggered in him by having to maintain such an uncomfortable position. He received me without getting up, his "Come in" came clearly from behind the closed door.

All week long Mauro and I have spent our visiting time in the clinic's garden, watching Giorgia take her walks. The nurse says that she always wants to go out at four o'clock: she gets out of bed and goes to the door on her own; if the nurse didn't run after her to dress her, she'd even go out in slippers. She doesn't feel the cold. The nurse also told us that the doctor ordered that she not be held back, unless she were to do something dangerous. But Giorgia has no strange intentions, her only interest is to wander around the garden for a couple of hours. She still isn't speaking, still doesn't notice us. After spending six days observing her walks, I decided to ask to see the doctor.

"Give me one more minute, I just have to finish this notation and I'll be right with you," he says, glancing quickly at me through the metallic rims of his glasses.

The monitor's bluish light seeps into old scars, amplifying pitted furrows in the pockmarked skin. He must be around sixty-five, proliferating wrinkles being one of the signs—two deep grooves on either side of the mouth, a vertical indentation between the eyebrows, an ascending ladder of folds lining the forehead below his thick gray mane. His eyes are clear and still, they examine the subjects of his interest briefly, never lingering. When standing, his posture is erect, the coat open over his dark clothing.

I remember our first meeting very well: it took place in here, in the company of a bewildered version of me—"Think of Giorgia's mental state as a changing entity," he'd said. "Her pathological condition began as a psychosis but now, due to factors that we will assess, it has evolved, it has crossed the border into paranoid schizophrenia." *Schizophrenia.* I had thought instinctively of a Bergman classic discovered at the film lab, the screams of the protagonist unleashed by the hallucination of a huge spider.

The doctor's fingers are long, flexed over the keyboard. When he finishes typing, he closes the laptop with a click and makes sure the tablet is on standby.

"So," he says. "Giorgia."

"Yes," I say. "What do you make of the developments?"

"Motor awakening? A good result, of course. However, Mr. Bonini, I must caution you."

He smiles at me kindly, not showing his teeth, like a caring teacher to a naïve pupil.

"Giorgia has regained her motor functions—nevertheless, we are not here to heal her legs."

"I know."

"Of course, you know. I don't want to dampen your enthusiasm, naturally it's a step," he adds, spreading his big hands out on the desk. "But in the present circumstances, we don't know where this step will lead us. A patient incapable of moving is a patient difficult to manage, especially if we think of future discharge; it is also true that a patient capable of moving, in the absence of valid clinical conditions, is a risky patient. Especially if we think about future discharge. Do you see what I mean?"

"Yes," I reply.

"Unfortunately, today I have to get back to San Paolo. Do you want to walk me down?" he asks, getting up.

He hangs the coat on the clothes hook behind the desk, picks up his black leather medical bag from the floor. Moving slowly and precisely, he puts objects back in their compartments in strict order. I follow him into the third-floor corridor, which is occupied only by administrative offices.

"I don't want to scare you, believe me. It is possible that a complex transition phase is opening up for her," the doctor says, walking unhurriedly. "In cases such as Giorgia's, when the patient partially regains possession of his faculties, begins walking again or even speaking, it is difficult for loved ones to resist the hope of a return to normality. It's a battle against memory. I ask you to resist the temptation. Free Giorgia's stages from the idea of improvement."

"Do you mean the fact that she's walking again is not an improvement in itself?"

We start heading down the flight of stairs. I was not counting on an enthusiastic reaction from the doctor: from the first moment he'd been clear with regard to Giorgia's condition—"I am not here to reassure you, I am here to help Giorgia. To help her, I must be patently clear. We are making our way through a labyrinth: we will evaluate tried and proven paths and formulate new ones." I thought there was no more fitting image to describe what was happening.

"The problem is that you attribute significance to Giorgia's motor activity," the doctor says now. "Undeniably, Giorgia is walking: but she is not walking as you and I are able to walk, from here to my car, to reach our respective destinations. There is no intention in Giorgia's walking."

I think about the circles that Giorgia traces in the clinic's garden. Now it's almost always the same sequence: concentric rings around the fountain, then an elliptical orbit among the bare trees, then over and over again, until a switch is turned off. She stops suddenly, tilting her head, her eyes blank. The nurse retrieves her like an empty shell deposited on the sand.

"Giorgia still displays behavior that indicates she is dissociated from reality."

When we reach the ground floor, the doctor nods goodbye to the receptionist. We stop near the entrance. Through the glass I can see Mauro smoking a cigarette and pacing back and forth in the parking lot. He chose to let me meet with the doctor on my own.

"That's not to say we can't act. Giorgia's new symptom offers us a starting point. In the next few weeks we will review the dosages," he says, taking the car keys out of his pocket.

"All right, thank you."

"It's possible that with a decrease in the dosages we may see some acute manifestation," he adds, looking me in the eye. "We don't yet know how Giorgia will react. Be prepared."

I nod. "I will be. Thank you very much," I say.

He says goodbye with a polite nod, and as I watch him walk away, I repeat that I'll be ready. When I join Mauro, we get in the car without talking.

"How'd it go?" he asks once the clinic is behind us.

I search for a reply, but all I come up with are a few doubtful sounds: I end up trailing off, leaning against the window, looking out at the street. Mauro doesn't press it. I turn down the invitation to the event we were supposed to attend, but he insists on having dinner with me, so we end the day on Corso Porta Ticinese, with a kebab.

* * *

Giorgia does not react to the reduced dosages. In the following ten days there is no breakdown, and no change in her walking routines either. The first few days Mauro continued to read, even in the garden, then his voice began to get on my nerves and I asked him to please stop. By now I know the play by heart.

I'm starting to feel the weight of repetition. The doctor is right: I let myself be dazzled by the prospect of progress. Seeing Giorgia walk filled me with hope, and no matter how hard I tried to stifle the thought, to suppress my relief, the instantaneous joy at seeing her first steps, the disappointment is searing.

I look at my reflection in the mirror in the entryway. I'm dressed and ready: Mauro will be here in minutes. We are invited to a birthday celebration for Sara, Amelia's friend. I fiddle with my cell phone, looking for Mauro's number. I should call him and cancel. I've done it a couple of times the past week, and he's been understanding. I don't feel like seeing anyone, just the thought of having to talk tires me out. I don't know why I accepted. I should have made up a story, another commitment, but Mauro would have immediately known it was a lie: the only social life I have involves his circle.

I'm about to call him and tell him the truth, but no sooner do I put the phone to my ear than the intercom buzzes. I recognize his two long, forceful rings. I think it's too late, I don't want to take a single step, and as I'm thinking this I'm already halfway through the courtyard.

Sara is as wealthy as Mauro. She also owns a house, in the Bicocca district, an open floorplan with a Scandinavian flair. There are about thirty of us at her birthday buffet: the mixed company of people from the Civic Schools and university colleagues is scattered here and there between the sofa and the living area, or crowded around the food trays. Mauro left me almost immediately: he recognized someone he hadn't seen for a long time and, after saying hello, he never came back. I approach a couple of familiar faces but everyone is busy talking and I don't feel like barging into their conversations. I end up in line for a drink: there's a real bartender, stationed behind the kitchen peninsula.

When it's my turn, I decide I'll finish the Negroni and

then leave. I'm pondering how to sneak out, the trip back on the metro, then everything goes dark. I feel two cold hands over my eyes, hear Amelia's laugh. She loosens her hold at once and leans over my shoulder.

"Mon ami!" she exclaims, then kisses me on the cheek.

I turn in her direction and find her heavily made up, her mouth hidden under dark lipstick.

"Why are you by yourself in a corner?" she asks, feigning a slight pout.

"I wanted a cocktail." I wave my glass as an excuse.

"Mauro says you're in a Macbeth mood tonight."

I look around for him and find him watching us from the other side of the room: he smiles and raises his glass of wine in a silent toast.

"Mauro should learn to mind his own business," I say, reciprocating the gesture.

"That's what I always tell him too," Amelia says. "I want something to drink."

I offer her my drink, which I haven't touched yet, then we order another one, then two more. We end up settling into the high stools around the peninsula.

"I'm sloshed," Amelia says, finishing her second Negroni.

"Can't you hold your liquor?"

"Of course I can hold my liquor, who do you take me for?"

I look at her: at about five foot two, she may weigh all of a hundred pounds; aside from the shiny eyes and somewhat flushed cheeks, however, she's not smashed.

"I had a terrible day at the university," she says. "The probe slipped and I injured a patient."

"What's a probe?"

"One of the instruments of torture dentists use."

"Studying dentistry?"

Amelia nods, taking another sip of the cocktail.

"Third year," she says.

I try to imagine her in a white coat and the idea makes me smile.

"What?" she says, annoyed.

"Nothing, it's just that I thought it would be something in the humanities," I admit.

"No, that's not for me," she says. "Anyway, university has never been high on my list. After graduation, I worked for a while. It was Mauro who encouraged me to study dentistry. He even prepared me for the tests."

"He cares a lot about you," I say. Though if it weren't for the alcohol, this is the kind of observation that I would never make—venturing into a delicate area, getting too close.

"He's like that with everyone he cares about," Amelia says.

She looks at me insistently, as if to emphasize the idea. I get it and feel the sting of guilt for tonight's defeatist thoughts.

Amelia suggests another round of drinks, after which we drift into a disjointed, patchy conversation made up of disconnected topics—her sad childhood in Buccinasco, my years at the university, her first performance. She began acting when she met Mauro, at sixteen: he was twenty-three and was teaching a class for beginners at a social center in Sesto.

When it's time for the cake, the luminous glimmer of candles files past us, and for a moment the light spatters our faces. There is Amelia, smiling as she joins the chorus of happy birthday wishes, there's me singing along with her, and twenty-five wax tapers burning on an enormous Saint Honoré. A minute later the choir has died, the candles are out and nostalgia shatters me—I feel my sudden, complete exclusion in images that affirm the seven years that separate me from Amelia, from her friend, from half the guests at this party. So when Mauro joins us and suggests a disco, I immediately say it's fine with me.

"I didn't know you were a dancer."

Mauro expels the smoke with a laugh.

It's a frigid, clear morning, and we're leaning against the side of his Alfa in the clinic parking lot. From the driveway entrance you can see the tranquil horizon of a rice field, and a strip of road where no one passes; beyond the horizon another identical horizon is repeated on and on, a rice field, an ash grove, a rice field, a rice field, ash trees.

"Every now and then you have to step out of character," Mauro says.

I look at him: he's bushed. From the first club we moved on to another, from there we drove back to Bicocca to bring Sara home and then waited for day to break over the hill of cherry trees—the sun swelled into a pink bubble, and we watched it in silence, me, Mauro, and Amelia, too drunk and exhausted to talk. Amelia fell asleep in the car on the way back; we didn't want to wake her. She's still there, stretched out on the back seat, covered with her overcoat and our scarves.

"You know what I mean? Deviate from the pattern of predetermined behaviors," Mauro goes on. "Think about it: what sets us apart from the character of a play?"

I'm thinking that I'm too tired for this. I rub my face with my hands, search for a sensible answer.

"Never mind, I'll tell you. A character operates within

a scheme of behaviors, and has boundaries; he has to have them, or it would be impossible to perform him. Real individuals, on the other hand, have no limitations, they can move across any set of parameters. Chekhov's Vanja can never be an enthusiast of life, for instance," he says, and takes a long drag. "I, on the other hand, being a real person—or at least I think I am—can be a director, take an interest in culture, be a former gambler and an excellent dancer. The possibilities are endless."

I picture him again on the dance floor, perspiring as he clutches Sara and focuses on elementary movements to the rhythm of a second-rate electronic piece.

"You are not an excellent dancer," I say.

He laughs again, chokes on the smoke and coughs.

"Certainly better than you are," he shoots back, his face still red.

"I don't dance," I say. "I've never danced."

Mauro shakes his head. "You see? You apply a pattern of behaviors to yourself. Yes to this, no to that. Essentially, you're a real person who thinks you're a character."

"I take that as an insult."

"It's not. I much prefer characters to people," Mauro tosses the butt on the ground, grinds it into the gravel. "What time is it?"

I check my cell phone. "8:27."

"It opens in a few minutes, right?" he says, nodding toward the glass door.

The idea of coming to visit Giorgia was his. He suggested it on our way home, at six in the morning. "Why don't we go see her?" he said. "As if she too had been out with us." We drove around aimlessly until eight o'clock, closer to the time for Sunday morning visiting hours.

I can smell the alcohol on me, my face is bleary with fatigue, and I'm a little ashamed at the thought of coming to see Giorgia in this state. When it's 8:30, I follow Mauro. The desk clerk greets us at the entrance, I nod in return, head lowered.

We find Giorgia awake, back in her old position, in bed, staring elsewhere. We take off our jackets in silence and return obediently to our habitual spots, me in my chair, Mauro at his windowsill. I wonder if not seeing her walking now seems strange to him.

I watch her and feel an intense desire to touch her. To stroke the back of her hand, see her react. The more I look at her, the stronger the desire; maybe it's still the aftereffects of artificial euphoria, maybe exhaustion, the lack of sleep: eventually I lean forward, start to reach towards the shape of her leg under the quilt.

Giorgia's eyes catch me in the act. She turns around and looks at me. She doesn't look through me, her eyes stop in mine.

I remain still under her vivid gaze and hold my breath; I can't believe it's possible.

The sound reaches me before I realize that Giorgia's mouth is moving: it's her voice. As if from a very distant dream, Giorgia is speaking.

"Have you any commission from your lord to negotiate with my face? You are now out of your text: but we will draw the curtain and show you the picture. Look you, sir, such a one I was this present: is't not well done?"

Before I can comprehend the meaning, a voice responds.

"Excellently done," Mauro says, "if God did all."

Giorgia's lips curve in a smile without warmth. Now she looks at Mauro, and my blood runs cold, as if my nightmare had slipped into reality. I recognize the dis-similarity: I know that the speaker is not Giorgia.

"'Tis in grain, sir," the one inhabiting Giorgia says, "'twill endure wind and weather."

CHAPTER FOUR

DIVERGENCES

There is a common room in the clinic: two long tables in pale-green laminate, a TV bolted to the wall. Tacked to the cork board are paintings by the patients, orgies of flowers in riotous brushstrokes, abstract motifs—in one of them a black background flaunts a red brooch in the center. The canvases are a panorama for Giorgia, who is sitting serenely in a chair, a plastic fan in her left hand. She looks around with a bored air, occasionally stroking the folds of her robe with the care she would give to a sumptuous gown.

There are three of us, me, Mauro, and the clinic's doctor, concealed behind the one-way glass in the observation corridor. From here we can see everything. At this hour the common room should be closed: they keep it open only for Giorgia, because it's too cold for her to take her walks outside, and when forced to stay in her room she tends to become fidgety. The attendants are showing considerable patience but I know that it is only thanks to the orders of the director that Giorgia is granted so much freedom. The evolution of her illness has captivated him. He studies her closely through the glass, silently, his hands thrust into the pockets of his white coat. This time I wanted Mauro with me, so that he can explain to him what I'm certain I can't explain.

"So then, you imagine that Giorgia is performing a script? That's your theory?" The doctor doesn't take his eyes off her.

"I don't imagine it," Mauro says. "I'm certain of it."

He is as worked up as he was a week ago, when Giorgia spoke and he responded with the appropriate words. He says he recognized the lines immediately, that there's no way he could be mistaken: in the last three months, during our visits, he has done nothing but read passages from *Twelfth Night* to her.

"It's the first major production we staged together," Mauro insists. "She's performing her role."

Giorgia hadn't spoken much the first time: the exchange of lines between her and Mauro hadn't lasted more than a minute—then she withdrew into herself again, and no longer reacted to his cues. Giorgia's voice stunned us, then disappeared so quickly that for a long while I thought I had imagined it after our night of drinking. We restrained ourselves, Mauro and I. He kept trying to prompt her with a few lines; I even went so far as to touch her at one point, taking her hand, but she showed no sign of wanting to be roused. On the way back in the car, neither of us had had the confidence to tell Amelia about it—and once I got home I talked myself into believing that Giorgia's response had been a fluke, that in any case there was nothing significant about what had just happened: her voice was the same, but it was still only an instrument of the something else that inhabited her. It seemed to me that this "something else" was becoming more powerful than Giorgia, so I hoped she would go back to not speaking again.

But Giorgia's voice had not stopped. On Monday, we'd found her arguing with the nurse because the woman had stepped on the skirt of her garment. We'd watched her from the door, without going in: sitting in her pajamas on the edge of her bed, she eyed the nurse with a disconsolate air. Mauro, huddled with me in a corner of the doorway where Giorgia couldn't see us, had said it immediately: "She's acting." I could hear my own disbelief and fear in his whisper, but also a detectable hint of excitement.

Now the doctor muses: "As if being exposed to the reading had reawakened in Giorgia the memory of her identification with the character ..." And turning to me he adds: "She showed no sign of recognizing you, I imagine."

I shake my head and look away. She treats me as if I too were part of the script, a walk-on: the more she looks at me, the more I stop existing. It's worse than the psychotic episode she'd had earlier. On that evening, Giorgia's Peter Pan had not held up for long—just long enough for her to go offstage and attempt to fly out the window. When we grabbed her and forced her to the ground, the seizure and the screams had started; Mauro and I were injured holding her still and all our pleas had been in vain. We hadn't yet realized it, but Giorgia was gone. I look at her now, serene, mesmerized by the white accordion folds of the fan that the nurses gave her.

"Is she following the script faithfully?" the doctor asks Mauro. "There are names she repeats frequently, people she looks for. We've been monitoring her this week and it doesn't seem like she's simply reciting lines from memory."

"No, as a matter of fact. Giorgia is doing what she should do: she's going along with the character. Acting is not about memorizing lines and then repeating them. Bringing a credible character to life on the stage means using the script to expand his or her identity, to develop it to the point of predicting how that character would react in situations and contexts beyond those contained in the work itself," says Mauro. His voice resonates in the silence. "Giorgia has always shown an instinctive talent in this. In *Twelfth Night*, as in any Shakespearean work, the subtext is almost nonexistent and all you can cling to are the character's words. Giorgia had succeeded in constructing a perfect, comprehensive Olivia."

"So, the character we're seeing would be a woman in a Shakespearean play?" The doctor is very grave.

"That's right, Giorgia is playing the part of the Countess Olivia in *Twelfth Night*."

We remain silent, observing through the window. The doctor rocks on the tips of his shoes and leans closer, practically touching the surface of the glass.

"It happened because of the decreased dosages, right?" I ask. "You'd said there was the risk of an acute episode."

"Partly, yes. However, the reaction to the new dosages is unexpectedly positive. Every previous attempt was a failure, we didn't obtain anything even remotely verifiable," the doctor says, his breath fogging up the glass pane. "From what I see now, though, the psychosis is acting within a partially predictable construct. Giorgia is following rules. Not mine, not hers, but those of a script."

"So you consider that an improvement?"

"Mr. Bonini, you know what I think of that word. We

are not talking about improvement, we are talking about a change in her condition. Giorgia has gone from a noncommunicative and essentially unmanageable psychosis to a structured psychosis. In other words, her world follows norms that we can at least discern. This gives us an unforeseen advantage."

In the room, Giorgia begins to stroll around the table. She holds her back erect, in an elegant posture that isn't hers. It's scary: it's as if someone has slipped into her skin, filling the space behind her eyes and bringing her body back to life. Mauro is not as taken aback as I am—maybe because for him the character is no stranger, he has already seen her performed by Giorgia.

"We'll review the dosages again. The new posology could trigger a crisis, or shatter Giorgia's current reality, or both. If we were to be successful in bringing about even a minimal detachment between her and the character, I might think of putting her in a psychodrama therapy group."

"What's that?"

"The theatrical framework of psychodrama observes the patient bring his own existential difficulty to the scene. It is not very different from the approach that Giorgia is already used to—except that in the therapeutic course a psychoanalyst chooses the scene to be performed and directs it using various techniques at his disposal."

Mauro lights up. "I think I've heard of it. There's a center for it, in the city."

The doctor nods. "I believe you are referring to the center operated by Dr. Fusconi. We have an open channel of communication with him; we've been working together for almost ten years."

"But is it really effective?" asks Mauro.

"It's been a valid alternative for several of my patients."

"How come you're only telling us about it now?" I ask.

The doctor barely glances at me. "Such a possibility wasn't even thinkable in the condition Giorgia was in just two weeks ago."

"Why not start now, if the therapy is effective?"

"It's not that simple, Mr. Bonini. Psychodrama requires a degree of contact with reality, so that the patient's experiences and traumas can emerge in the performance."

The doctor gestures, bidding me to look over at Giorgia. She is raptly studying the garden, whispering to herself.

"Giorgia is still prey to her psychoses. She would not be capable of acting out her pathology onstage and viewing it objectively. By forcing the therapy on her now, we would only trigger other serious psychotic episodes. Imagine if someone showed up at your door and told you that everything you consider to be your life is a stage production, a theatrical performance in which you are merely a character."

Giorgia closes the fan, puts it to her cheek, peers out as if awaiting visitors.

"And imagine if that same someone responded to your requests with conflicting stimuli: you ask for a glass of water, the stranger tells you that water doesn't exist, has never existed; you want to go out, and the stranger prevents you, reminding you that the outside world has been destroyed by fire—an event of which you have no recollection. Try to picture a complete reversal of every dimension that you believe to be true: you will have a vague sense of the kind of violence that Giorgia would be exposed to at this point if she is started on a therapy that is not suited to her state," the doctor explains, clearing his throat. "You know what I'm talking about: it's what happened at the first crisis, when Giorgia believed she was something and the world around her denied her that identity. Remember how she rebelled against the constraint."

I feel Mauro's eyes on me, and sense the same memory in him; the two of us realizing that Giorgia had been attempting to jump out the open window only after we instinctively grabbed her by the arms.

"We must be patient, observe her reactions and bring her as close as possible to the normality she knows."

"Do you think that will happen?"

"Are you asking me if Giorgia will recover?"

"Yes. Do you think she'll ever be the same as she was before?"

I don't have the nerve to hold the doctor's gaze while I wait for his answer.

"I was in Normandy, two years ago. Gorgeous scenery. You may have heard of Mont Saint-Michel: the bay is famous for its tides. The water rises and recedes twice a day, submerging then exposing everything. It's spectacular and treacherous," his voice glides over the window glass. "There is no before and after in Giorgia. We'll find a way to stem the tide, the water will carve out another route, and we'll curb it again. Giorgia has always been this. We can't choose a character for her to play."

"But isn't that exactly what she's doing, playing a role that she has been taught to recognize as hers?" Mauro's question trails off, his presence shrinks.

"So then you're saying we have only one option: to find a script that contains Giorgia's character, or something that at least resembles her?" the doctor asks caustically, with a cheerless laugh. "No. We can't do any more than what we're already doing. We must be patient."

I'm barely listening. I'm watching Giorgia imprisoned in the display case, and she's so far away she seems to grow smaller.

It's only when we get to his house that I notice Mauro's silence. After saying our goodbyes to the doctor, we didn't talk anymore in the car, and I can't remember why we're here. He shuts off the engine, lights a cigarette, then gets out. I feel so drained that I don't follow him right away; I sit there, staring at the folded scripts forgotten in the inner pocket of the car door. I'm as empty as if I'd been scooped out with a ladle.

After a few minutes, I drag myself out of the car and make my way past the gate and through the front door, both left open. Inside, Mauro is still smoking—it's the first time I've seen him smoke in a room other than the basement. I go to the couch and slump down. I close my eyes, I hear him walk around the dining table, then the smell of cigarette smoke comes closer and I feel him looking at me.

"I don't agree."

I open my eyes and find him standing in front of me. He points two fingers and the cigarette at me.

"He's wrong."

I can guess what he's referring to, as if during the drive back, in silence, we had spoken about it.

"I don't think he's wrong," I say.

"Not about everything, of course. He's the doctor. But he's wrong about Giorgia."

I feel edgy, I can't sit still anymore. I go around Mauro and walk over to the window.

"It's us," I say.

"What?"

"It's us, we're the ones who are wrong," I repeat louder, and my words bounce around the room.

"How do you mean?"

I sense Mauro close by again. I figure it no longer makes sense to avoid the subject we've been dodging ever since the meeting with Giorgia's aunt. As he stares at me from across the table that stands between us, I know he already knows.

"She's not well," I say. "We didn't realize it. What we saw wasn't the truth."

"You're wrong too. The illness isn't all there is."

"She was ill and we didn't want to see it."

"Giorgia exists."

Mauro snuffs out his cigarette in the crystal ashtray, doesn't look away.

"Giorgia exists. We didn't imagine her. I remember her, you remember her."

"I don't know what I remember anymore. I don't know if that was the truth."

"Don't even doubt it for a minute: Giorgia is who you and I have come to know, she's everything we've seen."

Mauro's eyes challenge me to contradict him.

"It doesn't matter anymore now," I say.

"On the contrary, it's essential. I've been thinking about it since the doctor said it: we can't choose a character to have her play. That's true. But we don't have to choose a character."

I feel as if I've lost his train of thought, or that he's left something out.

"What are you talking about?"

"Giorgia remembers: her memory must have endured, somehow. We need to help her remember the right things."

"I'm not sure I understand …"

"All I had to do was read the script to her, Filippo," Mauro says, now feverishly wide-eyed, an excited smile quivering on his lips. "It's about choosing the right script. It's about writing it."

I begin to see where he's going with this, and the absurdity of what Mauro is proposing floors me.

"You're not really thinking of …"

"Listen. Stop a moment and listen to me. Giorgia managed to be herself, without the illness, for a very long time. You've been together three years, and in three years she never slipped. Do you have any idea how much effort such a performance requires?"

I instinctively grab the back of the chair in front of me.

"She wasn't deceiving you, Filippo. She wanted to be herself, without the illness. She can do it. She remembered how to go back to being Olivia, she can remember how to go back to being Giorgia."

"This is science fiction."

"Why not try? She remembered a script she studied six years ago."

"She wasn't performing a script with me."

"No, she wasn't. She had learned to exist without the illness." Mauro places his hands on the table, leans towards me. "Let's try. She's still in there and maybe we can get her out. If you were lost, like she is, wouldn't you want someone to help you?"

My head is spinning. I'm exhausted, the room is closing in on me. I avoid Mauro's gaze and walk back to the couch a moment before my legs start to give way. It's terrifying, the idea that's beginning to take hold of me: I struggle to resist it.

"Let's try." Mauro won't give up, he follows me to the

couch. "What do we have to lose?"

"This is not one of your productions," I spit out sharply.

"No, it isn't!" Mauro kneels in front of me, on the carpet. "Listen to me: let's write it. Let's write the script as if it might work, let's kid ourselves that it will work and then we'll decide what to do with it."

We go on looking at each other in silence for a long moment. He knows right away that he's won, he knows it's because I'm desperate.

"What would you give to go back to how it was?" he asks.

"Anything."

"Let's start with this."

"I don't know how."

"I'll help you. I'll give you the form, the framework, and you give me the content, everything you remember about her. We'll reconstruct her together."

"It's insanity."

"Without a doubt."

I put my head in my hands, they're sweaty.

"I can't believe we're having this conversation."

"Don't focus on why, focus on how."

"Do you really think it could work?" I ask faintly.

Mauro shakes his head, attempts a cautious smile.

"I don't know," he says. "Meanwhile, let's write."

We begin in his basement the following afternoon. When Mauro hands me a sheet of paper and a pen, I tell him I can't. I look at the sheet, the pen, I think of how absurd it is and I freeze; so he brings down half a glass of poitín, tells me to drink but not too much, two or three sips to "warm me up."

"Just think about what you have to do, don't think

about whether it might be useful," he then says, taking the glass out of my hand and moving it near him. "Think of it as an exercise."

"An exercise?"

"Right," he says. "From now on this will be your exercise: to look for pieces of Giorgia in your memories."

"I don't know where to start."

"There's no need to proceed sequentially. Enter the first memory you find, like entering a room. Wait and see what happens and take notes."

"What should I write?"

"The details, the little things you're able to find. The tone of voice, the movements. We'll proceed in reverse, from the particulars to the whole, and from there work on constructing the character."

I watch him open the laptop that sits waiting and ready for us on the table.

"I'll deal with the script," he says, answering a question I haven't asked.

He too takes a sip of poitín, then his face gleams with the artificial light of a blank screen page and he quickly begins to write. He slows down, starts a new paragraph, goes back, hesitates, but doesn't look at me again.

I try to do as he's told me, erase the purpose of this insane project. I stare at the paper's grain for a while, the pen tosses as in a storm but remains stuck. I'm thinking that the exercise Mauro is talking about is familiar to me, because since Giorgia was hospitalized, I've done nothing but retrace the route that led us to this point—only now it's different, revisiting it scares me.

Giorgia exists: Mauro's words are an accusation. Giorgia exists and I had already started to separate her from the superficial layer. I grip the pen, suspend it over the sheet of paper. I want her back, and with her, our entire world.

The beginning is banal and eludes me, so I choose a very sharp memory midway along: it's the day we move to our apartment, a morning in the dead of winter. Giorgia enters the house before me, and I write about how she makes the new place her own, the ten steps in the hallway, her voice that continues to be heard where I can no longer see her.

* * *

Mauro subjects me to a strict discipline. We enter the month of December with the days of the week organized by activities: he's established a program that allows very few deviations. At set times—from seven to eight, Monday to Thursday, eleven to one on Saturdays—I have to write. I start writing under his supervision, at his house, with him urging me on when I think I can't do it. The first pages are full of just adjectives, some have scrawls that I myself can't make out. At first Mauro is satisfied, then he imposes a more methodical form on me, he makes me work at his computer. When I have moments of disillusionment, he tells me to focus on the exercise, he assures me that soon it will become an automatic action—from some point on, he says, the characters will begin to move independently, and in my case it will be a matter of choosing where to have Giorgia move, which memory to have her inhabit: all I'll have to do is describe what happens.

Before I know it, the exercise becomes a practice of monumental dimensions. The more I explore it, the more my memory expands, and Giorgia is everywhere, even where I thought I wouldn't find her.

"Are you nervous?" Amelia's lips are white from the cold.

"No," I reply.

Mauro has made me attend one of his beginner courses. He assured me that I will only take part in the workshops, I won't have to act: he says it's necessary for drafting our script, because it will help me understand how character construction works and what paths Giorgia also followed in the past.

"You look nervous."

Amelia pulls out a black veil, one of the metal hangers drops to the floor, and the clatter fills the empty room. Abandoned objects stare at us from all sides. Mauro sent us to retrieve some props before the start of the lesson: the storeroom is in the basement, inhabited by rickety clothes racks and the remnants of sets. One wall is occupied by the backdrop of a starry sky fading under the lights; I spot it now as Amelia goes toward it, looking for something.

"I'm not nervous," I repeat, and I can't seem to take my eyes off that backdrop.

Amelia notices, and stops beside me with a stool in her arms. We stand in silence, looking at the cardboard night, a ghostly clock tower taking up one side of the vista.

"How is she?"

As soon as Amelia asks, I remember where I saw this staging. It was in the first act of the play, on May 14: Giorgia had glided across it in the flight scene. I'd wondered how she could be so light, so natural, as if the harnesses and bruises did not exist—one would never have imagined them.

"Okay," I say.

In the clinic, Giorgia continues her performance: she is stable. Her hair is growing, she's no longer pale, she's gained some weight. I resist the temptation to think of her at a later stage, the one that Mauro and I are working on. I keep telling myself that it's not possible, it's only an exercise, a way to deal with the loss.

"I really like her," Amelia says. "I miss her." Her eyes are fixed on me, she looks at me as though to make me believe her. "I've always asked Mauro for news. Since I've known you, I've never had the nerve to ask you. It's strange."

"Why?"

"Because I'm usually bold. But this is an exceptional circumstance, right?"

I look at her, she's scared again that she's not up to the situation.

"It is," I say.

"You seem to be a little better than you were the first day, at the house." Amelia looks at the backdrop again, then smiles. "I really miss her."

"Me too."

"It's like when it happened the first time, when she left. I told you about that, didn't I?"

"Yeah."

"This time we won't let her go," Amelia says. "Sorry I've never gone to see her in the clinic, usually ..."

"Don't worry about it, seriously, I understand."

"I don't," she says. "Besides, without Giorgia there's no fun in it, no one to measure up to. Sometimes she did it on purpose: she challenged me to do better than her and I could never do it. Mauro enjoyed having us compete for parts."

"Really?"

"Yes, he always does that, he says it draws out the best from actors."

"No, I meant: did Giorgia really challenge you?"

Amelia raises her eyebrows and nods emphatically, like a little girl.

"She was very competitive," she says. "A constant spur."

I search my memories and find nothing that matches her description. I tell myself that maybe it's because I never saw Giorgia in her element. I shiver and Amelia notices.

"You're right, it's freezing down here," she says.

I try to offer to carry the stool for her, but she refuses and hurries to the door. When we return to the classroom, we find Mauro busy handing out photocopies to the students—a group of adults between twenty-five and thirty-five years old, the majority female.

"Can you handle the warm-up? I have to make a phone call," he says in a low voice when Amelia and I join him.

Amelia agrees and motions for me to join the class; some greet me with a nod, then we're invited to randomly arrange ourselves in the space, filling the entire room.

"You're still working on the body's presence and spatial awareness, right?" Amelia asks, closing the classroom door behind Mauro.

The class nods, a few confusing replies can be heard.

"Okay," Amelia says. "Now I'll turn off the light. You have to keep moving through space until I tell you to start searching for a partner. The first person you come across, in the dark, will be your object of study. Use touch, memorize enough details to recognize that person. Close your eyes if it doesn't bother you: it will increase the effectiveness of the exercise."

I glance around, looking for signs of the embarrassment I feel at the idea, but everyone is focused and serious.

"When you think you've gathered enough information, you can start walking through space again. Then I'll turn the light back on and we'll talk about it."

Amelia catches my anxious look and bites her lips to hold back a smile.

"Everyone ready?" she asks, looking at me.

Before anyone can answer, she turns off the switch.

"Start walking, cautiously."

Amelia's voice redescribes the room's boundaries, but the transition is abrupt and I walk slowly, fearful of stepping on someone. When my eyes adjust, I begin to see shapes: the indistinct bodies all look alike, the streetlights' glow filtering through the window coverings is not enough to avoid clashing. We wander silently through the space, aimlessly. When I gradually get used to the dark, I realize that no one can see me and the thought relaxes me.

"Now look for a partner: when you've found one, stop and close your eyes."

The shadowy figures quicken their pace. I stretch my arms out in front of me, instinctively, but other arms are speedier than mine: someone makes out the form of my back and politely invites me to turn around by taking me by the shoulders.

I close my eyes. Two unfamiliar hands hesitate around the crew neck of my sweater, try to recognize the texture or maybe the edging of the fabric, then continue to the sides of my face. The fingers are light and cold, they follow the trail of my long beard as far as my lips. The contact breaks off and the fingers begin moving again along the nose: the stranger—a woman, now I have no doubt—looks for irregularities in my profile and doesn't find any. She measures my forehead with a fingertip, up to the hairline, ascertains the hair length by touching the ends; the contact stops again, the hands return to my shoulders, go back to my face. The stranger takes my face in her hands, runs her thumbs over my cheeks; I sense her surprise when a fingertip stumbles onto the scar on my left cheekbone: the finger follows it from side to side to memorize its almond-shaped contours.

The scar provides the proof the stranger was looking for. Now that I know she can recognize me, I feel nervous. I follow her arms, encounter the elbows and move up. I find she's shorter than me, with thin, narrow shoulders, and I can feel the symmetrical points of the taut collarbone under her T-shirt. The neck is thin: I encircle it with one hand—finding the nerve to do it only thanks to my closed eyes—but I immediately feel a vein throbbing and I draw back, maybe too abruptly. She takes my hand and guides it back, this time directly to her face. I let her do so and resume my exploration, unsuccessfully looking for earrings on her ear lobes; I linger on the high, pronounced cheekbones, then the eyebrows, and the small, straight nose. I don't dwell on the hair, which is shoulder-length and soft to the touch.

I try to picture one of the unknown women I barely glimpsed entering the classroom, but I don't remember any of their faces. With a stretch of imagination it could be anyone, even Giorgia, provided I refused to remember her short hair, her height—if it were really her, I'd be able to feel her breath on my face. It's not Giorgia. I think of Amelia—I don't know who to attribute this identity to and I have a foolish need for a clue.

The figure could be hers, the height, even the hair and maybe the fingers, still cold from the trip to the store-room. Before I can look for more evidence, the stranger moves away—I feel the absence of the heat of another body in front of mine, I reopen my eyes and again I see only shadows.

"Everyone ready?" Amelia's voice startles me: it's very far away and suddenly I don't know where I am any-more.

Murmurs of assent are heard. When the light comes back on, I reemerge from a trance. I find myself a few steps from a wall.

"How did it go?"

Amelia's question finds us all confused. She makes us go to the center of the room, walks in front of us. I notice a few glances directed at me; I examine the female faces but the only one I can distinguish among them is Amelia's, as if it were the only possible option. It's absurd: there are at least four or five other girls with similar physical traits: same height, same weight, same hair length, yet I can't get the idea that the stranger might be Amelia out of my mind. I avoid her gaze, afraid to find the answer in her eyes.

"Can you recognize one another?"

A few individuals join other people, forming three couples—they say they recognized their partner by a necklace, the curly hair, the logo stamped on the front of a T-shirt. The others go on studying one another, with some embarrassment, and no one remembers my scar.

"It's important to be able to recognize yourself in space. Awareness of your body and that of your fellow actors, onstage, is fundamental. Mauro must have al-ready repeated it to you ad nauseam: it's from awareness of the body that a balanced stage layout is achieved."

As if conjured up by Amelia's words, Mauro opens the classroom door. Amelia reports the results of the exercise, then he takes over. Halfway through the class, when it's time to run through the monologues and I can finally bow out of the rehearsals, Amelia says goodbye to the class and leaves.

I write until late at night with Mauro, at his house. While I devote myself to accounts of my memories, he prepares his course material, does some research, or studies in silence. He always makes dinner, refuses my offers to contribute, and says he's content with free coffee at the café. I don't have the energy to make up for the disproportion, I know that he is doing much more for me than I am able to do for him and that, most likely, I will never be able to repay him—I don't have the means. The thought bothers me but the truth is that I can't think about it: since we met, he has filled almost every moment of my available time; him, his activities, his friends, and now, the project we're both working on.

Every now and then I am reminded of what Amelia said at the party—"He's like that with everyone he cares about"—and I think that there is no more distorted and, at the same time, fitting description. Mauro is all action, no apparent feeling that is not related to the theater; he moves nonstop and he registers the world around him only as a kind of anthropological observation. I see him gathering data on whoever is around him, sometimes I catch him processing them while, on the surface, he continues talking. Amelia is the only person for whom he has an obvious affection, expressed in mental code: there are no physical impulses in him aside from the attentions he infrequently devotes to women—Sara, most often, but also two other casual relations with members of the company.

I watch him grab one of the empty plates from dinner: he scoops up the sauce left on the bottom with a finger, then puts it in his mouth and stares at me. I suspect this is the only useful measure by which to gauge his affection: to constantly feel his gaze on me, even when he's not there. I don't want to know the reasons for his attention—my guess is it's the pity I must arouse in him, and his esteem for Giorgia.

"Did you understand what I meant when I talked about unconvincing characters?"

I break away from the monitor and squeeze my eyes shut. I feel a kind of fatigue that I haven't felt since my university days and my time as a freelancer. On the screen, Giorgia is telling me about her past on the way back from a concert at a club one Saturday night: the more I explore, the sharper the memories become—like her way of conducting the conversation in fits and starts: I thought it was shyness, what if instead it was the effort to lie?

"Tonight, the monologues in class," Mauro prompts me.

"I know," I say. "I get it, to some extent."

"What were the jarring notes?"

I save the document and close the laptop. He does the same and stretches out in his chair.

"Well, some were blatantly artificial. For example, the second-to-last girl was impossible to listen to."

"I agree, she was terrible."

"But can these things be improved?" I ask.

He runs a hand through his hair, which is getting long; he's started gathering it in a knot at the back of his neck.

"It depends a lot on the actor's cooperation. Some, for example, just feel blocked, as if the performance triggered a short circuit. They're shy about being themselves, but also about performing. That's why they take the course."

"But there were some who were better. The girl in the green T-shirt."

"True, she's not bad. But let's keep to the subject. The point is: as spectators, what makes us realize that a performance is awful?"

"It's not convincing, it sounds false."

He nods. "Exactly. And it happens even when actors memorize all the lines, when they observe the intonations and wear stage costumes. Why? You say that some performers seemed artificial, but in reality they all are: the same monologue recited by a capable actor doesn't become real."

"Sure it does."

"It becomes real for you," Mauro smiles; he loves to counter for effect. "The problem lies in the divergences. The variance between voluntary verbal expressions— the lines of a script—and involuntary ones—the tone, the tempo of the voice. Or, if we want to be more discerning, the variance between all verbal expressions and body language, what a person says and what he does as he's saying it."

Mauro pulls a cigarette out of the packet, lights it and looks at me, as if asking if I'm too tired for this. I motion for him to continue.

"A very important part of the performance is in the body. Think about how Greek theater was born: no scripts or dialogues, just mimicry, gesticulation, and acrobatics borrowed from sacred performances. Think about the mimiambi, but also about the optical theater of the nineteenth century. Think about where the illusion of a person who is lying fails."

The last reference is the only one I get.

"Convincing the body of a lie is a painstaking job," Mauro says, blowing out smoke. "The actor's internalization must be complete, his character must contain the information necessary for the creation of a new pattern of movements: the physical spaces where the performance takes place, the attitudes, the postures."

He flicks off the ashes.

"I started putting the script together," he says.

"When?"

"A while ago, ten days maybe. I'm drawing on your material."

We look at each other across the table.

"Is it adequate?" I ask, trying to maintain a neutral tone.

"It's perfect," he says. "I didn't expect so much care. Of course, the earlier facts are a little inconsistent, but the latest accounts are impeccable, full of details."

"Is it realistic?" I press him. "Do you recognize her?"

He sees my fear and smiles at it—again with the corners of his mouth turned down.

"Yes, Filippo, it's realistic!" he says. "And yes, I recognize her: she's your Giorgia."

I watch him smoke for a while longer, and he doesn't look away. In the end, I'm the one who gives in.

"I'll take you home, " he says then.

In the car, he explains that he's constructing the script without leaving anything out, that afterwards, when it's ready, we'll go over the story line together. Halfway there he decides to make a detour and we set off along Corso di Porta Ticinese. He drives slowly; the roads are practically empty.

"Look at the shops: aquariums, aren't they?"

I agree, and for a while we're silent, staring at the empty premises behind the windows, bathed in a watery green and blue neon light.

When we reach my house, Mauro parks and turns the engine off.

"Can I use your bathroom a second?" he asks. "I don't feel so good."

I look at him: he looks lifeless, his face pale. We don't make it to the apartment in time: Mauro throws up in the courtyard, in a flower bed.

"Maybe you should stay," I say, when we go inside. "No, I'll just rinse my mouth and be on my way."

He uses the bathroom for quite a while. When he comes out, he says he thinks he may have a fever. He decides to stay only when he realizes he's not clear-headed enough to drive. "It's those damn kids at the school," he says.

I find him one of my sweat suits, and he undresses on the bed that was mine and Giorgia's—thin body, tense muscles, a scar on the abdomen that wrinkles as he shivers with the chills. When he finally surrenders to sleep, with an empty bucket waiting by his side, I leave only the bedside lamp on. I observe his back for a while, then I fall asleep on the wrong side of the bed, the one that holds Giorgia's shape.

During the night, I have a dream: Mauro is stalking back and forth down the corridor like a ghost, an unlit cigarette in his mouth. He stops at the door and looks at everything, he studies the doorposts, our furniture, he searches unsuccessfully; then his eyes stop at me, the hostile half of his profile hidden in the dark.

Mauro is sitting in Giorgia's place, by the window. He must have woken up very early: I found him waiting for me in the kitchen when the sky outside was still dark.

"What time do you start work?" he asks me, watching me drown the cereal in milk. He has two dark circles under his eyes and his eyes are shiny, he must still have a fever.

"At seven," I tell him. "Do you want a Tylenol?"

He shakes his head and rests his forearms on the table.

"I did a lot of thinking tonight, I couldn't sleep," Mauro says. "I want to finish the script as soon as possible. We need to see if it works."

"What's the story about?" I ask, trying to shift the conversation to neutral ground—I'm not yet ready to discuss that likelihood.

"What story?"

"The plot. What happens?"

"Absolutely nothing," he replies.

"Nothing at all happens?"

"No. Excuse me, what would you like to have happen?"

"I don't know ... Still, we should organize the material with an objective."

"Filippo." Mauro smiles wearily. "Are you asking me if we're creating a character with a purpose?"

His condescending tone irritates me and he knows it, he used it deliberately.

"I understood that the character has to be believable. How do we convince her of a character without a purpose?" The implication of what I said dawns on me a minute later, and again the premise makes my head spin.

Mauro picks at a hole in the plastic tablecloth.

"Don't you think it would be riskier to give her one?" he says. "Look what happened with the Peter Pan role. Besides, what could be more realistic than a character without a purpose? Can you imagine anything that comes closer to reality?"

I make an effort to swallow a spoonful of cereal, and study the bottom of the bowl.

"No," Mauro continues. "The script will be a long description, a series of spoken lines interspersed with subtext."

"And the other characters?"

"You, me, people she knows."

"Don't forget my parents," I say, automatically.

"Don't worry, we'll go over everything together as soon as the draft is ready," he replies. "The narrative will be one of Giorgia's long days, a summation of her life in twenty-four hours: encounters with the people she loves and cares for, her thoughts, her movements from when she wakes up to the time she goes to sleep. If we're lucky, she'll adapt to the script and expand it on her own, proceeding by deduction."

The more I think about it, the more I know it can't work. Viewing us through an outsider's lens, I see us exhausted and disorganized, hostages of a delusional plan. What are we going to do when it doesn't work? What will Mauro do? I think, watching him trace invisible patterns on the table.

"Another thing I thought about tonight is that we have to pay close attention," he says, without looking at me. "I think it's possible that something unexpected may happen, and we have to be ready. I wrote for the theater, a long time ago, but I'm a director, not a playwright: I know the structures like the back of my hand, but I'll have to be cautious, and you'll have to follow me step by step."

I want to ask him if he thinks we should stop. He raises his head, as if he'd heard the question.

"There are things I can't envision," he says, as if to apologize.

When I leave to go to work, I tell him to stay as long as he wants. The day passes quickly, and on my return I catch myself hoping to find him still in the house. Instead a note from him awaits me, stuck in the mirror frame beside the door: "Thanks. I'll call you as soon as I'm better."

* * *

The first draft of the script is ready by Christmas week, the result of fifteen days of extremely intense work. After he got over the flu, Mauro resumed prodding me. Together we created the array of walk-ons, a brief, concise description of names that formed the background, then the characters directly involved in the action: my parents, Amelia, himself. I was the last to be written in: Mauro described me as a co-star. The work was concluded in utter secrecy—in answer to Amelia's questions, we fabricated a sudden interest of mine in writing a play. When I go to my parents' house at Christmas, I take the script with me. I read in the breaks between meals, during lazy mornings, between my mother's pampering—she treats me as though I were recovering from a long convalescence—and my father's cautious questions: "How are you doing?" and "What can you do? You have to be patient."

Mauro and I talk almost every day on the phone. A backdrop of voices and music can be heard on his end, and one evening, with this soundtrack, we decide on Giorgia's love for me. We opt not to make it explicit, to leave it up to her body in the subtext, to her improvisations. The crucial scene lies in the description of our first date: the pub on the Naviglio, the first kiss in a narrow street alongside the canal. On the eve of the new year, I wonder if it will be sufficient: whether that moment really was enough to determine us.

* * *

Mauro rolls the script in his hands and the stiff paper crackles, echoing our footsteps on the icy gravel path as we walk from the car to the clinic.

The clerk at the reception desk greets us with a smile. "Giorgia is in her room," she says. Mauro wanted me to start by myself, but I refused and, as we climb the stairs to the first floor, I don't regret my decision: today I would not have found it in me to read. My hands are covered in a cold sweat, there's a hard lump in my throat. He is calm, and strides decisively towards the room.

"Wait a second," he says, stopping in the middle of the hallway. "Whatever happens, let's keep in mind that it's just an experiment. An attempt to help Giorgia remember."

I nod. He starts walking again, then stops a second time, and comes back.

"We'll act as we always do: we'll play along with her. I'm going to try a little trick to get her to listen to me while I read, you follow my lead."

"All right."

I'm filled with impatience. In recent times I have cut down on visits to Giorgia due to writing the script, but also because of my own form of exasperation. I can't stand having to nurture the monster for long—every reply, every absurd phrase is an encouragement to that abusive tenant; and then to see her so free and easy in the character, to find her a little better each day in an identity so far removed from the one I knew.

When we walk through the door of her room I'm already afraid of failing, but there's no time to think about it for long. Giorgia is standing in front of the window: it's her favorite activity, whiling away the time waiting for someone. She doesn't turn around when we enter. Mauro speaks up first.

"My lady."

Giorgia barely flicks her head, as if disturbed by the buzz of an insect.

"My lady," Mauro repeats, this time louder.

Giorgia gives him a distracted glance.

"Have you seen him return?" she asks.

By now I too know the script by heart. I drag the guest chair against the wall and slowly sit down. Now that we're here, our attempt seems silly and desperate, and I feel all the accumulated pointless weariness of the last month.

"What does Malvolio say?" insists Giorgia. "The messenger? Did he see the messenger arrive?"

"No, my lady," Mauro replies, deadpan. "Malvolio says that he will be here soon. He sent us to entertain you."

Giorgia turns in my direction, bored. "Where is my clown?"

"Indisposed." Mauro waves the script. "But, as I told you, we are here to entertain you."

"Are you good at wordplay?"

"Absolutely. I propose a reading."

Giorgia's gaze sharpens, she weighs the idea, then she goes back to looking out the window.

"A reading is not enough," she murmurs. "Uncertainty consumes me."

Mauro bows his head toward Giorgia, goes on speaking amiably.

"Believe me, my lady: this is not a reading like the others. It will make you forget the apprehension of waiting."

"He should have been here already." Giorgia taps the folded fan against her chin. "What does Malvolio say? Did he tell you when he will arrive?"

"The messenger is expected shortly, my lady. You will not be disappointed. But now I'd best fulfill the task of entertaining you, or I will soon find myself indisposed like the clown."

She heaves a sigh, then walks back to the bed, holding the hem of her dressing gown. She sits serenely on the edge of the bed, folds her hands in her lap.

"So then, as you wish," she says. "What reading be it?"

"The story of a great love."

Giorgia, wound tight as a bowstring, raises her eyes. "You would have me dead, then."

For a moment I'm afraid she's going to throw us out of the room.

"May such an abominable thought never touch your lips," Mauro replies, fervently.

His performance is impeccable: he doesn't lose focus, he keeps his character grounded in Giorgia's world as I could never do.

"You say it's the story of a great love. How great, then?"

"Twice the size of Illyria," Mauro replies, taking advantage of the opening. "But let me read it."

"The messenger will come, won't he?"

"Yes," he says. "The messenger will come."

He opens the script, returning to his usual spot

against the windowsill. He discreetly observes Giorgia's reactions, now that she has finally resigned herself. When Mauro starts reading, she doesn't really listen.

"Giorgia is thirty-one years old, with a slim body, big dark eyes. One morning in January she wakes up very early."

Giorgia starts fluttering the fan, and Mauro goes on reading. I replace him when he gets tired, but Giorgia seems not to notice; her gaze is lost in space. I read until visiting hours are over. When we're about to leave, Giorgia asks again about her messenger, and we reassure her that he will arrive soon. Then the usual nurse presses us and we are forced to go.

In the car, Mauro says it's better than nothing, though I can't tell; I feel like I'm sinking back into apathy, but I don't have the heart to admit it to him. I don't know what I expected: when I arrived I was torn between doubt and uneasiness, and now I don't feel anything. Mauro reminds me that it's only an experiment, an exercise. But an exercise for what? I want to ask. The thought of giving up crosses my mind, but he says something will happen. "All those memories," he says. "Something is bound to happen."

CHAPTER FIVE

TWO ACTS

I see Mauro coming from a distance; I recognize his long stride. He ends the phone conversation when he's halfway here. His coat is unbuttoned and his shirt is open, leaving his throat exposed. I'm freezing in my jacket, standing in front of the closed café for forty minutes, waiting for him.

"Sorry I'm late," he says, as soon as he reaches me.

"I called you."

He shakes his head and pulls his hair back; he's got bags under his eyes and he's puffy, as if he'd just woken up.

"Yeah, sorry, I had a tough day."

"I could have taken the bus, it wouldn't have been a problem."

"The car is over there," he cuts me off, nodding for me to follow him.

"It's pretty late. Maybe we could skip it for today."

He puts his hands in his pocket, annoyed. "Why? Let's go."

"By the time we get there, we won't have much time left."

"I said we're going," Mauro says flatly, putting an end to the discussion, without looking at me.

I think maybe he's had enough of our constant visits, too. We've been reading for a month with no results, but neither of us has the guts to honestly admit that our plan has failed: it was inevitable. I think Mauro feels guilty, as if he were responsible for the failure, and I don't have the energy to convince him otherwise.

When we get to his car, I start to open the door, but stop midway: someone waves to me through the window, and I recognize one of Mauro's girlfriends. I try to meet his eyes for an explanation, but he avoids my look and gets in without saying a word.

"Ciao!" the girl says, turning towards me between the seats, when I'm inside.

"Ciao," I answer.

"You've met Giulia before, haven't you?" Mauro exits the parking lot without looking for cars; someone honks his horn and he snarls an insult.

"I don't know," Giulia says. "We may have met once, at the theater."

She smiles at me and shrugs, her full breasts squeezing together in the low neckline. My eyes drop to her legs, veiled by stockings, below the short skirt. The back seat is cramped and uncomfortable. I look at Mauro in the rearview mirror, but he keeps ignoring me.

Until we get on the highway, I'm hopeful that we'll be dropping Giulia off somewhere before going on to the clinic, but Mauro doesn't deviate from the route. The closer we get to our destination, the more agitated I feel. I grudgingly reply as Giulia bombards me with questions, thinking she is being courteous. I answer in monosyllables and watch her fiddle with her hair, curling the long, brown strands around her fingers.

Encouraged by my passive participation, she tells me about one of her university exams, about Musil. By the time we reach the clinic I'm so nervous my hands are shaking—Musil, the girl, me staring at her hungrily, Mauro being late, Giorgia waiting for us.

"We'll be back in half an hour" Mauro says in the parking lot. "I'll leave you the keys."

She nods, playing with the car radio's controls.

When we're in the clinic, I grab Mauro by the arm.

"Do you mind telling me why you brought her here?"

He looks at me aggressively. "What's your problem?"

"Did you think you were taking her on a joyride? *I'll introduce you to the loser with the schizophrenic girlfriend?*"

Mauro jerks his arm free. We've attracted the attention of the receptionist. I try to calm down, but I'm too worked up. I put two steps between him and me.

"All this because I was twenty minutes late?"

"Forty minutes. Anyway, you know that's not it."

"So, what is it? Are you pissed because I didn't answer the phone?"

I start up the stairs, determined to keep my distance.

"I don't want you bringing anyone."

"Giulia doesn't even know why we're here. And what if she did? Are you ashamed of it?"

I turn to look at Mauro and find him still on the first step, staring at me. I can't shake off his eyes, they reproach me for the petty thoughts I had along the way. I decide to ignore him.

On the way to Giorgia's room, we don't talk anymore. As we go inside I feel nauseous. I look away from Mauro and the script, which by this time is tattered from being carried back and forth. When he starts reading, after the usual pantomime with Giorgia, I close my eyes. I feel like I'm back to the day we met, in this same room, and that I've done nothing but go around in circles: the poles of my world are still reversed. I'd like to shut out the sound, instead I listen to Mauro read. It's the same story rewound, Giorgia and I meet; Giorgia and I continue to meet, she's thirty-one years old, has the same large dark eyes, slim body, and every day we occupy the same imaginary space. I no longer know where it was we existed, and Giorgia is no longer thirty-one years old: a fact I realize a week late.

"Would you stop, please?" I ask Mauro.

He looks up from the script for a moment, slowly enunciates a line, then continues reading, as if I hadn't spoken. Giorgia stares out the window, lost in her universe.

"I told you to stop," I repeat.

"Excuse me?" says Mauro.

"Enough."

"Would you mind telling me what the hell is eating you?"

He's still holding the open script in his hands: I can feel my pent-up rage mounting just watching him.

"It's absolutely pointless. You realize that, right?"

Mauro gestures towards Giorgia, as if to tell me to watch what I say. I can't even look at her.

"It's of no use."

"You don't know that."

"Do you know?"

"I see," he smiles insolently. "You've decided to have a showdown?"

I lean toward him, gripping the arms of the chair. "You're only insisting because you don't want to admit you failed. You'd go on reading for the next thirty years."

"Do you have a better idea?"

"We should never have started. I don't know why I went along with you."

"Went along with me?" Mauro's face is transfigured: the storm cloud that passes over him is savage. "What else do you want to unload on me? You think it's my fault our attempt hasn't worked? It's my fault that I can't perform a miracle and cure her?"

Giorgia remains motionless at the corner of my eye.

"Well? Maybe the job you hate is my fault, too, how about it? Or the fact that you don't fuck? Maybe that's your problem."

I leap at him without formulating a single thought, my hands already on the script: I grab it and throw it on the floor. Mauro laughs in my face, a loud, cheerless laugh.

"I can try to do something about that too, if you want," he says.

"It's a game for you, right? You're amusing yourself."

"A game? Do I have to remind you how I found you, Filippo?"

Mauro takes a step forward and I'm forced to back away to avoid contact. The effort to control my anger paralyzes me.

"Do you really want to hear a pitiful account of everything I'm doing for you? I welcomed you into my home," he keeps at it, "I introduced you to my friends. I gave you the social life you never had."

"No one asked you for anything."

Mauro's lips form another frosty smile. "There you go, finally. Come on, Filippo, muster the last shred of miserable courage you have: for once, say what you think."

I catch a sidelong glimpse of movement, but Mauro is too close, I can't resist the desire to hurt him.

"Say it, Filippo: it's my fault. Before me, Giorgia was fine, wasn't she?"

Mauro moves closer, I can feel his breath on me.

"Get away from me."

"Say it, Filippo: it's my fault that Giorgia got this way."

"You think I don't know why you're doing this? You want your plaything back, don't you? It's her you want."

Mauro grabs me by my jacket collar, pulls me so close that I can't bring him into focus.

"Don't you dare ..."

The scream freezes us. It starts outside of us, and drags us violently back into this room. It's coming from Giorgia, shrill yet at the same time deep enough to vibrate in our throats as well. When we finally turn to look at her, her eyes are wide open, darting around in all directions, as if an enemy were quickly advancing. When the scream dies in her throat, she huddles in the center of her bed, and begins digging her nails into her pajamas.

"Don't lower your guard, don't lower your guard," she repeats over and over, without stopping for breath. "From all sides, from all sides. I've seen them."

Mauro lets go of me, but we're both frozen in place. Giorgia screams again, grabs her head in her hands and closes her eyes. I instinctively rush towards her as she starts pulling her hair, and Mauro joins me. We both fall on the bed, I hold her wrists, she kicks out, Mauro grabs her legs and pins them with his weight.

"THEY'RE EVERYWHERE!" Giorgia's scream explodes straight into my stomach; again, the panic.

I restrain her wrists, press her tightly to me—"EVERYWHERE"; I'm thinking I can hold on forever. The nurses find us tangled up, a crab-like monster, capsized on the bed.

They immediately drive us out of her room and confine us to the third-floor offices. In the absence of the chief doctor, the facility is under the supervision of the health director, a woman in her fifties whom I've only glimpsed a couple of times: it is she who relegates us to the waiting room, she again who returns to tell us that Giorgia's crisis has reemerged, that they have put her under sedation, and that it's best not to expose her to any further stimuli for today. She sounds like someone who has been reciting those words her entire life.

When we leave, Mauro heads to the car without a word, and I set out in the opposite direction.

"Where are you going?" I hear his question, then his steps following it on the gravel.

I'd like to simply disappear or abruptly fall asleep; I don't want to process what has just happened. I wish Mauro would ignore me, that we would both remain silent, as we did during the wait. For a while Giorgia's screams had risen up the stairs. I kept listening until they stopped, torturing myself at the thought of having contributed to triggering the relapse. Was it our argument? And what if it was the script?

"I need to walk," I say, when Mauro blocks my way.

He too is distraught, I picture him facedown on the bed, his eyes squeezed shut, holding Giorgia still.

"Don't be an idiot. Get in the car."

I ignore his order and keep walking: he doesn't budge, and I end up bumping into him. He grabs me by the shoulder, preventing me from continuing.

"Do you want to start up again?" I ask.

I'm drained, terrified, not for a minute could I summon up the energy for a fight. I look at him and hope he understands that I'm surrendering.

"No," he replies, letting me go. All of a sudden he's depleted too. "I'm sorry."

I'd like to tell him that I'm sorry too, and that my regret begins far back in Giorgia's past—a past that I know nothing about, where I wish I could intervene and reshape the memories to accommodate a normal present, the kind that doesn't involve painful exercises, or suffering of this magnitude. I really wish I could write a new script and I know that, for different reasons, he would like to as well.

"I'm sorry too," I say. "Let's drop it for a while, okay?"

He looks at me, not understanding.

"The script, all the rest. I need to think."

He puts his hands in his coat pockets, keeps looking at me, and I do the same. I want him to know that this is my final word.

"All right," he says. "Sounds reasonable. But let me drive you back."

I shake my head. I can see him staging one last maneuver in the car in front of his new girlfriend maybe, or intoxicating me with his words at my front door.

"No. I need to think, starting now."

He hears me. "Whatever you want," he says.

As he walks away, I set out along the shoulder of the road, headed for the bus stop. The last I see of Mauro is the rear end of his Alfa as it passes me and disappears around the first curve.

* * *

The beginning lies in a distant world: the crystallized moment in which Giorgia's lips widen in the first smile. We are captive in a pub on the Naviglio and the music is so loud we can't hear our own voices. I've gotten into the habit of revisiting this memory often, sitting behind myself on our first date and observing. The details haunt me.

Some particulars are more elementary, like Giorgia's hands, which were always moving gracefully—first behind her ear to tuck back an unruly imaginary strand, then down along the neck. The appearance of the smile, however, is complex and tricky: it always turned up in places where I wasn't expecting it. At first I thought she was laughing at me, then, as I got to know her, I realized I was wrong. Nevertheless, Giorgia's smile remains a mystery. It was contained, fragile. It was rare. Now that it's gone, I like to sit in this corner of memory that is warm and comforting and so different. A moment forever unchanged. Unrepeatable. Unreproducible.

I'm unable to set aside the exercise: in my memory I'm duplicated, I start existing in two acts. I am in what is happening to me in a specific, pointless present, and in another scene as well, in the sphere that was Giorgia's. And so, after a while, reality begins to fade and I live in a dream. In the dream Mauro does not look for me, we stop seeing each other, and he too dissolves.

* * *

My mother has a strange way of laughing in response to my attempts at being humorous: she brings her hand to her chest, leans forward, and casts her laugh like a fishing line; she tosses the bait and sees if anyone—my father, a relative, a friend—will bite at the possibility of her son being brilliantly amusing. Often, the laugh comes back empty-handed until it dies in her throat: then she looks at me with an alarming tenderness.

I watch her as she separates the linen to be ironed,

standing halfway between the hallway and the dining room so she can keep an eye on the television. She follows the Saturday-afternoon talk shows, while I enjoy making a few jokes and seeing her seek my father's complicity; he reliably ignores her and, sitting on the sofa, impassively continues his battle with the crossword puzzle. Since they retired from the café, they have become extremely sedentary, as if to recuperate from thirty years of constant contact with the outside world. My father doesn't even like to go out for walks: he says that when one is not behind a counter, people are strange. "Is it because of your legs?" I asked him today, and my mother burst into one of her ill-fated laughs.

I think I stopped feeling at home, in this house, from the time I went to live with Giorgia. I remember exactly the spaces that I'm now a stranger to, my mother keeps everything in the same place, her care and cleaning rituals are manic.

"I don't mean you should come back to live with us," my mother says, steaming my father's underwear. "I just mean I'd like to see you a little more settled."

The topic of the day has been one of her three favorites: my precarious economic situation. She persists in treating the problem as if it were due to my lack of enterprise and not to a more general, structural crisis of which I am a product.

"You won't believe this but I wish I were more settled too."

I see her stiffen, scrutinizing the close-up of the show's hostess. I know she's thinking about Giorgia, even though she'll never say so out loud: she does that with everything she can't handle, she pretends it doesn't exist. Watching her steam the undershorts softens me, and at the same time I feel a strong sense of nausea—it occurs to me that our worlds differ only in their content and that our hereditary flaw is the same.

Since the crisis, I haven't been back to see Giorgia. I count the days in the crochet stitches of the doilies scattered on the furniture: two weeks without setting foot in the clinic. I'm still divided, Giorgia burbles in my subterranean springs, it is a current that I have learned to navigate. On the surface I adjust to those I'm talking to; when I'm home alone, I lose my configuration.

I have started visiting my parents more often again. They have stopped asking questions; they welcome me on weekends and let me regress to my adolescent state. Giorgia is something that we're all aware of and that no one talks about anymore, like my father's heart, which continues to beat fitfully, or the still unresolved tax demands from the Revenue Agency—all subjects to be discussed only when it's inevitable.

I get up and go to the kitchen for a glass of water. From this angle, I see my parents squeezed into the door frame: just as in my memory, they contract, get smaller and smaller, and their world could fit in a shoebox.

When my cell phone rings, I don't recognize the sound; I let it play until my mother turns to me—"Is that yours?" she asks. I slip my hand into the back pocket of my jeans and retrieve the phone in time. The screen blinks on and off with an unknown number.

"Hello?"

"Mr. Bonini?"

I immediately recognize the clinic director's voice and my blood freezes.

"Is she all right?"

"Calm down, Mr. Bonini, everything is fine."

I suppress a sigh, turn my back to my mother, who is watching me from the doorway of the dining room; I go over to the window.

"What's happened?"

It's Saturday afternoon, there must be a very serious reason why he's calling me. My thoughts turn to another breakdown, an accident that he's hiding from me.

"I apologize if this is an inappropriate time, I missed a weekly visit and had to make up for it today," the doctor says, his tone still calm. "Were you planning to drop by this afternoon?"

Maybe he wants to know why I've deserted the clinic: he must think I'm a monster.

"Actually ..."

"Are you able to change your plans? I'd like to have a talk with you. Today."

"What's going on?"

I sense the doctor's hesitation.

"Take my words with all due caution, keeping in mind what we've been talking about these past months," he says slowly. "Giorgia is asking for you. She wants to see you."

After ending the call with the doctor, I acted without thinking: I called Mauro. The phone rang and rang for a long time. When he answered, I did not go into complicated explanations: I told him that it was urgent, nothing to worry about but urgent, and that there was no time to wait for the bus. He replied in monosyllables, and had me dictate the address. Fifteen minutes later he was at my parents' house.

"Didn't he tell you anything else?" Mauro asks, getting on the highway.

"No," I reply. "He said to meet with him for a talk before seeing Giorgia."

We sink back into silence. Neither of us mentioned the argument we had two weeks ago; the news about Giorgia has left us speechless.

When we reach the clinic, Mauro parks crookedly against the hedge, and we both rush to the entrance, then up the stairs to the third floor. The director's office is closed; when I knock firmly, the door opens: it was unlocked. The doctor looks up from his desk, and smiles kindly when he recognizes us.

"Mr. Bonini," he says, motioning for us to come in.

I'm reluctant to sit down. I don't want this preliminary meeting to last longer than it needs to. I remain standing in front of the desk, and Mauro follows suit. The doctor understands our hurry.

"Just a few words, before you go to her," he says.

I nod, impatient.

"Sit down, please."

I grudgingly comply, tension making my hands sweat. I take a seat and Mauro sits next to me.

The doctor folds his hands on the shiny screen of his tablet.

"It appears that Giorgia has started remembering some things."

"When did it happen?" Mauro asks.

"A few days ago. I chose to have her monitored to make certain it wasn't an isolated incident."

I slump back in the chair.

"How did it happen? I mean ... she had a breakdown just two weeks ago," Mauro says.

"I can't say for sure. We can theorize that the decreased dosages resulted in the breach that we were hoping for." The doctor looks at me gravely. "It is very important to proceed with caution. Giorgia is still fragile."

"Of course," I say.

"Do you mind if I observe your visit? I won't get in your way. Today's information will be useful to me when considering the new treatment."

"No problem."

"Good, let's go."

When the doctor stands up, filling the room, we do the same and follow him into the hallway. We go down the stairs in silence. I feel the blood pumping into my body cavities, my heart is deafening.

"Try to control any manifestations of emotion," the doctor says when we reach the first floor. "It is preferable not to excite Giorgia with exceedingly intense stimuli."

I clench my fists, breathe deeply. When we are almost at the door, the doctor steps aside for me, then stops Mauro behind me: "No more than one at a time."

Coming from inside is the voice of the nurse: I recognize it before I appear at the door. Giorgia's voice is lower. Still hidden by the wall, I stay there listening and the words form a confused whole that I am not able to untangle. I'm thinking that the voice is hers again; it has the same tone. For a moment I don't feel I can do it. Then I push myself to go in, one step at a time.

"Oh, Giorgia! Look who's come to see you." The nurse's smile blends into the whiteness of her uniform, I don't notice her anymore.

Giorgia is in the chair by the window, one leg folded to her chest, as in one of my best memories. She turns to me. Her eyes find me and she recognizes me. I see myself appear in her eyes, and it restores me, along with the smile she gives me. I have it all back again, my name, my identity, a context.

She gets up with an agile leap and rushes over to me, hugs me. "Filippo," she says.

I'm afraid of collapsing under her, so I feel for the bed with one leg, sit on the edge, and she follows me. She's sitting right by my side, as though it were the most natural thing in the world. I can't believe it.

"Why did it take you so long to come?" she asks me.

I try to formulate a coherent response, to control my desire to hold her tight to me again.

"I told you, Giorgia, remember? Filippo was busy with his parents," the nurse steps in.

"Are they all right?" Giorgia looks at me, concern carving the usual furrow between her eyebrows.

"Yes," I say, clearing my throat. "They're fine. Routine visits."

"I missed you," she says.

"Yes, I missed you too."

"How much longer will I have to stay here?"

The nurse, standing behind Giorgia, looks at me purposefully.

"For a little while longer, Giorgia. Filippo will come to see you every day."

I nod, I'm afraid of saying something wrong.

"But why am I here?" Giorgia is calm, she looks at me quietly.

"To get better, dear," the nurse continues. "You'll stay here a little while longer, Filippo will come to see you every day, and afterwards you can go home."

Giorgia rolls her eyes, then shrugs and looks at me as if to apologize.

"She says it's only for a short time," she repeats.

"Sure."

She reaches out and runs her fingers through my hair, rediscovering the remembered path.

"Are you all right?" she asks.

"I'm okay. I just have to go to the bathroom," I tell her. "Excuse me a minute?"

"Go ahead! I'll be here, waiting."

I leave the room avoiding the doctor's shadow, a moment before it's too late. Out in the hall, Mauro is waiting behind the door. I meet his eyes, I find them as round and shocked as mine.

"He's not well," we hear Giorgia say.

"He's had a lot going on, with his parents," the nurse says.

"He's haggard," she insists. "Will I really be able to get out of here soon?"

"Of course, dear, it just takes a little patience."

"I want to take a walk, it's a beautiful day today."

I break down and weep silently: I cry on Mauro's shoulder, breathing into his coat without a sound.

Will I really be able to get out of here soon?

* * *

From the hallway, I keep an eye on the door of the director's office. Giorgia is talking with the doctor; I don't want her coming out and catching me on the phone.

"Do you need me to join you?"

"No, it's not necessary," I say. "It's just that she did it again this morning, with her clothes ... Like when we went to the park together."

I sense Mauro thinking, at the other end of the line.

Giorgia's return has been traumatic for both of us. We were under a lot of tension during the fifteen days the doctor prescribed to observe her condition. On her first day out, we took her to the nearby town for coffee. She sat at the café table as if nothing had happened, as if the clinic had never existed. We watched her talk, look around at her surroundings, straighten her hair. I don't know whether Mauro too felt an intense dread of looming disaster that day—seeing her touch the glass of her tumbler and fearing an explosion; foreseeing a crisis triggered by the barista's shouted goodbye, and hearing her respond with a polite "Bye now." The disaster did not materialize, the only absurdity was Giorgia's order: peach juice, a drink that, before her hospitalization, she would never have liked.

A schedule has been established and the time allowed for our visits to the outside world has gradually lengthened. Giorgia is responding well to the stimuli, as the doctor says, yet he proceeds cautiously, and urges me to be on the alert. The hours spent with Giorgia are still quite stressful: the sequence of possible occurrences is constantly on my mind. Most of all, I'm afraid of losing her again at any moment. I can't look into her eyes for long, before I quickly reach my limit of endurance and panic at the thought of seeing that she no longer recognizes me—I still dream about her turning to me as if I were someone else, almost every night.

I am sensitive to the warning signs, I look for alterations in her behaviors. There was a faulty moment a week ago, when Mauro and I planned the first walk in the city center. For the occasion, I'd brought some of Giorgia's clothes to the clinic—it seemed like a good idea to me to allow her to choose what to wear, instead of being limited to the usual jeans and T-shirt. On her bed I laid out the dark-green shirt that she said she loved, the two dresses I often saw her wear for our dinners, the gray-and-black nylon stockings. Giorgia stood there looking at the clothes for a while. "I don't know what to wear," she said. "Whichever one you like," I replied. "I don't know which one I like, I really don't know." I'd had to choose for her. Then at the park, in the city, as we watched the children throwing bread crumbs at the ducks, she'd burst into tears. "I don't know how to dress," she said. Her crying had shaken us, we'd immediately brought her back, but it had been nothing more than a passing dejection.

"She didn't want to choose her clothes again?" Mauro asks now.

"Yeah. I did as you said, I tried again, offering her only two options: blue T-shirt or red T-shirt. She was that close to crying again."

"Did you tell the doctor?"

"Yes. He says it's normal, that she's in a period of adjustment and we still have to determine how far the illness has retreated," I say, repeating the doctor's words by heart. "I'm not so sure, Mauro. What if ..."

"What?"

I lean further into the hallway, lowering my voice. "What if we forgot ..."

"We still don't know if that's the case."

"I know. But what if that were the case and we forgot this particular ... instruction. And what if we forgot something else, something more important?"

"I already told you that it's no use formulating hypotheses, we have to monitor her patiently, as the doctor says," Mauro replies, calmly but firmly. "However, since it's not the first episode, maybe I could try to reread the script."

I contain my relief. "Good, thank you."

"Giorgia's improvement might not depend on the script."

"I know."

"But then again it might well depend on it."

"I know," I say again. "I don't want to talk about it anymore, I just want you to check that it's okay."

"All right. Do you want me to come today?"

"No," I say, staring at the light reflected on the hallway's linoleum. "I think I can do it."

"It'll go well, you'll see. It's your first solo outing, just the two of you. How do you feel?"

"We won't be alone, technically."

"How long can this lunch at your parents' last? Not more than a couple of hours."

"I just hope everything goes smoothly."

"Don't worry. It's going to be fine."

Mauro says it as if he already knew the day's outcome, and I have no choice but to believe him, to rely on his certainty to compensate for my doubts.

"I'll bring the car back to you around five."

"See you later then."

I end the call at the sound of voices approaching. I recognize the doctor's heavy, cautious way of proceeding through the conversation, then Giorgia's brief, polite replies. When they reach the door, she smiles at me. After being on the verge of tears in her room, she is now calm. The doctor decided not to immediately address the details of her condition with her: for now their sessions are limited to a general exploration of her state of health, an observation of her reactions. Giorgia knows that she is here as a result of severe psychophysical exhaustion, and has no memory of the period spent in drug therapy at the clinic, nor of her most recent state of delirium.

"Thank you very much", Giorgia says, leaving the doctor.

"Remember the notes, for the next visit," he says, his arms behind his back. "Now enjoy your Sunday."

We both say goodbye. As we go down the stairs, I feel him watching us, a sensation that fades only when we are definitely out of his sight, in the car and on the road.

Giorgia is sitting quietly in the passenger seat, watching the landscape stream past.

"My parents are all excited," I say, after a few minutes of silence.

I feel my hands sweating on the wheel, I'm scared that the conversation will wind up at a dead end; you'd think it was our first date.

"My mother cooked for an army."

Giorgia smiles: I can't see her, I have to focus on the road, but her smile opens up at the corner of my eye, it's like being able to see it directly, and it has the same power. I think about her legs: she's regained the weight she had a year ago, before the last months of the rehearsals, and the pants she's wearing emphasize her body's curves—even though I thought I knew them by heart, the time spent without any contact has erased the familiar trails and I have to relearn everything from the beginning. I swallow hard, turn my mind elsewhere with an effort.

"I'm a little sleepy," Giorgia says.

"You can sleep if you want. I don't think we'll be there for another twenty minutes."

"But I don't want to sleep when I'm out. Maybe some music ..."

She turns on the radio and starts looking for a station. When she comes across one of her favorite songs, I feel a shiver run down my back: in the five seconds it takes her to make up her mind whether she likes it or not, I think of Mauro, and decide that we will have to reread the script carefully, regardless of what we believe or don't believe we've brought about. Giorgia lets the song continue playing, but she's not wild about it—I tell myself again that maybe it's just my impression, but all the same I feel the anxiety rise in my throat.

"Is it in such bad shape, your car?" she says, running a hand over the Alfa's dashboard.

"Yes, but maybe I can have the mechanic look at it, in a week."

"I can't wait to get out of there and start working again."

"We have to be patient," I say, thinking of the supermarket.

She nods.

"I'm glad Mauro isn't here today," she says. "You two have become inseparable."

"He's helped me a lot."

Giorgia slips off her shoes, brings her legs to her chest. "I hardly remember anything," she says. "I have vague sensations, sometimes, as though I were thinking something and were unable to speak."

I exit off the highway and, under the pretext of checking the rearview mirror, I take the time to formulate a safe answer.

"You weren't well," I say. "But, as the doctor says, we have to focus on the present. How do you feel now?"

I turn to look at her when we've stopped at a traffic light. She rests her head on her knees and looks at me drowsily.

"All right," she replies. "Every now and then I get confused."

"I think that's normal."

"And you?"

"I'm fine," I say, I look at her a moment longer, not noticing that the light has changed until someone honks his horn.

I shift into first. She keeps looking at me.

"Every now and then you get confused," she says.

I gave my parents instructions: what to say and what not to say, what steps to take. I prepared them for the possibility that Giorgia might do something strange and asked them to please control their reactions. She is stable, she is still under constant pharmacological treatment, but the doctor has urged us to pay attention to signs of agitation and to comply with her, except in the event of actual danger.

When we reach our destination, Giorgia doesn't seem to remember the way too well—she turns at the wrong corner, then she catches up with me, laughing when I point out that she was going to someone else's house. Though she clings to my arm and doesn't let go until we're at my parents' door, as if afraid of getting lost, she is not anxious: she looks around contentedly, smiles at passersby, she even says good morning to a woman we encounter.

I'm thinking I've never seen her so spirited, except maybe a long time ago, in the early days; she's not drowsy anymore. I imagine it must be due to her being let out from her mandatory confinement in the clinic. I try not to think about when I'll have to bring her back later on.

Standing outside my parents' door, there's no time to even ring the bell: my mother opens abruptly, surprising us on the landing. A burst of ceremonial greetings, kisses, hugs, caresses; my mother is emotional and hides behind my father's back. Giorgia's presence in my parents' foyer is like a Klimt woman in a neoclassical painting: she is beautiful and out of place; I remember thinking the same thing the first time I brought her here.

Around the table, my mother arranges us customarily around the four sides, then overwhelms us with her chatter, her stew, her roasted potatoes, while my father simply adds or subtracts two or three words at a time from her conversation: from their years at the café they are used to talking with people simultaneously, and now you can only easily understand them if they talk together. After the observation phase, my parents relax. Giorgia interacts normally, and is an active participant. Her composure encourages my mother, who expands her running commentary. As she talks, she slips compliments into the line of fire; I see that in her typical way she feels guilty, her cheeks are flushed and her tongue is loose, she wants to make it up to her. I think of her silence, the unspoken urging that I give up and move on, but I can't manage to feel any kind of rancor. Every now and then, my father raises his head from his glass of wine and looks at me, but I don't return his look.

Giorgia's leg presses against mine under the table, and doesn't move the whole time. During our lunch she puts a hand on me, on my arm, on my shoulder, she touches me again like a surface that belongs to her, and I find it difficult to follow the thread of the conversation.

"I'm so happy," my mother says after the espresso and liqueur. "We missed you."

I look at her, her skin is shiny and her green eyes, which everyone describes as my eyes, are teary from the wine.

Giorgia smiles, and puts a hand to the back of her neck, fingering her short hair.

"Thank you," she says.

There is a distinct moment of peace, I can see it clearly: the one where everything falls back in place. My footsteps are once again in front of me and all I have to do is follow them; my footsteps are right here, in a place that has known me since I was born; in the eyes of the person I love, whom I've come to know.

There is a distinct moment of peace, then Giorgia stands up.

"I want to wash the dishes," she announces.

"No, no, sweetheart, sit down. I'll do them later," my mother says, waving a hand.

"No, I really want to wash the dishes," Giorgia repeats.

She starts gathering up the empty cups, glasses, teaspoons. My mother tries to take some of them out of her hands with no success. Giorgia marches to the sink, ignoring our protests, turns on the faucet. My father shrugs and gestures to my mother to let it go. We watch Giorgia gradually empty the sink, and we keep chatting, but she doesn't join in. When I see her get busy on the stove, once the dishes and pots are done, I start to worry.

"Giò," I call her. "That's fine, come and sit down."

She gives no sign of having heard me. I get up and go over to her.

"Giò?"

She whirls around, as if I've distracted her from a thought.

"Yes?"

"That's good enough. Will you come back and sit with us?"

She smiles at me, then turns to my parents.

"It'll just take a minute," she says.

"You don't have to," I say. "Leave something for my mother to do, for later."

"But I'm considerate," she says, confused.

"Of course you're considerate. But there's no need to do spring cleaning."

"But I'm considerate."

I start getting nervous, but I pretend to be calm: I feel my mother's eyes boring into my back.

"That's right, Giò, you're considerate."

"I want to clean up."

"I'm sure my parents prefer your company to a clean kitchen," I say, taking her gently by the hand. "Come on back."

She looks at her hand, then at my parents, then at me; by the time I spot the tears it's already too late: in no time, Giorgia begins to cry. I feel the temperature in the room plummet.

"But I'm considerate," she repeats, looking at me as if I had accused her of an atrocious crime.

"Of course, of course, Giò!" I say, placing my hands on her shoulders. "Look at me. Of course you're considerate."

I try to stifle the panic, but she continues to cry; her sobbing grows more intense, and her face starts turning red.

"Why don't you want me to clean up?" she sobs, wiping her cheek with a sleeve.

"I just wanted you to enjoy dinner."

"But I want to clean up."

She says it with such anguish that my father gets up from the table.

"So let her clean, then," he says, standing beside her. "Where's the harm?"

"I'm considerate," Giorgia says again, turning toward him.

"Of course you are, I know that."

"We know that, Giorgia," my mother chimes in.

"I want to clean up."

"Okay, all right, look, I'll give you the cleanser, the sponge for the stove top."

"Are you mad at me?" Giorgia asks, looking at me.

Her eyes are swollen and her face is streaked with tears.

"No, not at all, Giò. You're right, go ahead and clean," I tell her.

My father takes me by the arm and makes me sit down again. My mother offers Giorgia the cleaning supplies, then, after trying to help her and seeing that she was not wanted, she joins us at the table.

We watch Giorgia scrub the kitchen; the more she cleans, the more her good mood is restored. When it's time to clear away the bottles and linen from the table, she is radiant. My parents are relieved to see her smiling again; I fidget in my chair. She seems normal, present in this reality, but it's obvious that something is wrong.

"We should sweep the floor," says Giorgia, hands on her hips, studying the tiles.

I feel a shiver run down my back. There's no time to intercept her before she's already armed with a broom and clears us out of the kitchen, bumping it between the legs of our chairs.

"Giorgia, sweetie, do you want a hand?" my mother asks, in a querulous tone.

"No, thank you, it's no problem," Giorgia replies. "Do you happen to have a toothbrush? The cracks are a little dirty."

My father, troubled by the crying fit, immediately gets her a toothbrush. "But it's yours," my mother objects. "So what's the problem? I'll buy a new one." Before we know it, we're watching Giorgia bent over on the floor, scouring between the tiles with the soapy bristles. My mother takes me aside, dragging me into the dining room.

"Filippo!" she murmurs sadly.

"She's just having a bad moment," I say, taking care that Giorgia doesn't turn towards us.

From here I see her derriere rocking, but any erotic urge has wilted.

"Are you sure she's all right?"

"She's still recovering. It takes time," I say.

I use the tone she likes to hear, firm and confident. She believes me, yet she turns to the kitchen again, then back to me.

"But what should we do now?"

"Nothing," I reply. "We'll let her clean."

As my father watches her from the doorway, Giorgia goes on scrubbing. After the toothbrush she wants a rag, a bucket, wax: she doesn't stop until the kitchen shines.

On the way back in the car, Giorgia is blissful. She tells me that she missed my parents, that they are exquisite people: this day really made her happy.

We listen to the radio together, and once again she is my Giorgia, so I want to believe that the crisis was only a momentary thing; I keep telling myself that I can't expect a complete recovery overnight and that her improvement is already in itself a kind of miracle. When we get back to the clinic, she clouds over. I walk her to the room, then inside.

"I'm really happy," Giorgia repeats.

When the nurse looks in the door to remind me that I have twenty more minutes left before the end of visiting hours, Giorgia stares at me with a pout.

"I have to be patient?" she asks, once we're alone.

"Yes," I say.

She curls up like a cat on the bed, and looks at me. I sit

down beside her. When I'm close enough, she takes my hand, guides it to her hip.

"Cuddle me," she says.

The revelation hits me with the force of a shove. I recognize my memory. She uses the same word, the same childlike tenderness, and for a moment I don't know where I am anymore, the two acts of my life overlap.

In the past world, my fingers are under her T-shirt, tracing circles around her navel, inching up to a breast —in the memory, I feel Giorgia straining under me. In the present, my hand is fainthearted, it isn't able to go beyond the ribs. I see the two acts come together as one, and my actions and reactions differ in the two dimensions.

In the present, Giorgia looks at me: I see the past materialize in her eyes. Trying not to disregard her expectations, I force myself to pursue the same touch, but I fail. My fingers are awkward, the invisible trace blocked.

"The nurse will be back soon," I say, drawing away.

I feel my heart beating loudly in my ears and I recognize my excitement: it does not come from Giorgia's body. It is the thought that she is actually taking her cue from our script, that this is the proof Mauro and I had hoped to see.

"You're right." She's disappointed but she smiles.

"I'll be back tomorrow," I tell her.

Somewhere, our memory ends in a kiss.

CHAPTER SIX

INCONSISTENCY

Little by little as we watch, the garden slips into darkness. The warm light of the living room clarifies the shapes of things: the sofa, the dining table, the kitchen peninsula. From here we can see Giorgia, sitting on a stool, and in front of her Amelia. We can't hear them talking, the window glass is too thick, and they exist without sound.

We came out using Mauro's cigarette as an excuse, but now the butt has been stubbed out and he holds it by his side, spent, clenched between his fingers. Giorgia and Amelia can't see us, we're protected by the shadows of the maples, and the darker it gets, the safer our hiding place becomes. We won't be able to stay here for long: the guests are coming.

"What do you think?"

Mauro doesn't take his eyes off Giorgia.

"Overall she's fine, but she still does those strange things every now and then."

"What does the doctor say?"

"He says that it could be a period of adjustment, or

that this could be the new Giorgia: it will take more time to figure it out."

Mauro raises a hand to his hair and fusses with a strand at his temple.

"Her aunt wants to see her," I add, filling his silence. "The doctor informed her of the developments."

"When?" Mauro asks, searching my eyes.

"I don't know. She agreed to the days out, but she doesn't seem in any hurry to see her herself. Maybe she's afraid that this state of grace isn't destined to last."

He nods slowly.

"We have to consider all options," he says.

"Meaning?"

"It could be that this is actually the physiological course of the pathology," he says. "Or it might be that we were the ones who triggered the process."

I glance around; I have the irrational fear that someone will surprise us from behind. The idea again occurs to me that our secret is dangerous or maybe wrong, that we shouldn't talk about it, that it shouldn't even exist. At the same time, the thought that our efforts may have helped Giorgia elates me.

"How do we establish it? It could all be the power of suggestion."

Mauro smiles his downturned smile.

"Reality is all suggestion," he says. "In any case, we can't be certain. We have to consider the possibility as if it were the only one imaginable and, at the same time, be aware that the cause may have nothing to do with us. Do you see what I mean? It might or it might not be us, but let's act as if it were."

I take a deep breath, prepare to take the leap.

"All right," I say, as if we had sealed an agreement.

"All right then," Mauro repeats. "I reread the script, as I'd said."

"And?"

"I found the mistake we were looking for. Nowhere in it did we talk about her clothes. We were too focused on individual scenes, on interactions, and there's no mention of stage costumes, not even half a line in the subtext. I can't believe I made such a gross slipup."

"You think her confusion is due to that?"

"I think the problem could be deeper," he says. "We bombarded her with information and she responds appropriately. For example, what do you think of her movement?"

I turn instinctively to look at her, and Mauro does the same. Giorgia leans over the marble counter, arms hugging her body, and watches Amelia up close as she opens a bottle of wine.

"There's nothing wrong with her movement."

"I think so too, it's faithful," he says. "All the same, I'm worried that I left something out, as if she weren't complete. If we really did a good job, even without clear instructions, she should be able to intuit what she likes and what she doesn't like. But if our mistake was not endowing her with taste ... well, it's more complicated."

The thought gets me agitated.

"What other effects have you noticed, apart from the problem of clothes?" he asks.

"There's the thing about being considerate: she takes it too seriously, I don't understand why," I say.

"We may have gone too far."

"But how do we know for sure?"

"We need to read it again more carefully," he replies. "How about coming over some evening? We'll take another look at it."

"But what's the point? Isn't it too late?"

Mauro's face is slowly vanishing into the winter

darkness, so when he looks at me, I can't make out his expression.

"We can step in and make adjustments where we need to."

"Rewrite it?" I explode, already panicked by the prospect.

"No. Supplement it, and only where necessary."

"And then?"

"Then resume reading it to her."

He watches me shake my head. I take a few steps back into the garden, moving away from the window. This new idea is too much for me to take.

"It would also be a great way to verify the method's effectiveness," Mauro adds. "A kind of acid test."

"The idea scares me," I find the nerve to say, finally.

"Me too." Mauro fishes out another cigarette, finds the lighter, and for a moment I see his face light up again, before quickly disappearing in the shadows. "We've come too far, don't you see? If it really is working, we can't risk leaving the job half-finished. Giorgia's happiness is at stake."

We've come too far.

"Tomorrow night?" Mauro suggests.

"All right."

Headlights interrupt us: the cars have arrived, their beams illuminating the driveway outside. It's six o'clock, and the winter afternoon ends in darkness. Without another word, Mauro gets ready to welcome the guests.

The group is handpicked, four longtime friends, people who have worked with Giorgia and Mauro or attended the same classes in the past. They have been prepared: it's Mauro who has told them about Giorgia's convalescence and our attempts to reinstate her into the real world. The idea that everyone Giorgia interacts with has somehow been placed on alert disturbs me—it underscores our precarious equilibrium.

Today, too, Giorgia was unable to overcome the clothing impasse. She practically broke down again. I tried pressing her more than usual, and all I got her to choose was which scarf to wear. The fact that she chose it herself must have impressed her, because she hasn't taken it off. She's sitting at the table, in front of a plate of pasta, with the blue wool scarf still knotted around her neck. I don't know whether to tell her to take it off or pretend not to notice. The others seem at ease so I decide to let it go, even though the heat is turned up high, and beneath her short hair a sheen of perspiration on her forehead gleams under the light.

Amelia, sitting in front of me, smiles encouragingly at me, while Mauro, at the head of the table, entertains the guests.

"When the framework of the costume begins to give way, it is already too late, and in any case Vanna is so absorbed in the performance that she doesn't notice it. Act Three, the big scene: the fabric slips off the underskirt and her fat ass bursts out onstage."

Mauro throws his head back in a resounding laugh and his enjoyment is infectious. It's not just the story, or the way he tells it: it's his participation in the narration. He's been drinking a lot since we sat down at the table, and I've never seen him laugh so extravagantly, or tell so many anecdotes. He's anticipated every treacherous lull in the conversation, deflected potential dangers.

The only one not impressed by his stories is Giorgia. She smiles faintly, toys with her spaghetti, looks at me as if to reassure herself that I too really find Mauro's tales funny. I know he's noticed. So far Giorgia's lack of response has pushed him to aim higher and higher, to exaggerate. All his efforts have failed.

By the end of the last story, he is drained—or maybe I'm just imagining the false veneer of his gaze, the weariness behind the excuse of one glass too many. He withdraws into his corner, the half-smile of a sad jester on his lips. I feel a prickle of enjoyment, and I don't want to. I chase the thought away as I follow the conversation.

It happens while Mauro and I are both distracted, him pretending to listen, his chin on one hand, me hypnotized by the beads of perspiration on Giorgia's forehead: my attention flits from the clock to the droplets dampening the roots of her hair. We notice that the discussion has become risky when it is already too late and Giorgia is involved.

"Remember? Paola had made that absurd scene, she showed up right in the middle of the rehearsal," says one of the guests, an attractive guy with a flashy watch on his wrist.

"Yes," Giorgia replies. "I remember it."

"Didn't she start yelling that the part was supposed to be hers, or something like that?" one of the two girls adds, shaking her head. "Unbelievable."

"Besides, it took some nerve. The comparison with you was pathetic. What could she have been thinking, not to see the difference?"

Giorgia turns to me, looks at me uncertainly.

"I'm honest," she says.

It's an assertion; I don't have a chance to reply.

"She didn't think she was better than me," Giorgia says, turning to the guests again. "Paola thought she should have the part because she and Mauro were having sex. I think he led her to think that, more or less."

A fork clatters onto a plate right then. Amelia apologizes and buries the forkful of pasta under a napkin. Mauro is frozen in place, a hand supporting his head; he's looking straight at Giorgia.

"I saw them too," Giorgia adds. "Once on Via San Mansueto, in the car. I was riding by on my bike. She was giving him a ..."

"Giò!" I try, clearing my throat. "Maybe you shouldn't ... It's a personal matter."

"No," Giorgia says serenely. "Everybody knew it. Mauro had sex with almost all the students in the intermediate course, and even with some of the beginners. They called it the instructor's ..."

"Giò."

"Baptism by fire."

Now we're all stock-still around the table. For one crazy moment, I feel like Giorgia is keeping us in check. She has no need to be violent, no need to raise her voice: we are all hanging on her every word, without the courage to even look at one another. I lower my eyes, stare stubbornly at the edge of the tablecloth.

"You forgot the senior group," Mauro says, breaking the silence.

"No, I haven't forgotten," Giorgia replies. "But the senior group was your last choice. You said you liked talents that could be shaped."

There is no provocation, no spitefulness in her voice, it is an atonal, impersonal analysis.

"You remember everything."

"Mauro ..."

I look up and see Amelia give him a warning look.

"Come on, you all already knew, let's not kid each

other," Mauro continues, ignoring her. "Do you remember any other details, for instance, about the female instructors?"

"Sure," Giorgia replies, undaunted. "You were dying to get to Gandolfi. She only went along when you took her to dinner for the third time."

"Gandolfi?" the guy with the watch can't restrain himself. "I can't believe it. Is it true?"

"I'm an honest person," Giorgia repeats, with an offended air.

"So, Giorgia, since you're an honest person," Mauro says. "Tell me, do you remember how it went with you?"

"Mauro!" Amelia exclaims.

"Don't you dare butt in!"

Mauro's eyes are fierce. I'm thinking I should get up and leave, take Giorgia with me, but I can't move.

"You're embarrassing me," Giorgia says.

"Forgive me, Giò." Mauro fakes a contrite smile. "But you're honest, right? Honesty always has a price. Answer my question."

"You're improper," Giorgia says calmly. "You've always been improper."

"Undoubtedly. Do you remember how it went with you?"

"It was after a rehearsal, we were alone. You put one hand behind my head, the other between my legs."

Amelia leaps to her feet. "I refuse to watch this spectacle!"

"Shut up."

"Filippo!" Amelia's eyes falter, looking for mine, incredulous, pleading with me.

I still can't find the strength to protest what's happening. I apologize with a look. The desire to know, at this point, is stronger than my will.

"Go on, Giorgia, go on. What happened next?" Mauro urges, leaning across the table. His eyes are shiny, his fists clenched.

"I said no. You let it go."

Giorgia's response has an explosive effect on those in the room. I feel my body loosen up, the tension dissolve.

"I have a lot of air in my belly," Giorgia announces, unconcerned with the disruption she caused. "I have to go to the bathroom."

She leaves us, perspiring in her blue scarf; Amelia follows her at once.

The silence is so thick I drown in it.

"She's not so bad," the boy with the ponytail offers. "I mean, apart from the intermezzo, of course. Generally, she seems to be fine."

"Yes," the girl beside him says. "We expected worse, from what you'd told us."

Mauro's friends, who are good people, weave a conversation around the two of us. Despite the fact that Mauro and I don't join in, we don't even talk, they continue, even after he and I are finally able to look each other in the eye again.

Slumped against the back of his chair, he looks at me as if to say, "You see?" And I look at him as if to say, "I'm sorry."

* * *

We took up the script again. We each read a copy, once more holding to a schedule, armed with a red pen. Rereading it, the errors multiplied. Mauro says that we mustn't get too fixated on the question of responsibility: it was a test, we treated it as such, and the result is excellent in any case, even though a significant revision will be necessary; he says this as his pen slashes dialogues, and adds entire paragraphs of subtext. I am not yet convinced of the effectiveness of what we are doing, nor that Giorgia's new eccentricities are caused by our poor attempt at being playwrights, but I have stopped saying so because Mauro can't stand my whining anymore.

Since the dreadful dinner, I feel a kind of pity for him. We have not brought it up again, nor have I felt the need to delve into it any further. I watched him shrink under Giorgia's merciless honesty. I wondered if, at the time, her rejection had been a blow to his pride—and I told myself no, he doesn't really get attached to any of his lovers, they come and go on the fringes of his life like walk-ons, in a constant turnover.

I asked Giorgia why she did it, but all she gave me were her unrevealing answers: "I'm honest"; "I'm considerate." I tried to explain to her that, sometimes, the two possibilities can't coincide; that, more often than you think, the truth excludes consideration and consideration can't contemplate the truth. She didn't understand: the assertion triggered another short circuit.

The day I bring Giorgia home for the first time, there's a downpour. The umbrella breaks as we rush from the car to the door of our building: just a few yards across the courtyard and we find ourselves drenched. Once we're under cover, Giorgia lets go of my hand, and squeezes the water from her hair; she starts laughing like a child and although I don't remember hearing her laugh like that very often in the past, I find I like it. It's an alternate version of Giorgia, or maybe just her echo, but it's still her.

"What crazy weather," she says, taking off her jacket on the landing.

"Yeah." I grumble, preceding her up the stairs.

We quickly reach our door, the first one to the left of the elevator. Even if it's the usual door, it takes us back to the day we moved in: I feel the same strange tension, as if, as soon as we get inside, something is bound to happen.

I step aside for Giorgia and she enters first. Once again I recognize the direction of my memory, the main scene. Though I've ceased being surprised at her fidelity to the script, seeing her follow it still strikes me, and I observe every move as if trying to catch her taking a false step. Instead Giorgia faultlessly replicates the ten paces in the corridor, and when she disappears around the corner of the living room, her voice is the same.

"I want to come back and live here," she says when I join her.

She touches the pieces of furniture, looks at the sofa where I helped her rehearse her part.

"You'll be back soon," I say.

"Do you really think so?"

"Sure."

The thought of the script is now a fixation, I can't get it out of my head. I know what happens next, because I've been here so many times before, during my exercise. She reaches towards me, just like she's doing now, then pulls me to her, and the kiss is identical: it is in physical, temporal dimensions. A precise memory that revisits me.

Giorgia takes me by the hand and leads me to the bedroom. The past rematerializes, I know the urgency, the sound of her clothes slipping to the floor when she undresses. I see her naked, pale, superimposed on her ghost. We make love in the same way, in the same position, the mouth sinks into its same groove, the tongue registers the same taste. Even the pleasure is identical, and the cum on her has the same consistency, the quilt is stained in the same quadrant.

When it's over, anguish grips my throat and squeezes. All of a sudden I want to get out of here.

"Are you happy?" Giorgia asks, following her lines.

I don't have the courage to abandon my role.

"Yes."

"Today I thought of something," she says then, and it's her first deviation.

I lie on my side and look at her. "What?"

"I realized that I don't have a purpose in my life," she replies. "A goal. I get up in the morning and there's nothing I want."

I'm still thinking about the script, the idea won't go away.

"Everyone has a purpose, don't you think?"

Mauro's bedroom is in the attic, it occupies the entire third floor. There is no door, the stairs lead directly into the room. On the floor there are still signs of drywall that must have been removed to enlarge the space; a carpet covers them, but not completely. Besides the bed, arranged against the back wall, there are a clothes rack and a built-in wardrobe. It's clear that this is not the place in the house where he spends his time: unlike the basement pub, here the order of things is observed. Clothes are hanging on the rack, sheets are tucked under the mattress, and there's no sign of the attributes that follow him everywhere—no ashtrays, books, or papers stacked in the corners.

When Mauro comes back up, he's naked. We started our discussion on the ground floor, and we continue as he's getting ready: tonight we're going to an opening. He rubs his hair briskly with a towel, swipes it awkwardly between his legs, then tosses it on the floor.

"As we were saying," he says, opening one of the wardrobe doors and picking up the conversation from where we left off. "I thought about it while I was taking a shower: you're right, we followed your memories too closely. We should have expanded on them and set them in an original context."

"Right," I confirm, as I watch him choose a jacket and a pair of pants. "This way it's like a continuous replication. I can't concentrate, I'm losing my mind."

"Maybe it's the path we should have followed from the beginning," he says, throwing the clothes on the bed. "Maybe we should have constructed a story line. Nothing too complex, but *something*."

"And how about what she said today? 'The purpose of her existence' ... I wouldn't want it to become another fixation or, even more serious, make matters worse."

"It's resolvable. We just have to give her an aspiration, everything will follow accordingly," Mauro says, slipping on his briefs.

I remain seated on the edge of the bed, watching him put on his clothes.

"Are you coming like that?" he asks me, as he buttons his shirt.

I instinctively lower my eyes to my matted sweater. Shaken by the morning spent with Giorgia, I hadn't even thought about wearing something more appropriate.

"I had a change of clothes at home, but I forgot," I say.

Mauro tightens his belt and returns to the closet, chooses a dark jacket.

"It'll fit you for sure," he says, tossing it at me.

I don't even try to object, I take off my sweater and put his jacket on over my T-shirt. I'd like to tell him about today, explain about Giorgia, because since I brought her back to the clinic my disquiet has grown and I feel incapable of controlling it. Then I think back to the dreadful dinner and her revelations, and I don't have the guts to say anything.

"We were in too much of a hurry to finish," says Mauro, gathering his wet hair in a ponytail. "Are you ready?"

"Yes."

We go down the stairs, already fifteen minutes behind schedule.

"We stopped at the first draft," Mauro continues. "Giorgia's character, as it appears in the script we wrote, is still a rough sketch. Developed, full of excellent openings, but still a sketch. It shouldn't surprise us that she's acting strange: we put her in a state of disequilibrium."

We both skip over the last step, which still has a gaping hole.

"Then too, as I mentioned to you yesterday, we went too far with feelings," he picks up the keys from the hall shelf and we're quickly out the door. "She's described too romantically."

The air this March evening is cold and dry. I vaguely sense what Mauro means—but it's too late to go into it any further: we decide to put off any conclusions until tomorrow's meeting.

The theater is at Porta Romana. We have to wait in line at the underground parking lot, and by the time we get there, the lights are already lowered. We join Amelia and Giulia, whose seats are next to ours, a few minutes before the room goes dark. The front rows have been removed, replaced by a circle of tables and chairs occupied by the public. The scene opens on a level with the audience, there is no clear boundary, and the actor appears unannounced, almost slinking in. The stage costume is plain: a dark sweater, pants with worn knees. After ten minutes, I recognize Pasolini's words in his voice; I realize that as usual I've come here totally unprepared.

Halfway through the play, by which time we've already reached a fair level of misery, the script suddenly soars, the actor is transfigured and, after that, undresses. We watch him become the killer; his body is the same as ours—when I dare turn to Amelia and Mauro, I see the same body reflected in their faces, the shadows identical to those defined by the rib cage. Then terror grips me: it's in the words that the actor recites. He is transfigured and his words choke my lungs. I'm grateful when it's over, because I feel like I'm suffocating.

On the way out, Mauro has an endless stream of acquaintances to greet; we are among the last remaining groups, but we don't linger to offer our compliments to the actor: the girls are hungry, they've already met him and seen him elsewhere. We end up in a nearby restaurant, but none of us wants to talk about the show, and we avoid the subject. Giulia entertains us, chattering on about herself, about the guitar she plays, about the poetry she writes, about the art films she likes. Amelia and I know that Mauro isn't listening to her though he stonily pretends to be, and meanwhile keeps filling our wine glasses. We're all drinking for different reasons: Amelia because she's in a good mood, Giulia to show that a woman can hold her liquor, me because since making love with Giorgia again, rather than finding myself I've lost myself completely.

When we leave the restaurant we're drunk. A moon that looks like an orange accompanies us under the arch of Porta Romana, or maybe it's a street lamp. Mauro loads us in the car like teenagers on a school trip.

"It was really tiny," Giulia continues to giggle, and Amelia follows her. "It was teeeny, teeny weeny."

"What do you expect, Giulia? A phenomenon of Italian theater and well hung as well?" Mauro teases her, looking at her in the mirror.

I turn around, drawn by the high spirits their silly laughter inspires, and I see Giulia sprawled on Amelia's lap, laughing uproariously, her bra peeping out of her loose neckline. Amelia is hooting, her head thrown back, and all you can see of her is a very long throat.

Mauro looks at them hungrily in the mirror, so even though I'm drunk, I'm not surprised when he says he wants to take us all to his house, right away. When we get there, he drinks what he didn't drink to be able to drive. Our conversation unravels and makes no sense, punctuated by Giulia's shrieks—"I can also play the guitalcle!" When he's tired of hearing her talk, Mauro drags her up the stairs and the two of them disappear.

Left alone, Amelia and I happen to glance at one another.

"Do you want to put on some music?" she asks, at one point. "I have a turntable."

"Okay," I say.

"It's upstairs in my room."

"Okay."

Despite the altered state I'm in, I remember the trap of the first step and skip over it behind Amelia, who goes up the stairs without making any noise. From the top floor Giulia's laughter can still be heard. We go into Amelia's room, which is larger than the guest room. One wall is covered with polaroid photos, idiotic faces in faded glossy ink, and she was telling the truth: the turntable is on the floor, in a corner, under the shelves where she keeps the vinyl records.

"Almost all of them were given to me by Mauro," she says, pointing to them. "In the beginning, when we first met, I didn't even know what kind of music I liked. I only told him I wanted a turntable because to me it seemed like something sophisticated. Something he would appreciate," she says slowly, in a lowered voice.

She pulls her blonde hair back in a ponytail, then immediately loosens it to one side. As she moves, I'm suddenly aware of her short dress, in a green that now gleams, of how white her skin is, and of a vein at the base of her neck, like a comma.

"You know how it happens?" she says, choosing a vinyl.

She crouches on the floor, on her high heels, and slips the record carefully out of the cover. Then she repeats a gesture she has down pat: she lifts the arm, chooses the track; who knows how many times she's heard this song.

"What?" I ask.

"Huh?" she says, standing up again.

"How what happens?"

"I don't know, I have to go to the bathroom."

I watch her leave the room; as soon as she's gone, I don't know why but I'm sure she won't come back. I sit on the bed, which is barely higher than a futon, and has a rustling duvet on top. I wander off a moment, in the wake of Jefferson Airplane, and maybe it lasts a very long time, two or three days, or it ends when Amelia comes back.

She's no longer wearing stockings and her dress got caught in her panties, so the skirt is hiked up unevenly on one side. She turns on another light, the bedside lamp. From this spot on the bed I am very close to the turntable, so, when she bends over, with no shoes, no stockings, I clearly see the drop of water left on her thigh that is sliding down to the inner fold of her left knee. It's like the first day here with Mauro: everything gets sharp before it blurs completely.

Amelia changes the track, but it's still Jefferson Airplane.

"I remember," she says, sitting next to me.

She has tiny feet, clear eyes.

"What?" I ask.

"How it happens."

It happens in her mouth, in this bed and in her body. It's all sharp before it becomes a complete blur.

I'm late for my afternoon appointment with Mauro. I even thought about canceling it, pretending to be sick, because the thought of going back to his house terrifies me.

This morning dawn woke me. Amelia was still half on top of me, her head sunk into my pillow, the fine skin of a breast glued to mine, collapsed as if she had been shot in the back; the sweat on my body had cooled, but I only started to feel it when I got up. I gathered up my clothes, careful not to make a sound. My temples were pounding from a headache, but I didn't pause, not even to go to the bathroom. The house was the kind of aquarium that Mauro likes, with its dense, whitish artificial sea. I didn't remember the trap of the last step:

I ended up putting one foot in it and got a bad scratch on my ankle.

When I got home, I decided not to think. "I can't afford to," I told myself, "if I do it will all be over." So I went back to sleep, in my own bed, and, when I woke up, I walked through the scenario of any other Sunday: hangover, black coffee. At ten thirty, I called Giorgia at the clinic and told her about the show the night before; she already knew we wouldn't see each other again before Monday. At the sound of her voice I had a brief breakdown, and the image of Amelia's spine, its imperfect curvature, came back to me. I drove the memory away with a sip of water, and my sour breath with it.

At dawn this morning, I was alone in the silence. Now, in front of Mauro's door, as my world threatens to collapse again, I hesitate one last time before ringing the bell. I imagine Amelia coming to open the door, like the first day we met, but I resist the temptation to mentally come up with apologies. I keep my focus on my situation and I am rewarded: Mauro opens up.

"Goddamm—" he says, as he stumbles over the shoes left at the entrance. The coffee he's holding tilts along with the cup and spills to the floor, splashing the toes of his bare feet.

For a few seconds we stare at the mess.

"Come in," he says then.

In his mouth is a cigarette that burned down during his creative ferment—by now I've learned to recognize it—and he doesn't seem to know it. I study him, while he wipes the parquet with a dishcloth, then I watch him wash his hands in the kitchen. When he's repaired the damage, he looks me straight in the eye and I don't see anything in him that tells me I've been discovered. I decide not to think about Amelia, about if and when I might confess to him.

"Want some coffee?" Mauro asks.

"No thanks."

"Shall we get right to it?"

"Let's," I reply.

In the basement pub, we go back to our places.

"Let's take stock," says Mauro, retrieving a sheet of paper and a pen. The script is ready and waiting on the table, he turns the pages to the mark he left. "I found a passage that could be the source of all our problems. It's the scene in the street, before the kiss, when you're walking away from the crowd of people lined up in front of the gelato shop. She says: 'I'm always honest.' And you: 'Always?' Her: 'I'm always honest and considerate.'"

He looks up and scowls at me.

"Okay, it's not the greatest," I say, intimidated by his look.

"It's awful. I haven't read such bad dialogue in a very long time."

"I thought you'd see to the form. You know I'm not a writer ..."

"You're not responsible, in fact," Mauro says. "I wanted to respect your memory of Giorgia, I tried to render her faithfully and conform to your recollection, without asking myself if what I was reading was credible in narrative terms. The result is a shaky character. I mean, these two phrases alone are full of holes. Who's always honest? Nobody. How can we put that thought in her mouth? Do you think Giorgia would really have said, 'I'm always honest'? Or worse yet, do you think she was completely honest?"

His questions come at me too fast. I watch him inflict two more red slashes on the paper.

"I don't think she was completely honest. But she was, she is honest," I say.

Mauro runs a hand through his hair, then rubs his eyes, leans back in his chair.

"Filippo," he says. "Giorgia lied to us about her illness. We can't describe her as an honest person, it would be completely inconsistent with her character."

Though he says it kindly, it's a blow.

"Do you understand what I mean by character consistency? We make her say that she is always honest, then, in the subtext, we explain that she has an illness that she doesn't talk about to anyone, not even you, and you're the secondary lead of this play. The fact that we've described her as capable of concealing and dealing with her illness, as she was during the three years of your relationship, is irrelevant: omission is a lie. And this is a big lie."

"I still think she was honest, despite that lie," I insist.

I feel as if I've been backed into a corner, as if Mauro were trying to block my way out.

"You think she told you the truth about everything else? That the only exception was her illness?"

The chair has become uncomfortable, and I look for a position that doesn't force me to face him directly. I pick up one of the sheets of paper that he had ready, then a pen.

"I think she did what we all do," I say, as I start scribbling.

"What we all do is different from being honest. It's choosing acceptable truths."

My thoughts turn back to our evenings, the ones before she was hospitalized, and the long weekend walks in the center, when we followed the return route from my winter courses at the university: Via Torino, the detour to the Colonne di San Lorenzo, skirting the side of Piazza Vetra. Along Corso di Porta Ticinese, Giorgia would look at the shop windows, at the clothes she would buy at another time, and that time never came. In Piazza Ventiquattro Maggio, as we stood like children at the traffic lights, Giorgia instinctively gripped my hand and didn't let go as we walked on the wrong side of the Naviglio. I begin my exercise automatically, by now I can visualize our conversations, I remember them episodically and as one, the story we told each other in those conversations, a story, constructed for the other, of a life that never fully existed. Each day brought an imperceptible variation in our version as, step by step, we created two incompatible worlds, in one of which we pretended to be living.

"Maybe it would be more accurate to say that Giorgia lied so as not to hurt anyone. That all her lies followed the criterion of kindness." Mauro speaks cautiously, but all the same I can't look him in the eye, and my inky doodle expands.

"The second point: consideration," he continues, pretending not to notice my discomfort. "I agree, Giorgia has always been considerate, but let's moderate this trait a little, let's make it a normal thing. I think that, for both qualities, we should eliminate the mention in the subtext: instead we'll expand the dialogues and make them more natural, and we'll show actions that describe her more faithfully."

"Terrific idea."

"Great. For the oversight of the clothes, we can simply describe the stage costumes called for in the three acts," Mauro goes on, paging through the script. "And about her having a purpose … do you think her theatrical aspiration will do?"

I'm thinking that, before she ran into him again, I'd only heard Giorgia mention the theater in passing, as a marginal element in her life, and that she never spoke of it as a particular dream to pursue. She knew about my ambitions to be a journalist, and I knew nothing about her passion for acting.

"I don't know," I say. "You tell me. How important was it to her? I mean, before she was with me."

Now it's Mauro's turn to avert his eyes, scribbling in the margin.

"Essential. I'd go so far as to say that, when we met, it was the only thing she really cared about," he says.

For a moment or two we remain silent. Now I see an alternate version of Giorgia sitting by his side, someone whose identity I only partially intuit. The idea scares me, and I try to file it away, but that filing cabinet is full since last night.

"All right, let's put it in," I say.

Mauro nods, serious, and fusses with the corner of a page, but I see him relax. When he looks at me, he smiles.

"We'll get there," he says. "We just have to keep in mind that it all already exists inside her: the memory of everything that has happened, of what she likes and what she doesn't like, of who she really is but also of who she would like to be. We just need to fine-tune the formula."

Hearing his words, I am reminded of a possibility that, before today, I'd only had the courage to consider once, the day of the lunch at my parents' house.

"Speaking of fine-tuning," I tell him, "let's say our plan works, that she gets better thanks to the script, and let's suppose that all the assumptions we're not sure about are right."

"Get to the point. What?"

"Do you think we should revise her past?"

As soon as I say it, I realize the import of my proposal. I see it develop in Mauro's eyes. He doesn't get ruffled, on the contrary, he becomes excited.

"Explain what you mean," he urges me.

"We can't change what happened to her, but maybe we should at least try to lessen its impact. Maybe she wouldn't be ill if she had gotten over the trauma of her mother, her father."

I see the wheels start turning, as he furrows his forehead, weighs the proposal carefully.

"How could we incorporate something like that, in a script?" he says then.

"That's your department."

"Still, you must have an idea if you've suggested it to me."

I go back to my doodling, which soon becomes a muddled black hole.

"Maybe we could describe her as being a little more confident, more resolute, less fragile."

"Didn't you like her fragile?"

Mauro's question makes me look up, startled.

"Of course I liked her," I say, and feel my face redden. "I just want her to be happier."

His eyes are still, indecipherable.

"If this experiment is really working, we have a chance to make life easier for her. It's too precious an opportunity," I add.

I don't want him to misunderstand; I'd feel like a monster to have considered such an extreme proposition.

"I just want her to be happier," I repeat.

"We can try," Mauro says. He pulls his hair back into a knot, takes a sheet from the stack of clean paper. "But here we're taking a step further, we're no longer following a track. We're creating."

He searches me as if asking me if I realize it, if I really want to go down this road. I don't have the gumption to say yes aloud but all the same he understands. He nods approval and starts writing.

"Is there anything else you'd like?" he asks.

There's no judgment in his voice, only the usual recognizable hint of excitement.

"No," I say. "No, that's fine."

"I'll work on it this week. As soon as it's ready, I'll give it to you to read."

The words sound like we're sealing a pact, but all I say is yes, thank you, that will be fine. When Mauro closes the script and puts it aside, I feel freed from a weight.

He finally lights the cigarette that had been waiting on the table during our talk, and slouches in his chair. He's wearing faded pajama bottoms, and a previously worn shirt buttoned hit-or-miss.

"How'd it go last night?"

I think if I look away, he'll know something happened, so I don't break eye contact, not even for a second.

"Amelia and I listened to records. I fell asleep. I went home early this morning," I tell him.

He blows out the smoke. My version of reality doesn't buckle, I hold it solidly together and repeat it to myself; I tell myself that if I believe it firmly enough, my body will also believe it. I'm careful not to fidget any more than I should.

"And you?" I toss back. "With Giulia?"

He gives a half smile. "You know how it is, right? After you eat it awhile, all food tastes the same."

I can't resist, I see Amelia's body again, a different drop, thicker and slower, sliding to the back of her neck and dissolving into her hair. Mauro looks away to flick off the ashes, and I'm finally able to clench my fists where he can't see them.

I decide to go talk to Amelia before it's too late.

"I'm going to the bathroom a second," I say.

I'm surprised at the improvisation but I'm already on the stairs, it's too late to regret it.

CHAPTER SEVEN

A GREAT JOB

Amelia is sitting at the middle table, her beret tilted to the left. Yesterday, when I went looking for her upstairs at Mauro's house, I didn't find her; today she showed up at the café without any warning, right at rush hour, that is, the hour between twelve and one when customers on their lunch break converge. She came in behind two first-year students from the university, while I was busy making cappuccinos. She said hello, and smiled equably. "Can I sit down?" she asked, without approaching the counter. She took a seat in front of me, with the look of someone who had wandered in by chance, and since then she's been looking around or sliding a finger over her cell phone, with the same serene expression on her face.

Customers keep coming and I keep messing up the orders, frothing milk already frothed, giving people the wrong change. A store of still frames entered the café with Amelia, all her angles from the other night. As soon as I saw her again, my scripted version fell apart: as I grind the coffee, I am reminded that it actually happened. Two espressos, a macchiato—afterwards we collapsed into sleep almost without talking—a sandwich to warm up, "How much for an orzo?"—had we looked at each other? I'm gripped by the groundless fear that Mauro will show up any minute, or that she'll tell me she immediately told him about it—they're very close, it's clear. What if yesterday Mauro had been pretending not to know?

When the place empties out, Amelia is busy reading a manual she pulled out of her bag. She reads quickly, marking her place on the page with a finger, and isn't aware that we're alone. I rub my hands on my apron, stumble on the rubber mat behind the counter, and when I go around it, she doesn't notice.

"Hi," I say.

She looks up from the book, smiles.

"Hi."

"Would you like something to drink?" I ask.

I figure that if I act as if everything were normal, maybe everything really will be normal; then I realize that there's nothing normal about what's going on around me, that I've spent almost a year in a state of dejection and that I'm worn out. So I don't wait for her answer before sagging into a chair in front of her. "I'm sorry."

She closes the book unhurriedly, and folds her hands on the cover: "Lindhe, *Clinical Periodontology*." When I look up again, she's looking at me, not at all embarrassed.

"You're sorry?" she asks, in a flat tone.

"Yeah," I reply. "You have to excuse me."

She crinkles her eyes in another smile.

"Oh, no, my friend!" she says. "Not the role of the shattered penitent."

There's no rancor or sarcasm in her voice, and the teasing is good-natured. She looks at me: my awkwardness amuses her. Worse, she seems to guess my effort not to think about the other night, to separate the two images I have of her.

"I mean, I should never have ..."

"Next you'll say it was because you drank?"

Her question silences me. She isn't smiling anymore, but she's not angry.

"We're both adults," she adds. "It was clear that when I asked you to come up and see my turntable ... Well, the turntable was comparable to 'come up and see my etchings.' Do we agree on that?"

I nod yes, warily.

It doesn't seem like she's laying a trap.

"And is it clear that it's not something that happened by accident?"

"Yes, it's clear."

I think about the day we did the exercise during acting class, how I thought I recognized her in the dark.

"There was an attraction and we acted on it," she says. "That doesn't mean that you and I have to make any decisions as a result."

"What do you mean?"

She crosses her legs and leans over the table. "I mean the situation is complicated enough as it is, and I don't intend to assign a name to what happened. It just happened, period. It was a one-time thing."

I conceal my relief, afraid of offending her.

"That's a good idea" I say.

"I thought it was great."

"Me too," I admit.

"I didn't tell Mauro," she says, putting the book back in her bag. "I think it's best we keep it to ourselves."

"Amelia ..."

"Don't say you're sorry again, because I'm not a patient person," she jokes.

"No ... can I get you something?"

She thinks about it for a second, checks the sunny morning.

"Is it still cold enough for hot chocolate?"

"It's always cold enough for hot chocolate."

"Hot chocolate then."

She stays for another half hour, drinks her hot chocolate while I watch her from behind the counter. We talk about innocuous things: the play that has now taken shape, her upcoming exam. The other night has been put away in an indefinite past, we're both over it, like a seasonal fever. All the same, I'd like to ask her if it was her, in the dark, that day at the acting school, but just thinking of the question makes me feel guilty. A customer comes in to use the bathroom and distracts me.

When we're alone again, she says she has to get back to the university. I point out to her that she has a chocolate mustache on her mouth. She leaves it there, says she likes to take chances, then says goodbye and marches out the door. *It just happened, period*, I repeat to myself, *it was a one-time thing*—and I watch her walk away.

"I've got two busy weeks ahead of me," Mauro says when we get to my house.

We're back from visiting Giorgia. Today it rained so hard that we had to remain indoors. He stayed with us for half an hour, then went back to the car to wait for me. I think there is something about this Giorgia that unsettles him, but I have the feeling that if I tried to probe, I wouldn't get an honest answer—his uneasiness is unrelated to the episode at the dinner, it must have to do with the nature of their relationship. She treats him politely but unintentionally keeps him at a distance; he is indifferent to her. When she's alone with me, she sometimes complains about his presence. In just one year our roles have been reversed: now I have to convince her of Mauro's kindness and the help he's giving me.

I watch him take the script out of the door pocket.

"I did all I could, in some places I stepped in directly and cut the misleading parts. In other passages I left you instructions," he says. "Complete it yourself. We'll reread it together when it's ready."

"Complete it?" I ask.

"The laptop," he says, retrieving the case from the back seat. "It's easier if you work on this."

"What do you mean, *complete it?*"

"I mean I've thought about it and I want you to work on it this time."

I stare at the laptop, the script, then him. I feel the disorienting sensation of having just been abandoned.

"I can't work on it alone."

"Of course you can," he says. "Afterwards I'll give you a hand with the editing."

"Why are you dumping this thing on me?"

I can't conceal how let down I feel, and he shakes his head, irritated.

"I'm not dumping anything," he says. "I just think it's only fair that you have a free hand this time. I don't want to act as mediator for you."

"But I need your mediation. I don't have the skills."

"All you need is formal consistency, that's all. I don't want to intrude in the matter anymore, I want you to handle it. All in all, I don't think I got that great a result with the first attempt."

"Exactly: it was an attempt," I argue.

His stepping back scares me. The script is a lead weight on my legs. I know I'm not ready for this, I'll never be able to do it.

"This too is an attempt," he says. "I'll help you fix it up afterwards. But this time you have to do it on your own."

"When did you decide this?"

He looks at me, he's exhausted again; I haven't seen him like this in months.

"I didn't decide anything, it's a practical matter. I have workshops to teach over the next couple of weeks, my calendar is so full it's crazy. I'm asking you to take over for a while, at this point."

I have no response.

"You'll do fine," he says, taking a cigarette out of the pack on the dashboard. "Listen, I called my friend. He's coming to pick up the car tomorrow morning. Make sure the registration and all is in it."

"What?"

"If you leave it out on the street a little longer, it will be good for scrap. He'll fix it for you."

He lowers the window, the rain drips into the car but he doesn't care.

"It's not necessary."

"It *is* necessary. You need the car."

He lights the cigarette, and we remain silent for a minute or two.

"You're making it bigger than it is, I'm telling you to try to work on it yourself for a couple of weeks. It'll go well, you'll see, don't be afraid," he says, after taking a drag. "It's easier than you think."

His gentle, even tone leaves no possibility of appeal. He's already made up his mind and I have the impression that any objection I might raise would do no good.

"Call me if you run into difficulty," he concludes, dismissing me. "At any hour. I'll do what I can."

"All right. Thanks."

I get out without lingering over the goodbyes. Soon I'm alone again, and the script is sitting on the kitchen table, looking at me from its white cover. I ignore it. I brood over Mauro and his defection, pick up my dirty clothes, and launch into an epic bathroom scrubbing. I clean until it gets dark, feeling like Giorgia, hostage to a sudden obsession. I eat supper in the living room, taking the plate with me, and turn up the television volume—it's as if someone were waiting for me sitting in the other room, an unavoidable guest. In bed, the thought of the script is so insistent that I find it hard to close my eyes. I imagine Giorgia, in there, and I fall asleep counting them all: all the possible Giorgias contained in the script that has yet to be written.

I wake up, the digital clock flashing red: 5:30 in the morning. I try to go back to sleep, but after a few minutes I give up. I feel lucid and wide awake, as if someone had spilled a bucket of water over me. I get up; after a slow ritual of heating the milk and choosing the biscuits, it's still me and the script, facing one another. I reach out, move it closer, but don't open it. I search for a strategy and as I usually do, construct it by following the path of an acceptable reality. The script is just an illusion, I tell myself as I raise the cover; it doesn't really work, it can't change Giorgia. It's a way of dealing with a problem that presents no solution. It's ineffective and therefore harmless.

I peruse the notes printed in red by Mauro and leaf through the script unsystematically, from the middle to the end and then the beginning, before I start looking at it as a whole and not in bits and pieces. After a while, the notes take on a shape, the path left by Mauro makes sense. I begin to consider the requested modifications, one after the other; then I finish my breakfast and let things settle.

As I see it, there's only one way I can do what I've been asked to do, and that's by expanding my acceptable reality. Maybe that way I can write about Giorgia, build her a new world to live in, one in which the harm that's been done to her is corrected, and imagine what she would have been if the order of events had been shifted, if a hand had been offered to her.

It won't work, I keep telling myself as I look for a pen. It won't work. I make a note on the margin of the script.

* * *

I resume my two parallel lives, the outward facade and the deeply interior one that's invisible and mine alone, in which I begin to sift through the memories again. This time I'm not unprepared and I start my exercise with confidence. Some memories are city flats without an elevator, others cramped closets, waiting rooms, endless parks; I orient myself in my memory by following a temporal development, from the beginning to its end. From some point on, I start looking for Giorgia even where she isn't, in the afternoons before I met her, in high school. I look for her in me before I do in her.

The exercise is everywhere, it pursues me. Our ghosts have remained in the places where Giorgia and I had been, I can't avoid them, no matter where I go here in the city I come upon the imprints our bodies left. The only place I can't find us is at the clinic. I continue with my visits, and the days out that she's allowed. The more I'm exposed to the present Giorgia, the more I fantasize about her future version, and when I get back the volume of my notes increases.

Since I've been writing in the spaces that Mauro has laid out, the script has become my alternative dimension. In this dimension, Giorgia has overcome the pain of loss and abandonment, and from this nucleus a chain reaction is triggered: the new Giorgia is everything she could have been and wasn't. As I work on the script I realize that this is what I'd like someone to do for me: rewrite me from the beginning, more resolute, taller, more confident. I figure that, since the script won't work, I might as well exaggerate, create the rosiest version of a reality that can never exist.

I work at the new Giorgia for two weeks. I don't call Mauro, I don't answer his phone calls, I shut myself up in the creative process. At the end, I don't read it over. In the script the new Giorgia is a strong, happy person, she loves me and I love her, and her dream is to become a great actress; in the script Giorgia is able to choose her own clothes, she likes the kind she never would have worn even before her illness, though they would have looked better on her; in the script Giorgia has a different way of walking, the way I only saw her walk once in the time I've known her: straight and confidently towards a goal. The new Giorgia, the new Giorgia ... the way she likes to please me when we make love, with creative, unpredictable moves; I imagine her in my world, I imagine touching her, and I yearn to touch her, as if she were already real. In the new Giorgia my memories pale, and the exercise takes on another form.

I can't sit still. I pace around the bookshelves, while Mauro, behind me, finishes reading the script. After our two weeks' separation, I find him thinner, his hair even longer. This morning, in the mirror, my face was as haggard as his. I'm tired, I think, taking a volume from the shelf: I glance at Aldous Huxley's Point Counter Point, and realize that we're wearing ourselves out.

I'm extremely sensitive to sound, I can tell immediately when the pages stop turning and there is a longer pause than usual. I pretend I'm still interested in the books and keep scanning the titles, but after another moment I turn around and make an effort to appear calm. He's closed the script and folded his hands on top of it. From this angle I can't see his face.

"Finished?" I ask, joining him at the table.

"Yes," he replies.

Now that I can see him, I have no clue: the voice is his usual, his expression neutral. I sit across from him.

"What do you think?"

"You did a great job, as I'd expected."

His stillness makes me nervous, I squirm in my chair. "I followed your lead," I say.

"No, you did a lot more, and you know it," Mauro gives a faint, one-sided smile.

"What do you think of the third act? A little lacking?"

"No, it's perfect."

"And the apartment scene? Do you like how I revised it?" I ask, gauging his reactions—and setting a trap.

I sense he's lying to me, as though I could see the lie through the barrier of his body. In the apartment scene, the sex between me and Giorgia is different from how it was in the original version, the one we used in the first script. I want Mauro to react, to tell me the truth, but he remains inscrutable.

"In line with the character," he says.

"I did a kind of compendium," I add.

"Yes, I guessed that, but the overall effect is not forced, it's consistent."

I slumped against the backrest, defeated. I don't know why I expected to have to face his criticisms. The script is exaggerated, the Giorgia of the script is overstated, yet that's all I was able to come up with. I'd like Mauro to stop me, to tell me that it needs to be completely revised, that we can't present it to Giorgia as it is. Instead, he's determined to like it at all costs.

"I'm not sure about it," I say, attempting the last card.

"What aren't you sure about?"

"I don't know, maybe I was too heavy-handed. I mean, Giorgia ..."

"You aren't sure about the character?"

"Yes, of course. I just want her to be happy."

Mauro nods understandingly.

"I just want her to be normal again," I go on, no longer knowing if I'm talking to him or to myself. "Not that she wasn't fine the way she was. But I want her to be able to live without being constantly haunted by her illness, by her past."

"Naturally, naturally," Mauro reassures me. "Listen, don't worry too much. Start reading it to her, and let's see how it goes."

He slides the script across the table, until it touches my hands.

"Right away, as is?" I ask, incredulous. "You really don't want to change anything?"

"Filippo, damn you!" he says, his voice distorted by a yawn. "That's right. I can't take your insecurity anymore. The script is fine as is, I already told you it's perfect. Now do me a favor. Do what you have to do, and propose it to Giorgia."

I pick up the script. Mauro's unprompted reaction mollifies me.

"Okay," I say. "When do we start?"

"I'm afraid you'll have to start on your own."

I watch him stand up, retrieve the pack he left on the couch, put a cigarette in his mouth.

"What do you mean, on my own?"

"The opening is in two months, I've stepped up the rehearsals and we're terribly behind. I have to use the time I don't have sparingly and I can't guarantee that I can be at the clinic."

"But I ..."

"I swear to God, if you tell me one more time that you can't do it ..." he threatens, waving the lighter.

"But what do I tell her, how do I convince her?"

"You don't have to convince her. You just have to tell her that you have a script for her to read, that you like it, that I told you to let her read it. Fabricate, improvise, lie," he says, returning to his seat. "And wipe off that penitent expression."

He persistently searches me with his eyes, and I make an effort to follow his advice, repeating his words to myself one by one.

"I'll keep an eye on you from a distance. You know you can count on me, should there be an emergency," he says, then smiles his turned-down smile. "When will you start?"

"Right away," I reply. "Tomorrow afternoon."

"See, you got my drift."

I watch him disappear behind a cloud of smoke.

Giorgia dangles her legs, sitting on a high stool at the restaurant. I took her to eat a kebab during our free time out.

"It's delicious," she says, wiping mayonnaise from a corner of her mouth. "Sure you don't want some?"

"I'm sure."

I smile at her and go back to looking out the window. The idea of the kebab was mine, this Giorgia doesn't have any ideas: she just goes along with me, wherever I take her, and adapts. Maybe it's apathy induced by her being confined in the clinic, knowing that the time spent outside doesn't totally pertain to her. Or maybe her submission is part of the Giorgia swept along by the current that I can no longer tolerate. I watch her eat the kebab with the same ecstatic expression already described in my exercise, the same way of chewing on one side only, with her mouth closed, and I wish she would tell me that the kebab is disgusting, that it's awful. I foresee her every move, she fulfills my expectations at every step, by now even when she has her short-lived breakdowns. I already know when she's going to cry, I know when she's going to link arms with me, I know when she'd like to kiss me; for every single move she makes, I know what's happened and what's going to happen—because what's happened is what's going to happen. In her character we stop living: there is no variant that I haven't already imagined.

When I focus on the thought of a whole lifetime, forever invariable, by her side, the idea of the new script immediately becomes a loving, unavoidable gesture. With every ounce of my being, I want it to work, I want it to be our impossible way out.

On the way back, she brings up the usual subjects, and I follow along. Listening to her talk is the only pleasure I have left—but I have to concentrate intensely only on the sound of her voice, and try to come up with alternate topics. When we park at the clinic again, I retrieve the script from the door pocket and take it with me. Once inside, she doesn't feel like going back to her room, and we still have an hour before visiting time ends, so we wind up in the common room, which is deserted.

"What's that?" she asks, when I place the script on the table.

I repeat Mauro's mantra: fabricate, improvise.

"A script," I say. "Mauro wants you to read it."

She picks it up, starts flipping through it.

"Why?" she asks.

There's no suspicion in her voice.

"He says it's good, he wants to know what you think," I tell her.

Giorgia closes the script.

"It's pretty urgent. Mauro needs your opinion," I persist. "He says that without your blessing on the leading role, he doesn't feel he can propose it to the company."

"I don't know if I feel like reading it," she says.

Fabricate, improvise, lie.

"If you want, I'll read it to you. I think we should help him. I've already told you that he's done a lot for us these past months."

Giorgia is not swayed, lethargic after the heavy food. For a moment I think I've already lost the match, but I conceal my edginess and reopen the script to the first page.

"You're considerate, Giorgia, aren't you?" I say, playing the last card.

It's like pressing a switch: Giorgia sits up straight in the chair and looks at me, surprised.

"Of course," she says.

I restrain my eagerness, I proceed cautiously.

"So don't you think we should do him this favor?" I push the script towards her.

"Yes," she says. "I really think we should."

She immediately bends over the list of characters, and dutifully reads the few lines.

"Why do they have our names?" she asks, not looking up, leafing through the pages with renewed energy.

I don't think the answer really matters to her, but I remind myself that I have to be careful not to push too hard.

"Mauro hasn't yet found suitable names, he decided to use familiar ones. They'll be replaced later when the draft is edited," I reply—and she hardly even hears me, she's already immersed in her new performance.

* * *

In Giorgia's room, the bed is made, the sheets stretched tight. I look around and I realize there is nothing in here that belongs to her: once her body has crossed the threshold of the place she's lived in for almost a year, nothing remains of her. It is the backdrop of a performance that is drawing to a close.

Sunlight sinks its talons into the doctor's scars and deepens them—his profile is irregular as he leans down, looking out the window, intent on the garden. Today as well there is the wheelchair patient and his love for the fountain. Then, on a bench, the unexpected variation: Giorgia is sitting, legs crossed, talking; her hand follows the conversation in measured gestures, then rests on her knee; her aunt is listening, leaning towards her. There's something strange about the two of us watching them—my observation is not an analysis but a kind of hypnosis, it happens every time I dwell on her too long, when I don't let my eyes slide over her like a normal occurrence.

"I repeat: be scrupulous about the medications," the doctor says, rousing me from my contemplation. "The dosage is mild, but it's essential that she follow it."

I nod, I can't hold back a frisson of excitement. I think about where we were, just three weeks ago: Giorgia sitting and reading the script from its first page. Since that day, she has read constantly—I just had to push her a little more, arguing the need to be considerate, the favor we owed Mauro, and she got carried away, she committed herself to it as if it were a matter of life and death. She read during the hours she spent outside the clinic, she read by herself. The new Giorgia has spread from fiber to fiber in a salutary, silent contagion. I watched her change before my eyes—the mutation was too pervasive to deny the influence of the script. She started feeling so good that it's like she'd begun to walk again. It didn't take long for the doctor to consider her request to be released. There were the sessions, the monitoring, leading to today's finishing line: the meeting with her aunt. If she consents, Giorgia can leave here.

I can't wait for Mauro to see her.

"I know that we have already discussed this in our talks," the doctor adds. "But I want to be sure that you do not lower your guard: keep your level of attention high, remember the list of dangerous symptoms, see to it that she keeps to the schedule of visits that we have established. Giorgia still needs to be medically assisted."

"I will," I tell him.

"Continue to treat her like an individual in recovery. The wounds are less visible now, but they're there. Don't be taken in."

I can't conceal my impatience. When he smiles at how

I'm fidgeting with the fringe of my beard, I quickly lower my arm and feel like I've been caught red-handed.

"So, the tide has retreated," he says, slipping his hands into the pockets of his white coat. "Enjoy the moment, Mr. Bonini, because tides are capricious, and that applies to everyone."

In the garden, Giorgia and her aunt hug each other tightly.

On the day she's released, it is Giorgia who leads the way when we get to our apartment. She insisted on dragging the suitcase herself, despite my offering to help her. It's as if she wanted to signal that this return was hers to manage. I let her do it. At home, I watch her repossess the spaces: she gets her bearings walking from room to room, studies details as if to quantify the time that has passed.

When it's time to unpack her suitcase, I join her in the bedroom.

"How do you feel?" I ask.

She looks at the open suitcase, the clothes inside it, consisting entirely of pajamas and socks.

"Good," she says, not looking up. She touches her hair distractedly, then shakes her head. "I hate this stuff."

She leaves the room, I hear her looking for something in the kitchen; she comes back with a garbage bag in her hand. She opens it up and starts filling it with the contents of the suitcase.

"Giò ..." I start to say.

"I don't want to keep this stuff, it smells like that place," she says.

When it's all stuffed inside the bag, she breathes a sigh of relief. She looks at me and gives a broad, dynamic smile.

"You have no idea how good I feel," she says.

"I can imagine. It's been a tough year."

"I'm not just talking about the clinic," she says. "It's also what came before, as if I'd spent the last few years of my life in a kind of sleep. I haven't felt so full of energy in a very long time."

She lowers her eyes to her T-shirt, then slips it off with a fluid movement; it too ends up in the bag. I don't have the nerve to protest. This lively version of her paralyzes me: it's like a perfectly successful performance, and I can't wait to know what happens next. I think about the miracle of the script, which no longer exists just on paper but is also embodied in Giorgia. And exists so intensely, it's real and I can touch it.

She gets rid of her jeans, and in her bra and panties, opens her side of the closet. She sifts through the clothes, appraises them, then turns to me, incredulous.

"I don't like any of these anymore," she says.

It's a hitch I hadn't thought about.

"We can buy something," I suggest.

"Good idea" she says, closing the closet.

There's a pleasant change in her voice too: it's clearer now, more precise, bolder somehow.

She sits on the bed, in front of me, crosses her legs. All I can think about is that I want Mauro to see her as soon as possible. He preferred not to show up during Giorgia's learning phase: he said he only wanted to see her when the process was completed. I didn't reveal any details to him during our phone calls, I merely informed him of her imminent release, and described a general improvement in her condition. I admit to feeling a flicker of pride, and I find it hard to hide it from myself; I am also haunted by the specter of a sense of guilt, the same guilt that I stifled when drafting the script. But Giorgia is doing so well, and she's so real ...

"Mauro wants us to go see him tomorrow," I say.

"Great," she says. "I have to talk to him."

"About what?"

"About the theater. I want to go back to acting."

I nod and pretend to be composed, though her request triggers an alarm bell.

"You know the doctor said to go slowly, you have to be patient," I tell her. "You'll start doing everything again, little by little."

"Sure, of course," she says. "I just want to get back on the circuit, even with a very small part, a few lines."

"You have to avoid overly intense stimuli," I add.

She smiles again, and this time it's yet a different expression, there's something in it that I can't decipher.

"I know," she says, slipping her fingers under the thin contour of her bra.

She exposes the skin where a dark nipple protrudes, runs a fingertip over it, and then displays herself, not taking her eyes off of me.

"I don't like my underwear anymore either," she says, and a deep current shoots through her voice, from her throat to my thighs.

"We can buy something," I say again.

She takes one of my wrists, pulls me close.

"Right now?" she says.

My hands are cold, I notice it only when I feel the temperature of her body.

"No," my voice cracks. "Not right now."

Giorgia opens her mouth on mine and takes all the words I can't say to her.

Mauro hands me a drink and for a moment I enjoy our interlude of silence, listening to the ice splinter in the Martini.

"What do you think?" I ask, after the first sip.

He glances behind me. He's opened the French door, from where you can see a corner of the garden. He's arranged a cocktail party with a few individuals selected from the company of the new production, people that Giorgia doesn't know well, some not at all. I don't know if she is visible or not from this angle, but all the same he has a self-satisfied expression. "Remarkable," he says. Giorgia has no flaws, she sustains the character magnificently. We're a long way from the day when, in this same house, she was perspiring in her scarf. She's enjoying the guests, chatting, she's completely composed. Every moment by her side, my excitement grows and my fear shrinks.

I know the doctor urged caution, but it's difficult to hold to a steady course. She is so faithful to the script and at the same time so original, she has the unpredictable predictability that was lacking in the first draft. And as I process this thought in my head, the words no longer seem strange—script, draft, character, are just other ways of signifying a recovery that is saving our lives.

"How is she with you?" Mauro asks, looking over his glass. "I mean, in private."

"No complaints there," I say. "On the contrary."

He deduces a different answer on my face and gives a feral smile, canines exposed.

"All that insecurity, such a waste of energy," he says.

When he steps towards the garden, I follow him. We stop at the edge of the door, from where there's a broader view. The scene is complete, the group engaged in lively, alcohol-fueled conversation. Giorgia and Amelia are sitting next to each other.

"What do you think about her clothes?" Mauro asks.

"Well ..."

"I don't mean she's dressed badly, far from it."

"I know."

"It's just different from her usual."

Giorgia is wearing a short skirt that exposes her long legs, and she's not wearing stockings, despite it being a pretty cool day. As she talks with Amelia, she fingers the edge of her low neckline.

"She wanted some new clothes," I admit. "She says she doesn't like the old ones anymore. She's going to ruin me."

Mauro laughs faintly, sipping from his glass.

"Isn't it remarkable?" he says then.

I know what he's referring to, and I nod. "It is."

"Over and above the miracle: being able to use her illness to cure her is obviously sensational."

"Yeah."

"But it's not just that. I'm talking about the character, the inferences. The way Giorgia deduced from your script even what wasn't written in it, how she processed and performed it. It's a phenomenon that always catches me unprepared."

"I know what you mean."

"No, you don't know."

His tone is suddenly distant. Mauro looks at me coldly, as if he weren't really seeing me. Before I can think of a reason for such an abrupt transformation, he immediately returns to normal: he points his finger at me and winks.

"Filippo," he says. "You're so expressive when you're scared, you should see yourself."

I suppose it's another of his strange ways of teasing me, and I indulge him, even if I don't like being his source of amusement.

"Were you offended?" he asks, taking me by the shoulder.

His eyes are kindly again, his smile friendly.

"No," I lie.

"Good," he drains his glass. "The workshops are over. We can see each other more often now, if you want. Maybe take the opportunity to ease Giorgia back into wider social contexts, see how she reacts. I think it's wiser if we're together to handle the situation."

"I agree."

"I imagine that sooner or later she'll have to go back to work," he says.

"Yeah, like it or not," I admit. "Our economic situation isn't rosy, and the new clothes, the medications ..."

"I can help you during this period, it's not a problem."

"I could never ..."

He shakes his head. "It will only be for a short time, you'll see."

We go back to watching Giorgia, who is now circling the table in the garden, choosing a few nibbles. She fingers her hair where it's growing, at the base of her neck.

"There's one thing ..." I say.

Behind Giorgia, Amelia looks in our direction. "Stop whispering together and come out here," she calls loudly.

"We're coming," Mauro says.

I look away. I'm not yet free of her memory, and seeing her so close to Giorgia scares me, as if two incompatible versions of reality were about to coincide. I know Amelia won't talk, she made it clear that day at the café, and at this very moment I keep repeating her words to myself—*a one-time thing.*

I don't want to spoil this day, so I too empty my glass in one gulp.

"There's the problem of her acting," I say. "She's going to ask you for a part in the show, I'm sure. She keeps talking about the possibility of a marginal role."

Mauro turns serious, considers my words. "I see."

"I'm afraid it might destabilize her."

"All right, let me think about it," he says.

Giorgia waves a hand in our direction, pouting.

"Go ahead, I'll catch up with you," Mauro says, pushing me.

I head into the garden before him. When I'm halfway there, I hear him call me.

"Filippo!" he says, raising his glass in a toast. "Great job."

CHAPTER EIGHT

GHOST

Swirling the remaining sip of coffee at the bottom of the cup, my mother considers an impression that leaves her doubtful. She casts yet another skeptical glance towards the living room where, on the sofa, Giorgia is helping my father with a crossword puzzle. She's wearing a skirt that leaves her legs exposed: one white thigh crossed over the other, cotton knee socks snug above the knee. My father, a little red in the face, makes a joke, and Giorgia laughs tossing her head back.

"But how come she dresses like that now?" my mother asks.

We are in the kitchen, sitting at the table, as on every weekend—after dinner, she always wants at least a quarter of an hour alone with me, to discuss whatever is worrying her. It is a ritual that no one has ever had access to; not my father, in the last thirty years, and not Giorgia either. My memories are full of these fifteen minutes during which I become hers.

"Don't you like it?" I ask.

She smooths out some imaginary wrinkles on the plastic tablecloth.

"She didn't dress like that before," she says.

We both look at her now: she isn't wearing a bra under her t-shirt, and when my father raises his eyes, he focuses on the tip of his shoes, on the corner of the carpet, on the base of the floor lamp—everywhere except on Giorgia.

"I like it," I say.

My mother makes a face as if an unripe fruit had puckered her tongue.

"She's dressed a little like a ..." she whispers, then giggles.

She says it without malice, in keeping with the cheerful mood of this lunch, and I can't take it as an offense. I wonder what this Giorgia would say if she heard: maybe she too would smile. Yes, I think, observing her as she points my father to a square, with a good-natured expression on her face—she would smile.

"Your father will have another heart attack soon, look how red he is," my mother adds, stifling a hiccup. "And I'll be left a widow."

She laughs, querulous. I'm thinking she's had too much wine and only now do I notice her shiny eyes.

"You seem like you're doing fine though," she says.

This conversation could continue even without my input, but I know she likes it when I reassure her aloud, and not just nod attentively.

"I'm much better," I tell her.

"I'm glad," she says, still swirling the cup. "So then, you like her clothes."

"I do," I repeat.

"There's something different besides that, I don't know," she goes on. "I remember when you introduced her to me: a little bird who'd fallen from the nest, she never spoke loudly."

Now I'm sure she's had too much to drink, because it's not like her to express herself so openly about someone other than herself. She has a very narrow perspective, as limited as the café where she spent her life polishing surfaces; my father and I are part of it, like extensions of her body. My mother's world is tailor-made, it has precise rules, physical laws that no one can evade. She'd formulated her predictions, made complex calculations that turned out to be all wrong. My father's precarious health and my professional failure had eluded her plan; the variations destabilized her and she still lives in two worlds that will never meet: the one that keeps following the track of what she would have liked, and the one in which she struggles against an inevitable state of affairs. There is no balance in how she sees things, it's all an idyllic future or an imminent tragedy. I'm moved when I look at her and think that, for more than twenty years, her life followed the plan that she thought she had chartered for it—and then, all of a sudden, when she was too old to contemplate a contingency, her reality had begun to crumble. I wonder if we are ever ready for it.

"I liked her right away," I hear her say.

When I reach out and squeeze her arm, I see her pretending not to be emotional.

"I know," I say. "Do you still like her?"

"She's different."

"More confident, right?" I encourage her.

I'm curious to know her impression.

"Yes," she replies. "The first time you brought her here she was someone you had to be careful not to hurt."

I understand what she means, because I remember having the same impression: for me, too, Giorgia had been vulnerable.

"I think being more self-assured is good for her," I say. "I think she was too defenseless before."

She doesn't seem to get it, and it's important to me that she understand.

"Wouldn't you want the same for me?" I ask her.

She looks at me, toys with the ceramic cup handle.

"Wouldn't you want me to be the best version of myself as well? More enterprising, more daring, more muscular," I persist, teasing her.

She laughs again, wiggles out of my grip and slaps my hand.

"That's not what I want," she says, side-stepping. "To me you're fine as you are. It's all the rest that's not right."

That's always been her problem: to want to change the sum of the addition without changing the addends; it's too late to tell her that.

"We have to go, they're expecting us at rehearsals."

She watches me get up.

"I wouldn't have minded having the kitchen cleaned a little, though," she says.

I shake my head, while she indulges in a naughty laugh. When I join Giorgia and my father in the living room, I find them still busy with the crossword puzzle.

"The opposite of crisis?" he asks, his pen poised over the paper.

"It's time to go," I say.

Giorgia looks up at me: "Right now?"

"We're late."

She nods and sighs theatrically, then smacks a kiss on my father's cheek. He stiffens even more. When we say our goodbyes, Giorgia hugs my parents warmly, as if it were a normal thing—the Giorgia of the past would never have done that. They're struck by it, and I can't resist glancing at my mother. "Okay, you're right," she whispers in my ear, when I'm already at the door.

I'm still not used to Giorgia's new energy. On the street, I watch her walk fast, two steps ahead of me, her hands in the pockets of her faux-leather jacket; I have a hard time keeping up with her.

"I can't wait," she says, turning around. A passerby turns to look at her, she notices and smiles at me. "I can't believe they're doing Wedekind: I adore him."

"Great," I say, as we reach the car.

The idea of having her attend the rehearsals was Mauro's and I did not object, but now I feel tense. I'm thinking this will be the last in our series of tests, and I hope that Giorgia successfully passes this one too.

"What's wrong?" she asks when I start the car.

"Why?"

"You seem nervous."

"Not at all," I reply.

She knows I'm lying, I can tell by the way she touches me—she slips a hand on the inside of my knee.

"I'm fine," she says. "I took my meds."

"I know."

The truth is that I watch her closely, even if there's no need to: she adheres scrupulously to the prescribed regimen, she never slips up. She's already had two weekly checkups with the doctor and both reported positive results.

We're late getting to the school. We slip into room twelve hoping to pass unnoticed, but we don't quite manage to. Most of the performers are gathered along the wall and the scene is occupied only by Amelia and one of the co-protagonists. Behind them, Mauro is studying them—he gives us a brief nod when he sees us come in, while the actors continue as if nothing had happened. We join the group of observers, and exchange silent greetings. Giorgia stretches her legs out in front of her, her eyes are lit up. After a few minutes she's already taken a script from one of the extras, and is paging through it distractedly, looking up from time to time to keep an eye on the action onstage. Seeing her with the script in her hand makes me nervous.

In front of us, Amelia is having a hard time: Mauro keeps interrupting her performance—"More confident, the voice, more confident," he repeats, pacing around the scene in ever tighter circles. She stops, picks up from where she should start changing her interpretation, but she can't finish a line without him criticizing her about leaving something out.

"I, Melchior, have never been beaten in my life—not a single time …" Amelia recites. "I can hardly imagine what it means to be beaten. I have beaten myself in order to see how one felt then in one's heart—It must be a gruesome feeling …"

"Amelia, for God's sake, listen to yourself when you speak!" Mauro raises his voice sharply. "Can you hear the pity you put into it? It's totally out of line."

He invades the space now, stands between Amelia and the other actor.

"In Wendla there is no request for compassion: don't prepare the audience to commiserate with her. She's about to ask Melchior to beat her with a switch, she can't wait for it to happen. No one feels the need to know your opinion about it."

"But I …" Amelia starts to say.

"Don't even try," Mauro cuts her short. "It's the same old story. I ask you to vanish and you intrude your body everywhere, look how you're holding your arms: your character doesn't want to be protected, I don't see why you should do it."

Amelia nods, tightens her lips.

"Look at me," Mauro orders.

She hesitates. Around me no one is particularly fazed by Mauro's outburst: some are rereading the script, others are enjoying Amelia's embarrassment as if she were part of the show. Giorgia, too, is staring at both of them, and for a moment I glimpse the hint of a smile at the corner of her mouth. Then she turns around and the smile disappears: I don't know if I imagined it or if it was really there, because she is as mortified as I am. She shakes her head imperceptibly, as if to say she's sorry.

"I said: look at me." Mauro doesn't let her off the hook, and finally, Amelia obeys. "Please do what I tell you, period. I'm tired of repeating myself."

She nods again, and doesn't look away. I wonder how Mauro can hold her gaze without blinking. "Let's continue," he says.

When he leaves the scene, Amelia attempts to get back into the character—I watch her relax her shoulders, breathe deeply, then nod at the other actor.

"I don't believe a child is better for it."

"Better for what?" Amelia asks.

"For being beaten."

She takes a step or two, as if following a tracing on the floor, until she reaches the thin switch, lying on the ground, waiting for her. She picks it up and, whether due to suggestion or as a result of Mauro's words, seems to shiver fearfully as she holds it.

"With this switch, for instance!" she recites, as though in a trance. "Ha! but it's tough and thin."

"That would draw blood!"

"Would you like to beat me with it once?"

It's not a suggestion: Amelia's voice now is uncertain.

Mauro bursts back into the scene, waving the script.

"I give up," he says. "A ten-minute break, we'll pick up from act two."

The pause is greeted with enthusiasm, many leave the classroom, and Amelia remains alone onstage, with the switch in her hand. I'd like to go to her, say something to her, but Giorgia's presence holds me back: sitting beside me, she is again immersed in the script.

"What are you doing?" I ask her.

"I think I see where the problem is," she replies in a low voice.

"Would you like to go get something from the machines?" I suggest.

"One second."

I see her get up to go and join Mauro, who is pacing around like a caged beast at the back of the room. He gives her a hostile look, then Giorgia says something that I can't hear from here, and he becomes tame.

Amelia walks across the frame, blocking them, then sits on the floor next to me. A girl touches her shoulder. "Want to go out and have a cigarette?" she asks. Amelia shakes her head and smiles uncertainly. When the girl walks away, she lets out a long sigh and rests her head on the wall. Back there, Mauro and Giorgia go on talking, she opens the script, he leans over to read, and I have to turn away.

"How are you?" I ask.

Amelia makes a glum face.

"I hate him," she says. "If I could, I'd stick this switch up his ..." She breaks off when a colleague walks by.

"I'm sorry."

"Don't be, he's right. I'm the problem. There's something that scares me in this script, and he knows it. I promised him I'd be able to overcome my reservations and I'm not keeping my commitment."

"I'm still sorry."

She reaches up, shifts her hair to one side of her neck, and the memory of the turntable night comes rushing back to me like a punch in the gut. I look away.

"You know what really irritates me? That he's always right," Amelia says.

We both watch Giorgia and Mauro talking seriously on the other side of the room. The script is between them like a battlefield: Giorgia wants to convince him of something at all costs. He gives me a sidelong glance, then quickly turns back to reading.

"He's not always right," I say.

"You don't know him well enough," Amelia replies, getting up. "I need to get some air."

I watch her walk away and disappear through the door, and I feel confused, as if I've been turned upside down. Only half an hour ago, my world was my parents' house, the sidewalk, the new perfect equilibrium; now everything is topsy-turvy, all it took was a gesture. I suppress my agitation, I tell myself again that it's the result of having gone through a long, difficult period and that the experience of Giorgia's illness was trying, debilitating.

Giorgia and Mauro go on talking until the actors drift back to the classroom, a few at a time. When the break is over, Giorgia comes back to me with a blissful smile on her face. I wait for her to sit down beside me, but she bends over slightly, leaning towards me.

"We're just giving it a try," she tells me, in a reassuring tone.

Before I can ask her to explain, she is quickly absorbed into the orbit of the scene, the script in one hand. When everyone is seated again, I realize what's about to happen and it's already too late.

"We're giving this a try," Mauro says aloud so that this time everyone can hear. "Amelia, sit down as well."

Amelia stares steadily at Giorgia for a long moment, without animosity, but Giorgia doesn't notice: her eyes are still fixed on the script. When Amelia obeys Mauro's order, she comes and sits next to me again, in the place Giorgia left empty.

"Giorgia and I had the opportunity to work together on this play, a long time ago," Mauro explains to the group. "Maybe her collaboration can help us get out of this impasse."

He is very serious, fully taken with his role as the stern instructor, and I wonder what he's thinking, what absurd idea made him think this was the right thing to do. Where is the caution we agreed to?

I restrain my nervousness, I realize that I'm thwarted by our secret.

"Let's resume," Mauro says, moving out of the scene. "When you're ready."

The other actor reacts readily to the change, adapts to Giorgia, waiting for her line: now she is at the center of the scene, with her cropped hair, her short skirt and knee socks, the buttons of her sweater open at the neckline, and for a moment I hardly recognize her.

"I, Melchior, have never been beaten in my life—not a single time," Giorgia begins. "I can hardly imagine what it means to be beaten. I have beaten myself in order to see how one felt then in one's heart—it must be a gruesome feeling."

As she speaks, she looks at the switch, back in its place on the floor, behind the other actor. Right away she's someone else, she's not the new Giorgia. The terror that I might not see her come back paralyzes me—how can I watch her and not be able to prevent it? It's like going back to the night of the opening.

She's taking her medicines, I tell myself—the tide has retreated.

"I don't believe a child is better for it," says the actor playing Melchior.

"Better for what?" Giorgia asks, still distracted by the switch.

"For being beaten."

Giorgia picks the switch up off the floor, completing the intention that drove her from the beginning. She runs it between her fingers, tests the sharp tip.

"With this switch, for instance!" she says. "Ha! but it's tough and thin."

Her touch is hypnotic, and avoiding the idea of pain is impossible.

"That would draw blood!" says Melchior, he too mesmerized by Giorgia's fingers.

She doesn't speak, the silence expands, quivers with her next line.

"Would you like to beat me with it once?"

I feel the tension explode—it explodes in my hands, clenched into fists, and in those looking on: there is no one who isn't staring, who isn't waiting for the next step. Giorgia, who is no longer Giorgia, draws us slowly to the edge of the precipice.

"Who?"

"Me."

"What's the matter with you, Wendla?"

Melchior takes two steps back, horrified, and Giorgia instantly bridges the distance.

"What might happen?" she says.

"Oh, be quiet! I won't beat you."

Giorgia clutches the switch to her chest like a cherished treasure.

"Not if I allow you?" she pleads.

"No, girl!" Melchior takes her by the shoulders, pushes her away.

"Not even if I ask you, Melchior?" Giorgia entreats.

Her eyes are wide open, she's braced against the young man's hands, she counters his push. Her cheeks are flushed with an unhealthy excitement, the same excitement I feel clawing at the pit of my stomach. I find myself hoping that he will satisfy her quickly, without putting up any more resistance.

"Are you out of your senses?" Melchior lets her go, he too now a victim of temptation.

"I've never been beaten in my life!" says Giorgia in a honeyed voice.

"If you can ask for such a thing ..."

Giorgia is a little girl begging for a spanking; she surrenders the switch to Melchior's outstretched hands, and he grabs it without protesting.

"Please ... please ..."

The young man clutches the switch in his hands, takes a step forward and she does not back away. For a moment he gauges her desire, then moves away just enough to gain momentum and lashes out, pulling back his arm.

"I'll teach you to say please!"

When the first whack strikes Giorgia's side, I catch myself sighing with relief. There's no time to check and see if others around me are experiencing the same disconcerting sensation, as if they've been released.

"Oh, Lord, I don't notice it in the least!" says Giorgia, her eyes wide open, hands pressed to her stomach.

"I believe you ... through all your skirts ..." Melchior pants, savagely.

"Then strike me on my legs!"

The young man obeys, the switch thwacks sharply on Giorgia's bare thighs, she bites her lips in pain.

"You're stroking me!" she cries. "You're stroking me!"

"Wait, witch, I'll flog Satan out of you!"

Melchior strikes her again and again, and, when Mauro grabs the switch, I find I'm holding my breath, waiting for another blow that doesn't come. The actor awakens from a state of trance: he looks at the switch, the red welts on Giorgia's legs, runs a hand over his sweaty, convulsed face—"I don't know what came over me," he says. "Are you all right?"

"Don't worry," Giorgia turns around and shows her radiant smile. "I'm fine."

An unnatural stillness has come over the audience. I can't look up, I feel as if all of these strangers are looking at me and, as they look at me, judging me for what I just wanted. Once again, Giorgia left her body and took me away with her, to another of her dangerous worlds. She came back—of course, I tell myself, after all she's taking her medicines; I recite the names, the doses, the containers by heart, and I wonder if the fear of us both losing ourselves will ever end.

"I hope that what I have in mind is clearer to everyone now," says Mauro, serious. "Wendla wants to be beaten. Masochism is inherent to her character, there is no Wendla without the desire for punishment. To deprive her of this desire would be to strip her of her identity."

Mauro now focuses purposefully on Amelia.

"Giorgia's Wendla craves pain so intensely that we want it too," he adds. "Now do you understand what I was talking about?"

All eyes are on Amelia and I can't resist looking at her either—I now know that there's something seductive about that discipline: the pleasure of not being its victim is irresistible. She acknowledges the defeat with a curt nod of the head, yields to Mauro and also to Giorgia who, at the end of the run-through, readily accepts the enthusiastic compliments of their colleagues.

At dinner, the purple streaks of the blows Giorgia received are visible on her thighs, but she doesn't care. We are guests at Mauro's place, for a get-together planned before the turmoil at the afternoon's rehearsals. Amelia is here: she isn't smarting from the lesson that Mauro inflicted on her. Still, she avoids talking much, letting others answer for her, and drinks: she's on her fifth glass of red. He pays no attention, and acts as if nothing happened. I don't know anything about how they handle friction over work, nor have I ever seen them argue; besides, I'm distracted by Giorgia. She's been holding forth since we sat down at the table: a series of anecdotes that she pulled out of a hat, whose existence I knew nothing about, stories dating back to her early days in the theater, to the beginner courses.

I look at her as she describes the disastrous collapse of a stage set. Sitting at the head of the table, she occupies the place that only a few weeks ago was Mauro's. He studies her, sitting across from me, and I wonder if he too is able to spot the similarities: she's appropriated his best role. He hasn't even tried to interrupt her monopolizing the conversation, he observes and lets her go at it, joining in with the laughter.

I wish this interminable day were over, I need to pause, to reflect. I can't escape Giorgia's new potency, this way she has of keeping attention on herself—and I wonder how I did it, in which detail of the subtext I endowed her with the superpower. I'm tempted to consider a rereading, out of caution.

"Giorgia was my crown jewel," Mauro says, at a certain point.

She stretches, clasping her hands behind her neck: it's a masculine gesture, yet at the same time charged with sensuality. For the first time since she left the clinic, I wish she'd behave differently.

Out of the corner of my eye, I see Amelia empty another glass.

"An inimitable performer," Mauro piles on. "Impossible to find another actress who can match her."

Giorgia does not hide her self-satisfaction, she looks at me for confirmation, as if expecting her measure of tributes from me as well.

"Excuse me a second," Amelia says, getting up.

No one hears her, the guests are focused elsewhere.

"Today was spine-tingling," someone remarks.

"Yes, extraordinary."

"How did it feel, that part where you offered Luca the switch? You were so intense …"

A profound fatigue comes over me, a sudden, strong desire for a little silence.

"Be right back," I say, and I too am ignored.

I go up the stairs, leaving behind the celebration of Giorgia's talent, her proud smile. When I reach the first floor, it's all a long way off.

Amelia's room is empty. I find her in the bathroom; she left the door open. She's standing in front of the mirror looking at herself; she's so still, it's as if someone drew her on the glass. When she sees me, her eyes are the only thing that move in the warm glow of the lamps above the sink.

"Did you need some air too?" she says.

I go in, and shut the door partway. "I can't take it any-more. Plus the way he treats you ..." I admit.

Amelia smiles bleakly, she turns to me.

"Why does he keep harping on that?" I ask her.

She hops up and sits on the marble sink counter.

"Every now and then he likes to act that way," she says. "Usually it doesn't bother me. I'm just tired of all this bullshit."

"I apologize for Giorgia, I don't know what got into her," I say.

She measures me with her eyes, motions to me to close the door. I put aside the fear of being caught, of the questions that might be asked, and I shut the door. When it's locked, I breathe again.

"She's still a little strange, don't you think?"

Amelia says it as if the thought saddened her. It's that melancholy expression that keeps me from getting nervous: it isn't really a question, more like a wounded observation.

"Maybe, a little," I say, thinking of my mother's words.

"Do you think she'll go back to being the same as before?"

I move closer to her with the pretext of seeing myself better in the mirror.

"Maybe she just needs time," I say, though I don't really believe it.

There's no chance that the past Giorgia will return, the script leaves no room for any of her old frailties. I wonder whether it's right to want her to embody our ideal in all respects, whether it isn't selfish to want her to be identical to how she was before the illness. Why not let her be different, improved?

"They all adore her, don't they?" Amelia goes on. The illuminated half of her face is uncertain. She dangles a leg slowly, lowers her head a little but doesn't look away. "I'm just jealous."

"You have no reason to be," I tell her.

She shifts her hair aside, baring her neck.

"But I do," she says. "At least one."

I think I should get out of there now, and I don't want to. I think of the perfect Giorgia waiting for me, I focus on her body during the last orgasm, but it's not enough, my brain is obsessed with another desire.

Amelia decides for me: in my moment of hesitation she slips down and walks out unsteadily, and when I follow her it's already too late, the door of her room is closed. Going down the stairs again I feel short of breath; I tell myself that nothing happened, nothing was about to happen. I'm too tense, I suppose, I get distracted and forget the trap of the last step: I stumble into it and the splinters of wood reopen the gash of the old wound.

My accident puts an end to the dinner; with the excuse of needing to attend to my injury, I persuade Giorgia to leave. During the drive home and even after we get there, she keeps talking about the performance, about how alive she felt while acting that one scene— she's distracted by her own chatter, so I have to dress the cut myself.

"Don't you think Amelia is inadequate for the part?" Giorgia asks, as I try to disinfect the gash.

Sitting on the couch, I have cotton, a Band-Aid, and hydrogen peroxide at hand. Trying to swab my ankle, I lose my balance and tip over the antiseptic. She barely notices, ignores my attempts to retrieve the bottle before it rolls too far. When I straighten up and lean back against the couch cushion, she starts up again.

"I don't mean she isn't good, I just think the part isn't right for her," she says.

"Don't you think that, in any case, it doesn't concern you?"

My response takes her by surprise: she stiffens, sitting on the other side of the sofa.

"Why do you say that?" she asks.

I leave aside the Band-Aid and cotton, I ignore the trail of antiseptic inching across the floor.

"Because it's Amelia's part," I say.

"I know that, I was just making an observation."

"A superfluous observation."

"Do you mind telling me what your problem is?" she says, arching her eyebrows.

She's beautiful even with smudged makeup around her dark eyes. She looks at me like a pouting child.

"Why did you have to do that today?" I ask. "Why did you have to humiliate her?"

She hesitates a moment, then chooses an innocent smile.

"It wasn't my intention."

"But that's what you did."

"No one was trying to humiliate anyone, it was just a rehearsal."

"Mauro didn't seem to think so."

Giorgia draws her legs up to her chest, revealing the blue crotch of her panties. I am torn between the scenario in which I wish I'd never started this discussion, and that in which I end it with a victory—but for who? Who am I defending?

"I'm more talented."

The old Giorgia would never have said such a thing out loud; just a year ago, here, in front of me, she was still unsure about her leading role.

"Meaning?" I ask.

"Why should I have held back if I knew I could do better?"

"Because Amelia is your friend. Because, like it or not, you mortified her," I reply. "It's her role, not yours."

Giorgia absorbs the blow, her cheeks flushed by the confrontation. Seeing her like that attracts me and at the same time repels me, as if it appealed to both sides of me. After a few minutes of silence, I bend down again and place the Band-Aid on the wound. I hear her move close.

"Are you mad at me?" she asks, stroking my arm.

"No," I say, not raising my head.

She slides to the floor, kneels in front of me, between my legs, forces me to look at her.

"Forgive me?" she asks.

I can tell she's not sorry: she still has a hint of that self-satisfied smile on her face, the same feeling of omnipotence that she must have had while doing the scene. When I don't answer, she puts a hand on my sternum and pushes me back. She raises my T-shirt, runs a finger over my jeans button, dares me to stop her. I couldn't even if I wanted to—and I don't want to. She pulls down the zipper, moves closer, never stops looking at me.

"Forgive me?" she breathes, over me.

I'm thinking there's something wrong and something tremendous and right; I'm thinking I should have begged the old Giorgia for the same impulsive attention. "Yes," I say, or maybe I just imagine it, or maybe it's not my voice but a simulation. She smiles down at me, she never takes her eyes off of me, even when I come.

* * *

The doctor's office has a pale-green waiting room, with a large window. Since Giorgia's visits here in the city began, we've never encountered any other patients either going out or coming in. The doctor admits us personally at every appointment, at five in the afternoon, without his white coat; the session with Giorgia never lasts more than an hour, sometimes even less. There are no magazines to read, nor do the two of them speak loud enough for me to hear them, and I can't sit still for more than ten minutes.

From the window you can see the two-lane driveway: it is early May and the linden trees are about ready to bloom. Just a year ago today it was also May seventh, and two years ago the same, whereas we were all different. Since the start of the exercise, my memory has become sharp and troublesome, at certain times it's so vivid that it flows on a plane equivalent to the present, as if all the memories were happening at the same time; I am here and at the same time I am in all the other May sevenths of my life, a single May seventh each year, thirty-two May sevenths altogether. Here, Giorgia has a self-awareness that she never had, and I feel a sadness, recently germinated, over her precarious equilibrium. Nostalgia emerges occasionally, at times when she is not too close to me, when she can't talk to me— the new Giorgia traps me in her body more than I would like. Most of the time, I manage not to think about the possibility of having made a mistake—how could that be so? This is the Giorgia who was released from the clinic and has started living again.

"Filippo?" the voice startles me.

Giorgia steps out of the hallway leading to the doctor's office; she laughs as she comes over to me.

"Everything okay?" she asks, scrutinizing me. "Did I scare you?"

"No. Yes," I say as she strokes my cheek. "I was thinking."

"The doctor wants to talk to you," she says.

"How come?"

"I don't know, he didn't say. He probably wants to ask you something about me."

She winks conspiratorially.

"Okay." I head towards the hallway, leaving her behind.

There are two sofas in the room, facing one another and separated by a low table: the doctor is waiting for me, sitting among the cushions, to my left. In front of me, behind the dark wood desk, is another window. I walk across the deep carpet. "Would you close the door, please?" he says, when I'm already halfway there. I go back, close the door, then he motions me to sit down.

"How are you?" he asks.

"Fine," I reply.

Away from the clinic he looks innocuous—it's the absence of the white coat, or maybe being able to talk in a normalized setting.

"What can you tell me about Giorgia?"

"She seems fine," I say.

"Seems?"

"She is fine."

He folds his hands on his knees, studies me silently for a few seconds.

"Giorgia asked me to support the revocation of the interdiction," he says.

The news takes me by surprise. She hasn't mentioned this issue since she was released, and I'm startled to only now realize that she is not yet truly free. The truth is that I didn't give any serious thought to the interdiction: I just wanted to see her come home. After all, Giorgia was returned to me thanks to the consent of her aunt, who could also have decided to prolong her clinical stay or force her to live with her. I wonder how it could not have occurred to me to discuss the matter with Giorgia.

"So what happens now, Doctor?" I ask.

"I'll have to formulate my diagnosis. Provide a medical report certifying her sound condition."

I can't divine his thinking: the doctor gives a polite, impassive half smile.

"I think you may be able to help me."

I nod, straightening my back. "What can I do?"

"What do you think of Giorgia?"

The idea that Giorgia's freedom somehow depends on what I'm going to say makes me nervous.

"I think she's fine."

"Manic episodes?"

"None."

"Resistance to drug treatment?"

"No."

"Unusual reactions?"

I hesitate, the question stops me.

"In what sense?" I ask, trying to buy time.

"Unusual," the doctor repeats. "Reactions that are not part of her pattern of habitual behaviors."

He straightens his glasses again.

Habitual behavior, I repeat to myself—but what typical pattern are we talking about?

"No, nothing unusual," I say. My voice is uncertain and he's aware of it.

"Anything you want to talk about?"

"Nothing in particular." I realize I've conceded when it's already too late. "It's just that there are differences."

"What kind of differences?" the doctor asks.

He slips off his glasses, starts wiping them on the edge of his blue polo shirt. I feel more at ease without his eyes on me.

"She's not the same as before. There are differences," I repeat, and, as I say it, I think I must be nuts: I'm the one who wrote this Giorgia.

"I understand what you mean perhaps," the doctor says, holding his lenses up to the light. "You mustn't be alarmed, Mr. Bonini, it's only natural that she should be different. Giorgia went through a very difficult period. In fact, I am amazed at the speed of her improvement: in the last month she has made great strides."

I nod, and instinctively finger the scar on my cheekbone.

"You must be patient, wait for the adjustment," the doctor continues. "But you must also begin to consider the possibility that Giorgia will not return to being identical to the way she was before."

The way she was before.

"I just want her to be all right," I say—the only words that don't cost me the effort of formulating a reply.

"That's what we all want," the doctor says. "We're close to achieving our goal, don't you think?"

"Yes."

"So then, you have nothing to report to me?"

"No," I reply. "Everything's normal."

"How come I don't have my own phone?"

Giorgia's heels strike the pavement at a brisk pace and, even though we're arm in arm, I still feel like I'm running after her.

"I lost it on the night of the opening," I explain—I don't tell her that I think I may have dropped it while I was in the hospital, but all the same she senses that I'm keeping part of the story from her.

"That's okay," she says. "I want to get one."

She looks around: we're crossing the piazza at Colonne di San Lorenzo and the only mobile phones available are already someone else's.

"We can buy one tomorrow," I tell her.

She nods, busy formulating some plan that excludes me.

"I want to talk to my aunt tomorrow," she announces when we're forced to stop for a red light.

"The doctor told me about the interdiction" I say.

"Yes, I think it's time to at least start discussing it." Giorgia's hand goes to the back of her neck, as if searching for her long hair.

"You're right," I say.

My memory is full of glowing sunsets like this one. We are following the route that we often took in the early days, when we had no direction to follow, no place we had to be. It was all potentially extraordinary; now that I saw it clearly, I often had the feeling that something decisive was about to happen.

The cars' headlights wipe away Giorgia's profile—forehead, nose, mouth—and she's lost.

"I can't wait to be my own boss again," she says as we cross the street.

"It's not that big a deal," I say, taking her by the hand.

She wraps her fingers around mine, smiles, but her smile is not only for me: it embraces the entire street, the passing tram almost stumbles over it.

"You don't really believe that."

Maybe I too would like someone to rewrite me, I think, as we cover the distance between us and Piazza Ventiquattro Maggio. The places are those we already know, everywhere I look I see our ghosts. I don't know what's happening to me, the talk with the doctor has made me vulnerable to uncomfortable thoughts. It is Giorgia and I, and with us all the others, our former selves who preceded us.

I quicken my pace behind her, anxious to leave this stretch of the way behind me.

"I really hope my aunt doesn't oppose it," Giorgia says. We pass in front of the local market hall, but she doesn't even glance at it, she doesn't say a word: in the past she would have made me go in; now it's two steps away and the market is already a distant thought.

"Don't you want to have a look inside?" I ask as we walk by. She looks at me, puzzled.

"No," she says, distracted. "Do you think my aunt will put up a fight?"

"Why should she?"

"I don't know," Giorgia says as she leads me along the high walls of the shipyard. "I'm scared. Maybe, if I behave the way she wants ..."

"The way she wants?"

"Yes," she replies. "She likes me when I'm composed, calm. I could change my clothes, maybe I still have something old in the closet. I don't want to start off on the wrong foot."

I see her picturing the matched sets. I let go of her hand with the excuse of letting her go ahead in the crowd of pedestrians strolling along the Naviglio.

"You don't have to pretend," I tell her. "You just have to be yourself."

Giorgia smiles at me patronizingly.

"What is it, Giò?"

"She will never agree unless I show her what she wants to see," she says.

The words leave me bewildered—she made it sound like the most normal thing in the world. Maybe it is, maybe those words are part of a normality that I don't know, but it's not hers, it's not Giorgia's, or mine. I can't have written anything like that. I swallow, my mouth dry.

"I could start working again," Giorgia continues. "You should think about a new job too."

"A new job?" I echo her.

"Yes, you don't want to be stuck in that café all your life, do you? You have no future if you stay there. You should get out there again, you can't expect me to do everything."

"Expect you to do everything, what do you mean?"

"Expect me to be the only one thinking about better-ing ourselves."

Giorgia is lost in her new dimension, unaware of me, and of the ever-wider distance that separates us: we're walking so far apart that passersby come between us. She's fine, I think, she has everything she needs for this life. Her legs climb the stairs of a bridge, I watch them go up ahead of me, in no time we're at the top. Midway along, as Giorgia goes on talking to me about her plans for the future, the memory becomes more real than the present actuality: I see the ghost of Giorgia, the mem-ory of the last time we were here, overshadow her—the two of us were looking over the railing where she's now standing alone. She's beautiful. She's as beautiful as she was then, leaning over to study the reflection of the streetlamps in the black water. She is everything that Giorgia would have been if the illness hadn't crushed her.

"Coming?" she says.

I'd like to tell her that she is perfect, I'd like to tell her that I wrote her to be better suited to a world that has always frightened us, so that she wouldn't be afraid, so that she wouldn't have to suffer—but it's already too late: in her arms I become a ghost.

CHAPTER NINE

DIFFERENT

Giorgia's aunt puts up resistance, determined to stand her ground on the interdiction until she's certain that her niece's condition is stable: she imposes a schedule of afternoons spent together, at her house, requiring me to change the open hours at the café.

Today, as I drive her to the appointment, Giorgia keeps adjusting her T-shirt: she's dressed in what's left of her earlier wardrobe, the pants and shoes that she always wore to work. I watch her slip two fingers inside her sleeve, scratch away an imaginary itch.

"I can't take it anymore," she says when we're almost there. "She's doing it on purpose."

"She just wants to spend time with you."

She holds back a sigh, shakes her head. "She's selfish. She's holding me back."

"Maybe she's afraid you'll exclude her from your life again," I say.

She stops a few steps from the door, slides her hands into the pockets of her jeans.

"She can't force me to include her," she says, not looking at me.

"She's your aunt."

"That doesn't mean anything."

The new Giorgia is not receptive to my efforts to suggest alternative points of view. She pulls me to her, stifles my regrets in a deep kiss.

"I'll be back to pick you up in a couple of hours," I say, letting her go.

I wait for her to close the door behind her, and return to the car with the same sense of emptiness that has haunted me since the day of our walk. Even Giorgia's body has become hostile, I touch her and immediately think of her earlier awakening, when another character, the Countess Olivia, possessed her. I expend a lot of energy driving away fear, I live my days underwater.

By the time I get to the café, I'm so caught up in the effort not to think that I don't notice there's someone waiting for me.

"Hey there, my friend."

Amelia is leaning against the rolled-down shutter, holding the piece of paper I left taped there before leaving. "You're back early," she says, reading.

"Hi," I say. I attempt a natural smile, feel it fall flat. "What are you doing here?"

She crosses her arms, glances around looking for someone.

"Where's Giorgia?" she asks.

"I took her to her aunt's," I say. "Why?"

"I have to talk to you."

I bend down to open the padlock, the keys are slippery in my hands, which have begun to sweat.

I follow her inside, she stops suddenly in the middle of the room, and I end up bumping into her. Five awkward minutes go by during which I keep apologizing to her, then I manage to move behind the counter. Amelia is still worried; she stands across from me and I think of asking her what's going on, but the truth is, I'm exhausted, so we end up looking at each other in silence.

"I have to talk to you about Giorgia," she says finally. "There's something wrong."

"I know. The doctor said to have patience, that she'll adjust."

"What do you mean, she'll adjust?"

I'd like to give her one of the ready answers I have, but when the time comes, I can't follow the script: I flub the line.

"I have no idea," I say. "Why are you worried?"

She hesitates, studies me for a few seconds. "She wants my part," she says.

"Your part?"

"Right, in the play," Amelia continues. "She told Mauro that she should replace me, that I'm not up to it. She said I'm not even half as good as she is, or something like that."

"When..."

"She showed up at rehearsal, two days ago." Amelia clenches her fists on the counter. "She insisted until Mauro was forced to let her perform in my place."

"Two days ago?" I calculate the dates, the times. "That's impossible, she spent the day at her aunt's."

As soon as I say it, I realize that this assertion means nothing: a day is six hours during which she could have been anywhere. "I went to pick her up, she was there."

Amelia rests her head in her hands, she too is exhausted, she doesn't really hear me.

"I don't understand what's gotten into her," she says. "That's something Giorgia would never have done. Since she was released, she's been a different person."

She looks at me hoping for an answer I don't have. I consider the possibility of confessing the existence of the script, but I immediately shelve the idea—she'd think I'm a monster, wouldn't she?

"Maybe it's the result of her being committed," I say. "She was in the clinic for a long time."

Her eyes keep probing me—could she know? When she looks away, the alarm is still tolling in my ears, one knell after another.

"I'll try talking to her," I say.

"I doubt it will do any good."

"Why?"

"I tried talking to her too," Amelia says. "She's not herself. The way she looked at me, what she said. I can't explain it to you, it's as if … as if they had replaced her with someone else."

"Don't you think you're exaggerating?"

"Exaggerating?"

"Maybe you're imagining things," I say. "You're too involved."

She stiffens. "You think I'm worried about my part?"

"I didn't say that. Still …"

"It's not the part, Filippo!" she leans towards me. "How can you not notice the difference? There's something wrong."

"The situation is not as bad as you make it."

"Do you mean to tell me that you see the same person you met three years ago?"

"That's not the point."

"That *is* the point."

"I'll talk to her," I say again. "I'll make her see reason, she'll give up the part."

"We're not talking about the part."

"I said I'll talk to her, you don't have to worry about

the part." I run a hand over the counter in an automatic gesture. "End of story."

Amelia remains suspended in the middle, between us, and I no longer have the nerve to look at her—I picture myself reflected in her eyes. I hear her leave in silence, then I figure that, if I try hard enough and long enough, I can pretend that this conversation never happened. Still, Amelia's questions come flooding back, in a slow tide that submerges everything.

Giorgia's eyes are closed. The yellow light of the lamp inscribes two half-moons under her breasts, a soft shadow between the abs. She isn't sleeping: after sex, she stretched out next to me; her breathing is regular, deep, she still has her new half smile at the corner of her mouth.

Her body has also begun to change, the metamorphosis is extending from the depths to the surface. The original Giorgia's insecurity constrained her within a cage, and she had assumed its form: in bed she lay huddled, taking up as little space as possible; she walked with extreme caution, not making a sound, calculating distances—she had already experienced the harm that a distraction could cause her. I can see her so clearly, now that she has ceased to exist.

"Amelia came to see me today," I say.

Giorgia slowly opens one eye, then the other, looks at me placidly.

"Good."

"She told me you went to rehearsals on Saturday."

She isn't fazed, she's made of wax. She rests her head on one hand, waits for my next move.

"Why didn't you tell me you wanted to go there?"

"You worry about everything. This illness thing has made you paranoid."

"I just want you to be okay. The doctor …"

"Oh God, not again, the doctor, the doctor," Giorgia says, springing up and sitting on the bed. "I feel like I'm suffocating."

She turns her back to me, hugs her knees to her chest; I'd like to touch her, reach out to her bare neck.

"He too wants you to be okay," I tell her.

"He too wants me to be *good*, you mean."

"Giorgia." I try to take her by the shoulder, she pulls away. "Giorgia, please."

I am forced to move around her on the bed to face her: her eyes stare into mine, motionless; there is a cold stillness in her gaze that frightens me.

"You all want me to go back to the way I was before," she says.

"What are you talking about? I'd just like to understand why you want that part at all costs. Amelia said …"

"I'm more talented."

"That's not a good reason to hurt people."

"So I should back off? I can perform the part better than anyone else."

"Amelia has been studying for the performance all year."

Giorgia gets out of bed, looks down at me. "That's irrelevant."

"No it isn't."

"It is to me."

There is a diabolical force in her body standing over me, the skin is sheer and transparent over the bones. It is my nightmare coming back to me—spreading sheets on this same bed, and realizing that the real Giorgia was hidden in the closet. The dissimilarity has reappeared, so terrible that I can't breathe.

"She … You would never have …"

"She? You mean, me?" Giorgia looms over me like a shadow, her voice strong and steady.

"Once you would never have had such a thought," I find the force to say.

The smile widens in a broad slash.

"I'm right, then. You want me to be the way I was before."

My silence doesn't scare her; she laughs at me softly as she pushes me down on the bed. Right away she's on top of me, straddling me, looking at me so closely that the light is eclipsed.

"I remember it, how I was before," she breathes into my mouth, her breath is warm, sweet. "More dead than alive, caged inside my body, paralyzed. Is that how you want me, Filippo?"

Her voice hesitates, trails off, and she rubs her body against mine.

"Do you want me to be like that again?"

"I …"

"How do you want me? You just have to ask. Don't you have the guts to ask? Tell me how you want me."

There's no space between me and her to formulate a thought, the light is completely gone, and I'm lost.

"Are you crying, Filippo?" she asks as if talking to a child.

She licks away the tear pooled in my scar, kisses the wet spot.

I slide my hand into her hair, if I close my eyes I can go back to my exercise, feel her hair long, the way it was in the time we had together before today. I'd like to tell her, I'd like to explain to her, I'd like to ask her if she can find the traces that I erased. In my fingers the memory falls apart, I along with her; we are lost.

"I want you to be okay."

"Do you really want that?"

When I open my eyes again she is still over me, but far away, her back straight: an unfamiliar goddess in the lamp's yellow glow.

"Yes."

"Then let me do it. I need to get back to the stage, Mauro can help me," she says. "I can't think about all the rest now: my aunt has agreed to sign and revoke the interdiction."

"Really?"

"Yes." Giorgia traces a line on my belly. "And besides, we have to make some changes: this place, your work, mine. I'm not going back to the supermarket. We have to get out of here."

She's drawn up a plan, like the endless circle she's tracing around my navel: only now do I realize that she already anticipated the next moves. It's how I wrote her, powerful, different, what I thought I wanted.

"Is this how you want me?" Her question is an echo, and I no longer know if she really spoke or if I imagined it.

Giorgia raises a hand to the back of her neck, grabs the long hair that doesn't exist and tosses it over her right shoulder, leaving her neck bare: the gesture is Amelia's, in her room, that night. In my script.

At Mauro's the gate is open, I'm free to enter the garden as the late evening turns to night. When the moment comes to ring the doorbell, I consider returning home to Giorgia, going to sleep, and deferring the anxiety and fear. I left her alone for the first time since she was discharged: I pretended I needed to take a little walk, after our disagreement. "Are you okay?" she'd asked.

"After all, what happened wasn't that big a deal, was it?" She used that simpering tone and caressed me again, to sweet-talk me. She's afraid I might talk to the doctor and interfere with her plans.

I'm still undecided and I can't stand still, I walk around the house. The dining room light is on, reflected on the maple trees, and also the yellow lamp, a muted gold. The French door is open, I can hear Mauro talking. I stop before rounding the corner and from here I can only see his long shadow on the ground. His voice stirs the flickering outlines of his body. "That same old story again, Valeria? Give me a break."

The voice that answers him is feminine and high-pitched, that of a mature woman. Only her fractured profile lies on the dark lawn, scattered among the bits of leaves and stones.

"I can't do it alone anymore, there are too many things to think about. And then the cancer, Mauro, you know the tests are continuous, exhausting."

"I wish you wouldn't do that."

"Do what?"

"Use your illness as blackmail."

The laughter in response is sharp, an abrupt beginning and end, like turning on a switch.

"Stop being melodramatic." The voice hardens. "I need your help."

"I will never step in as partner."

"All right. You want real blackmail? If you don't step in as a partner, I'm going to cut your annuity altogether."

"The heavy artillery. Is that why you brought the Sacher torte?"

"I have no intention of supporting your father's illegitimate daughter."

"Illegitimate. Holy Christ. Come back to earth. A little more gin?"

There's a long silence, then the gurgling of liquid in a glass.

"You shouldn't have to be the one to take care of her. She has a father. You don't owe her anything."

"Why do you do this? Why do you show up here from time to time, threaten me, and then leave? What did Amelia ever do to you?"

"Nothing, I'm sure she's a fine girl, but she's not part of my family. You are part of my family: only you."

"Mother."

"He abandoned you when you were six years old."

"I'm not the one he abandoned."

When silence falls again, I let myself slide to the ground. Sitting against the wall, I'm thinking that I'd like to stay hidden here forever. I wait, and listen to the rest of the conversation between mother and son: it's a trance in which they go on saying no, before the ritual of ultimatums, and finally the goodbyes. When Mauro's mother gets up from the table, I hear the tapping of her heels on the parquet. I picture her dark-haired, commanding; protected by darkness I watch her step out and walk down the driveway, illuminated by the light coming from the open door, and my fantasies are immediately disillusioned—short, with close-cut hair, she bolts out of the gate so fast that I barely have time to make her out.

"Filippo."

The sound of Mauro's voice is sudden but doesn't startle me. He's appeared in the garden; in the dark you can't see his eyes.

"May I ask what you're doing?"

"I was waiting," I say.

"I saw your shadow," he says, pointing to my outline on the ground. "Are you coming in?"

He doesn't wait for an answer, and goes back into the house without me. When I follow him in, he's already sitting amid the remains of the dinner—empty glasses, scraps of bread on the white tablecloth. He gestures to the other end of the table, and I take his mother's still-warm place.

Mauro lets me stew slowly, not saying a word; he picks up a wine glass, empties the last of a red, and smiles at me. His smile was waiting for me; I realize now that he's drunk a toast to me. I wonder how much of what I want to say to him he's already anticipated.

"What's up?" he asks.

The wine has left its bloodred on his mouth, his teeth are stained purple.

"Nothing."

"Nothing? You were hiding in my garden for no reason?"

"No, I don't know why ..."

"You don't know why you were hiding in the garden?"

"No, no. I meant ..."

"Do you want something to eat? You look pale."

"No."

"A little wine?"

"No, no!"

I raised my voice, but Mauro doesn't lose his composure, he keeps looking at me calmly, his long hair framing his face: a dark-haired Christ with a crooked nose.

"It's Giorgia."

He licks away the remnants of the last sip, his face expressionless.

"What about Giorgia?"

"She's not right."

"She's not right."

"No."

"Excuse me, I don't understand: you were thrilled with her."

"I was."

"You were." Mauro gets up, pads barefoot to the entry hall, returns with a pack of cigarettes. "What's the problem? More unforeseen twists?"

"Not really," I say. "But, well, the thing about the rehearsals. Why didn't you tell me?"

"Tell you what?"

"That she came to rehearsals, that she's trying to take Amelia's part."

"I thought you knew. You drove her there, didn't you?"

"No. I thought she was at her aunt's," I tell him. "It's not like her to behave like that."

Mauro sighs impatiently.

"Okay, she's very headstrong. Obstinate," he admits. "But I like her that way. The old Giorgia was often insecure, it slowed down the work ..."

"But she wants to push Amelia out of the role."

"Try to look at the situation from her point of view: she's really more talented, why should she stand by and watch in silence?"

Mauro lights a cigarette, takes the first drag and looks at me over the red glow.

"You can't let it happen," I say.

"Why not?"

"It's risky," I attempt.

"But she's following the regime, right?" Mauro volleys back.

"Yes, but it's not prudent."

"I don't see the problem, provided her condition is

stable, and it is. You know I would tell you if I were to notice any warning signs," Mauro says, flicking off the ashes. "Even on meds she's superior to any other performer I have. She can be an added value to the company."

"But Amelia ..."

"Filippo, I'm not following you!" Mauro snaps. "What's the problem? Giorgia is fine, she's been released, her medical checkups confirm an exceptional recovery, and you show up at my house at midnight, sweating like a pig, and whining about Amelia."

His eyes probe me: I'm afraid he'll see the secret, Amelia's blonde head on the pillow, the slower, thicker drop.

"It's not about Amelia," I say. "It's Giorgia. She's not ... It's not her, I don't recognize her. I no longer know ..."

Under Mauro's steady gaze, I pour water into a lipstick-smeared glass and drink it, while I try to calm my breathing. When I'm done, he goes on staring at me and doesn't let up; I feel like I'm suffocating.

"It's not her," I say again, wiping the water that dripped down my chin. "I don't recognize her. It's not just Amelia, it's everything. She wants a different job, she wants me to leave the café, she wants us to find a new place to live ... I ..."

"Filippo."

"I can't do it, she doesn't care, it's what she wants. These things she wants, I can't ..."

"Filippo, please calm down."

I obey the order; we end up looking at each other in silence from across the table.

"Isn't that why we had to see to a new script?" Mauro says then. "Isn't that why you rewrote her?"

"I rewrote her because the way she was before wasn't working. For her own good."

"Right," he says and looks away, restoring my oxygen. "What was it that wasn't working in the first version? It's odd. I can barely remember."

He looks for the answer in the mouthful of smoke he blows out, brushes a crumb off the tablecloth.

"She was too honest," I say. "Too considerate. She couldn't choose her clothes. She had no purpose in life."

Mauro smiles his wry, turned-down smile. "You've described at least seven people I know."

I can't sit still in my chair, I slide forward, my knee muscle trembles.

"This is no time for snappy jokes," I fume.

"No, Filippo, this simply can't go on," he replies, seraphic. "You have to calm down, I told you. I've already paid my dues for tonight. If you don't calm down, I'm going to throw you out of my house."

He says it without raising his eyes, his voice flat. His threat wounds my pride; I'd like to get up and leave on my own, but I can't. I attempt a deep breath, fail, try again, and the air goes down to the mouth of my stomach; on the third attempt, I fill my belly. I realize that if I don't abide by his rules, I will not get what I want from Mauro: it's like the new Giorgia says.

"Sorry," I say, controlling my tone. "I'm upset."

"There's no reason to be. It can all be resolved." Mauro takes another cigarette, lights it from the embers of the one that's almost a stub. "Let's start over."

I wait in silence for him to finish his pause for reflection.

"The first Giorgia was just a test; I agree with you, she was incomplete. A new script was essential," he says then. "But this one? You wrote it yourself from start to finish, my contributions were effectively nonexistent. I thought this was what you meant when you said you wanted her ... how did you put it? More confident, more resolute. Isn't that what you talk about in the script as well? About overcoming the trauma of her mother, of her father."

"Yes, but ..."

"And then the matter of having a purpose: you were the one who chose acting for her."

"Because you said it was the thing she wanted most."

"And that was the truth."

"But not like this."

Mauro shakes his head, irritated.

"That's not how it works," he says. "The Giorgia who wanted to be an actress when I met her is different from this one. You can't expect the same results."

"But now she's aggressive, she doesn't care about hurting anyone."

"It's extraordinary," Mauro smiles for real this time, without looking at me.

"What is?" I blurt out, exasperated.

He weighs his words, tortures me: I realize that I'm his plaything, an outlet to release his irritation after the encounter with his mother. He enjoys making me beg for him to remedy things.

"It's amazing how little it takes to alter a character," he replies. "What a person can become if relieved of their pain. The elimination of that single element cost Giorgia much of her identity, don't you agree? There is no longer any trace in her of the childish fear of getting hurt, or of hurting others. She's become an adult."

"You read the script before. Why didn't you tell me?"

"I had no way of knowing. Her way of interpreting the character remains an unpredictable factor."

"I just wanted her to be happy."

I am reminded of all the fantasies I imagined while writing the script, the moments I eagerly anticipated—an afternoon with her, a smile instead of the sad expression, her body no longer bent as though expecting to receive a blow, but straight-backed, her voice strong.

"But now she *is* happy," Mauro says. "I've never seen her so full of energy, so confident. It's a sight to behold."

"But the differences ..."

"Damn it, Filippo, the hell with the differences! There are differences, sure, but isn't that why we rewrote her?" He shrugs, and flicks off the ashes. "If you really want to obsess over the details, that's fine, I agree that she sometimes crosses the line. With her clothes, for example, we're not quite there yet, it's exhibitionism that pushes the boundary of good taste. I think you also went a little overboard with the seductive element. But that's normal, the characters of novice authors are always too intense: it's their beauty and their flaw."

I remain silent, going over the passages in my head, the scenes I edited without considering their impact in a broader dimension—not just the Giorgia in the script but the one outside, in the world; I gave very little thought to the latter as I wrote.

"You wanted Giorgia happy, and she is. You wanted her confident, and she is. You wanted her to be what you wanted: Giorgia is that. Now Giorgia is what everyone wants," Mauro says, in my silence.

"No. This isn't what I wanted," I say.

"You're the one who wrote her. You knew what you were doing while you were writing her. I read the script, don't play games with me."

I consider trying to lie, or at least disguise the truth, but he knows, it would be pointless. He wants me to say it out loud.

"Okay. Some choices were consciously made. Please, don't get me wrong, but it's so difficult ... having the chance to choose, knowing that afterward it will actually happen ..."

"Knowing that what you create will begin to exist," Mauro says.

"Yes."

"You got carried away."

"Yes."

"And now you find that what you thought you wanted is inappropriate, misguided, very nearly disturbing."

"I realized I just want my old life. I want Giorgia the way she was before. I don't want to change a comma of her anymore, she was fine the way she was, she was perfect as she was. Everything was perfect."

Mauro looks at me steadily, once more expressionless, and runs a hand over his face. He's tired, and I'm bent over double, in front of him, with the prayer he's already intuited.

"You want to rewrite her," he says.

"We have to."

"I need a drink."

I watch him get up and go to the liquor cabinet where he unerringly chooses a bottle: the poitín of my first confession, of the drafts written in the basement pub. He disappears behind me to the kitchen where I can't see him, and comes back with two clean glasses. He fills them both in a slow ritual, offers me one.

"There is no distinction," he says, sitting back in his place. "There is no distinction between what we think we know and what we know: what we think we know is all we know."

He's lost, absorbed in another thought; I can't follow him. He takes a sip, and I do the same to keep the body busy.

"It's a matter of simplification, reduction to the bare bones, a strategy that we apply without being aware of it. We are unable to tolerate the weight of infinite possibilities, so *we simplify, we reduce*; we choose a possibility that we sense is right for us; we simplify. We believe in the only one we've arbitrarily chosen. We believe in it to the point of denying the evidence." Mauro looks at me, waiting for a reaction.

"I'm sorry, I'm not following you," I say, wiping the poitín that dribbled onto my chin.

"You want Giorgia the way she was before."

"Yes, I'd like …"

"But what was Giorgia before, if not a product of your imagination?"

The idea freezes me.

"Hold on," Mauro quickly adds. "It's not an accusation, it's an observation of a set of circumstances. None of us is immune to the rule of simplification, it's our way of negotiating the world in order to survive."

"I didn't imagine Giorgia." I sit up straight in my chair.

Mauro's tone is gentle, his eyes kind, yet all the same I hear an alarm sounding, the icy grip of a hand around my throat.

"It's we who choose the identities of the people around us," he says. "The pattern of predetermined behaviors, remember? We treat people like characters, we construct on them a detailed list of what they can and cannot do, the wrongs that we are willing to endure if they inflict them on us, the weaknesses we can tolerate if they have them. Our characterizations are detailed and rigid and, the closer the character is to ourselves, since we are the protagonist of the story, the more demanding we are."

Mauro takes another sip, reaches out to retrieve the bottle.

"There's nothing wrong with any of this," he continues. "Reality passes through a filter, our own reflection in the mirror, the idea we have of ourselves. Imagine spending your whole life with the persistent awareness that those you love could do horrible things to you. The destructive potential of irreversible acts. The constant risk of a deviation from the preordained course."

"I know who Giorgia is," I say. I wish I could find other words, a more confident tone.

"You know the identity you chose for her, you constructed your acceptable model based on what she showed you. An effective and economical solution," Mauro says, filling his glass again. "Don't think it only applies to you. It applies to me as well, to anyone."

I think about the illness, about the list of omissions we built on in the three years we spent together. And yet, something, I keep telling myself, there must have been something authentic.

"I didn't impose an identity on her," I tell him.

"Every relationship is a game that involves acting: you perform your role until the last act. That's the way it should be," Mauro says, then downs a sip. "Anyway, I'm digressing, you're not here to talk about this. You're here for a new draft, and I'm going to help you. What were you thinking of?"

He looks at me, he's earnest and extremely exhausted, and the fault line opened by his remarks is too disturbing for me to be able to face right now—I don't have the time, the energy.

"I want Giorgia back."

"You're a broken record," Mauro says. "How can I help you?"

"You yourself have to write her."

He studies me from his side of the table, doesn't speak.

"I'm missing a piece of her life, the part before me. And you know what to do, what's needed," I add, moving my still-full glass towards the center of the table.

Mauro looks at the poitín, then at me again.

"I don't think I …"

"Look: you know what to choose. I think that's my problem, I always end up picking the wrong details, I don't have a clear idea of how to construct a character. You do," I tell him.

"I'm not a playwright, I told you that."

"You've been dealing with scripts for a lifetime."

"A lifetime, let's not exaggerate now."

"It's your area of expertise, your world."

Mauro slumps against the back of the chair, massages his temples.

"This time it's different, I'm too involved," he says.

"*I'm* the one who's too involved. I don't know what I'm doing anymore." I'm having trouble breathing again; I grab an edge of the tablecloth, the bread crumbs scrape my palm. "Since I started the exercise, there are so many memories that I can't distinguish reality from fantasy. The farther into it I go, the more lost I get. I need an outsider's eye, someone who knows Giorgia as well as I know her, who knows me well."

"I don't know you that well."

"You know me better than many I considered friends."

I watch him as he weighs the proposal, turning it round the bottom of his glass.

"It's complex," he says, without raising his eyes.

"I imagine it is."

"It's not just writing," Mauro continues, swirling the

poitín. "It's a question of reconciling three images: the one you have of Giorgia, the one I have of her, and the one that Giorgia has of herself. The risk of another failure is extremely high."

"I can't stay with her the way she is," I say. "Today it's complaints about my job, or stealing Amelia's part, but tomorrow? What happens if her ambition can't be restrained?"

He avoids my eyes, toys with the fringe of a napkin.

"Her aunt is going to revoke the interdiction," I continue, leaning towards him. "If we don't act as soon as we can, we risk losing her."

Mauro heaves a long sigh, crosses his arms over his chest. I wonder if I too look so old tonight.

"You'll have to reread it," he says, finally giving in.

I feel the first real relief of the day.

"Even a hundred times," I say.

"If you don't read it, we won't use it."

"No. Agreed. I'll read it. I'll read it as many times as you want."

"If something doesn't look right, you'll have to tell me right away. No bullshit."

"I will, I promise."

"I'll do my best."

"I'm sure you will."

"First draft in ten days?"

"A week?"

"Done."

Afterwards we hardly look at one another. The agreement hangs suspended between us like something that might easily be broken, and neither of us wants to upset the equilibrium. Instead we act as if our conversation had never taken place: Mauro urges me to empty my glass and I obey, then for half an hour we delve into a discussion of his inheritance, his mother, and his company.

When Mauro drives me home it's very late, the darkness occasionally pierced by artificial lights, and the world does not exist outside Milan. Sitting in the car, I'm thinking that my last hope is driving haphazardly in and out of the lane we're in, but my sense of solace doesn't fade, I feel as relieved as if I'd been told I'd suddenly recovered from a long illness. I already imagine Mauro's script, cleansed and perfect, faithful. I picture it and Giorgia is with me again.

Mauro is also in good spirits again—he sings a nursery rhyme, the same slow verses over and over, interrupted by a few drags of his cigarette: *As I was walking by the clear spring, I found the deep pool so lovely I stopped to bathe. I've loved you for so long, never will I forget you. I've loved you for so long, never will I forget you.*

CHAPTER TEN

THE EXERCISE

I look at Giorgia and to my mind she has the gift of a beauty that is out of place, that on the one hand composes her and on the other hand unravels her—her hair, her posture, her clothes, everything is constantly thrown off-balance.

We're at the café, the day is coming to an end, and she's sitting in her favorite place, the last table in my "theater," midway between the orchestra, the stage, and the wings. She watches me crouch over, polishing the counter tops. How many times have I revisited this memory in my exercise? I review the transitions, the variations differ in the color of the dishcloth, in the light—the first time it was day, now it's late afternoon; the temperature has changed, and I want it to still be cold as it was in the original. I am content with observing Giorgia when she's distracted, and reality regains its familiar contours in her, everything falls back in place.

There's hesitation in her now, fear. I've watched the third draft spread through her body, shrinking her movements, going deeper each day, Mauro's character-ization a precise tracing consistent with the prototype, and Giorgia's steps becoming more cramped, slower, her skirts longer, her voice a little softer—Giorgia reas-suming her recognizable form.

"Shall we go?" I say when I'm finished.

She nods, her smile is circumspect, it doesn't show her teeth.

Outside the bar, the shutter is hard to close in the muggy June heat.

"I thought I'd take you to the interview tomorrow," I suggest, as we make our way to the bus stop.

"But it's close by," says Giorgia, crossing her arms. "No need."

"Are you nervous?"

"No, " she says. "I just want to find a job. Interviews are exhausting."

I hug her to me, and she rubs her face against my shoulder. We slip unnoticed into the group of passen-gers waiting for the next bus.

I've found a new guilty pleasure: it's sweet, and harm-less; it's knowing to which side Giorgia will tilt her head, the prescience that I enjoy in our dimension. I think of her reading, in her short skirt, not raising her eyes from the script. Mauro managed to convince her by pretending he was offering her the leading role in a new play. Lying to her didn't bother us, we did it for her own good, and she went along with it without protest, yielding to her authentic identity. I like to think that, in her deepest recesses, she was conscious of it, that she knew she had to come back.

What is reality? I'd like to ask her. The three choices we have as the bus approaches: get on, wait for the next one, walk away. Reality is what we know.

"I could also try there again," Giorgia says during the ride, when the side of the supermarket appears around the curve.

The neon light is ugly, white, half of her profile becomes a mask.

"You could," I say, as I stroke her head.

Everything is falling back in place, yes, everything is going back to how it was.

* * *

Giorgia experienced a long dream: when she thinks about it, she remembers the exact measurements of the room—the rectangle of the floor, and inside that the rectangle of the bed, and inside the bed her body that had a rigid geometric shape as well. Together we went over the months of her clinical stay, the rules of the new regimen. Psychopharmaceutical drugs all have names that sound like Latin prayers, but *her empathetic problem with people* is resolved: whoever she meets stays in place, no longer tries to bore into her—she told me it's a relief, there's a lot less confusion inside her. For the first few weeks, it's as if someone has dropped her into the world from an extrasolar planet: Giorgia suddenly realizes that she is back one afternoon, sitting in front of a turkey breast that her aunt made for her. She recognizes the house, the silence within those walls with no television, which as a teenager drove her crazy; she recognizes her aunt, who eats with her mouth closed and resembles her mother. She understands that her aunt is not her mother, then bursts into tears over the turkey, and wonders why she chose to wear such a short skirt, why she's wearing such high heels, and why her mother closed the door behind her, why the door never opened again.

Since the afternoon of the turkey, Giorgia feels like she's had an out-of-body experience, or like she never existed. Even now that our world has regained its equilibrium, she's so light that she might be swept away with a little push, but she doesn't tell me: she soon begins functioning on multiple levels, maybe the second or third week, and from there on everything becomes simple—no longer rectangles but parallel lines that will never meet.

In life after the dream, I am familiar with the illness and I'm not afraid of it, nor is Giorgia afraid of it: each day has a scheduled time for a Latin prayer; from prayer to prayer she feels the monster settle into a thousand-year sleep.

* * *

"How are you?"

Mauro is filling in for me one afternoon: as a favor he's driving Giorgia to an interview while I'm on duty at the café. She gets in the car with an awkwardness that's unlike her, squeezes into the seat scattered with scripts and papers.

"Good," she replies, fastening her seatbelt.

Mauro doesn't start the car right away. He looks at her persistently, as if he were asking her permission to shift into first. Her hair is tied back; Giorgia measures the months since she's been out of the clinic by its length. Then he quickly looks away, focuses on the résumé she brought with her, held in a stiff, rectangular plastic envelope.

"Where are we going?" Mauro asks, starting the motor.

"Redecesio," she says.

He drives calmly. "Does it bother you?" he asks, lowering the windows. Halfway there, he puts on a Bennato disc, hums along. Giorgia finds that she knows this song by heart.

"What's the job?" he asks, when they slow down for a red light.

"What?"

"The interview. For what job?"

"Clerk."

"But where?"

"A supermarket."

Mauro doesn't say anything for a while and Giorgia worries that he's displeased. He continues driving; at another traffic light he slips an unlit cigarette into his mouth, keeps shifting it from side to side, then starts casting grim looks at her résumé. Giorgia rolls it up, trying to hide it. She'd like to ask him to stop it, but she can't accuse him of being grouchy, she'd seem stupid. She hopes the trip will soon be over.

"It's over there," she says, when they spot the neighborhood Esselunga market.

Mauro slows down, turns into the parking lot, then stops in front of the entrance.

"Thanks. It shouldn't take longer than half an hour."

He doesn't react. Giorgia unbuckles her seatbelt, opens the door. The car behind them sounds its horn, urging them to move.

"Sorry, could you close the door for a second?" Mauro says.

"I'm going." Giorgia is about to step out, but the car moves off.

"Just one second, we'll get out of the way," he cuts her off.

Giorgia obeys. When it's time to pull into an empty

parking space, Mauro accelerates, exits the parking lot going the wrong way, and speeds away from the supermarket.

"What are you doing?"

"Nothing, we'll just be a minute ... I mean, if we go this way ..."

"We're driving away."

"Of course, of course."

"My interview is in five minutes."

The résumé's plastic envelope slips out of Giorgia's fingers as her hand continues to grip the door handle.

Mauro smiles, lights his cigarette when forced to pause at a stop light.

"We're not going there anymore," he says.

"What?"

"We're not going to the interview," he repeats. "We're going somewhere else."

"But I have to go. The job ..."

"The job, the job." Mauro accelerates, driving farther and farther away from their destination. "There'll be another interview, it's not going to be the only one of your life, is it?"

"But ..."

"Oh come on, Giò, shitty supermarkets are a dime a dozen," he fumes, taking a drag and exhaling, irritated. "This city is full of supermarkets, there are more supermarkets than people, everybody shops in supermarkets, it's kind of a collective pandemic, they're all ..."

"Okay, okay. Enough." Giorgia lets go of the door handle, fastens her seatbelt again.

She remembers this Mauro clearly, the capricious, impulsive one. Something is bothering him, you can tell by the way he jiggles his left knee when his foot is off the clutch, by the ash on the cigarette as it quickly burns. Giorgia thinks about the interview, distinctly recalls the questions from her last one—*If you had forty emails to read and only twenty minutes to do it, which emails would you open? Who would you save if atomic missiles were about to reach your location in twenty minutes? You can choose only two of the following people to take to the bunker: a medical student who has dropped out, a five-months-pregnant black woman, a seven-year-old French boy, a priest, or a cabaret entertainer.*

"What do I tell Filippo?" she asks aloud.

"That it didn't go well," Mauro replies. "It's the truth."

Giorgia lowers the window, stretches an arm out in the warm June air.

"Where are we going?" she says, when Mauro turns off the radio.

"I have to make a stop someplace. I'll take you with me, if you don't mind," he replies.

They stop talking; Giorgia rests her head on the seatback, and gazes out at the world. She knows all the places that stream past, even the blind spots around the street corners; she is so intently focused on observing that at some point she sees herself, her body in all sizes, her hair in all lengths, her stops along the way, the day she lost her cell phone—*Who would you save if atomic missiles were about to reach your location in twenty minutes?*—she sees herself walking, running to catch a tram, resting her forehead on the grimy window of the bus—*You can choose only two people to take to the bunker.* Which of all of her selves would she choose? *A student, a woman, a child, a priest, an entertainer.*

"We'll walk a little way," says Mauro, after a complex maneuver to get into a tiny parking spot.

Giorgia doesn't object, she likes to go along with events, as if something wonderful might happen. She follows Mauro. It's another route that she's familiar with, but that she doesn't remember precisely. Parallel tracks on Via Cesare Correnti, the cramped opening of a narrow lane packed with Tuesday morning traffic. Sunlight reflected in the mirror of a motorcycle blinds her, Giorgia continues walking, with Mauro two steps ahead in the dazzling glare; when she loses him in a group of Polish tourists, he turns back to get her, takes her by the hand. It's a few yards to the entrance of the theater, but Giorgia braces her arm between them, maximizing the distance, and Mauro settles for dragging her.

In the courtyard, they meet two guys struggling with a backdrop. "Partacini is at the van," one of them tells Mauro, "he'll be back in ten minutes."

"Okay to go in?" Mauro asks, when they're already one step past the entry arch.

"Go ahead, I'll tell him to join you."

Giorgia is also familiar with the darkness of her first day in this place: she arrived there the same way, six years ago, with Mauro leading her by the hand. He walks onstage once they've entered, just as in her recollection; six years ago the smooth, silent floor was empty, now the frames of three cubes clutter the scene.

"In the thirteenth century, this was a church," Mauro says, touching a beam. "That's what I said, right, Giò? Do you remember?"

He's standing in one of the shafts of light coming from the windows above the high walls—glass openings in the ceiling. Giorgia is surprised to be thinking the same thought.

"Remember?"

"Yes," she replies, not stepping out of the shadows.

"Do you remember what you said?"

"Yes."

"Would you say it again, please? Would you say it as if it were happening now?"

It doesn't take Giorgia long to come up with the line.

"It scares me," she says, and her voice echoes back from the walls, from the past.

Mauro too vanishes into the shadows, slips out of the spotlight.

"Me too," he says—he takes two steps to the side, as if to turn towards the audience, but Giorgia remembers clearly the orbit of that movement, from alongside her to behind her. "All empty theaters scare me."

His voice is closer and he is invisible.

"We have to work together," he continues. "You have extraordinary potential."

Mauro grabs her right wrist, makes her turn around.

"Work together?" Giorgia repeats, forcing a nervous laugh. "But I have no training. I only started attending acting class because the psychiatrist said I needed to develop some recreational activities."

"You have to trust me, I know what I'm talking about," Mauro says, smiling. "I've never met anyone with a natural talent like yours."

Giorgia shakes her head, drives away the impossible thought of hope.

"It's not like volunteering at a social center," she says. "You're a real director. I know you only teach the basics at the center. I could never keep up with you."

"I say you can, Giò."

"And then too, can you imagine if I were to lose my sanity?" Giorgia squirms out of Mauro's grip, hastily scratches a forearm. "I'm there because I'm ill, have you forgotten that? I'm ill like everyone else there."

"You're not ill," Mauro says, smoothing a nonexistent

wrinkle on her shoulder—six years ago it was winter, she wore a sweater, now instead there's only skin, but he smooths it anyway, gives it the same care. "And besides there's always the emergency nursery rhyme, right?"

"You can't solve everything with an emergency nursery rhyme," Giorgia says. "It's not a magic formula."

"Oh yes you can." His finger slides along the profile of her cheek, his eyes searching for something in her hair, and Giorgia, like six years ago, can't move away. "Try it with me, will you? You'll see for yourself. It's magical."

"Don't be silly." Giorgia lowers her eyes, looks for a way out of the power that holds her motionless.

"*As I was walking by the clear spring.*" Mauro's voice comes from a hidden world, deep down. "Come on, Giò. *As I was walking ...*"

"*By the clear spring,*" Giorgia says, giving in.

"From the beginning. *As I was walking by the clear spring.*"

"*As I was walking by the clear spring.*"

"Very good." Mauro places an imaginary medal on her forehead. "*I found the deep pool so lovely I stopped to bathe.*"

"*I found the deep pool so lovely I stopped to bathe.*"

He is so close that his shape dissolves, the planes of his face lose focus; the closer he gets, the more he dissolves, and with him Giorgia: her body begins to crumble from the center.

"*I've loved you for so long, never will I forget you.*"

"*I've loved you for so long, never will I forget you.*"

"*... For so long ...*"

* * *

A week later, the morning is chaotic, the light excessive: the theater in which Mauro is holding rehearsals for the reruns of the play is the same as for the first performance. I get there in a heated rush, sweat making my eyes tear. I left all of myself behind: all the essential parts remained at home, along with Giorgia. An hour of frenzy and sobbing, a hibernating false calm stands between me and them.

No one stops me, the transition from outside to inside is abrupt—red velvet backdrops, linoleum, empty ticket offices. The hall is deserted, the stage animated: only two actors in the scene, no one to watch them, not a movement to give away the bustling taking place backstage. The script, which I'm gripping tightly, makes me unsteady.

One of the actors is masked, the costume covers his face, leaving his mouth free; he leans towards the young man who looks at him terrified, pale—"I will open the world to you," and his voice carries everywhere. I stumble among the third-row seats, reach the opening to the wings, where behind the curtain bodies are waiting along the stairs, murmuring. Mauro isn't there. I know even before I look for him, yet all the same I scan every single face to defer the moment of the encounter. Now that I'm here there's hardly any more fury in me, any more anguish; it's all been spent.

Amelia spots me before I can avoid her and comes towards me. "What are you doing here?" she whispers in the semidarkness. I can picture her eyes, the confusion: for a moment she thinks I'm here for her.

"Mauro," I tell her.

"He just went onstage," she says, hiding her disappointment. "Everything all right?"

I don't answer. I step on a few legs on my way, and

someone shoves me. From the curtain you can see Mauro, hidden behind the two actors.

"Who are you? Who are you?" I recognize Melchior's actor. "I can't trust a man that I don't know."

"You can't learn to know me unless you trust me."

"A step towards the audience, both of you," Mauro speaks aloud, then moves closer. "More forceful, more forceful."

I burst onto the stage without waiting for the scene to end, ignoring civility, shame, fear. He sees me, and immediately narrows his eyes, weighs the next move.

"Ten-minute break," he announces out of the blue, catching the actors off guard.

"But we just had one half an hour ago," Melchior's actor objects.

I can feel sharp glances thrown at me from those in the wings, pins in the back of my head, the sharpest among them Amelia's.

"Everybody out, go," Mauro cuts him off, casting a furious look backstage.

We're alone, even before the others leave us. He knows: I can tell by the cigarette he takes out of his pocket, puts in his mouth.

"Filippo," he says, an official nod of greeting.

I consider the few feet separating us, I decide not to bridge them—so where's all my rage, the world turned upside down, if all I can do is stand there looking at him mutely?

"Do you know why I'm here?" I ask, my voice frail, someone else's.

Mauro smiles his mocking smile, allows himself a moment's pause before making a sweeping gesture that encompasses us, the stage, the audience.

"The big climax," he declares, and the proclamation has a lengthy echo.

I think of Giorgia. I see her sit down on our bed, her back to me. I look at her, and I don't imagine anything; it's only her back. Instead it conceals the harshest truth—and her voice as she says it, as she says it I begin to fall apart.

"Where?" The script is still in my hand; I throw it on the floor, we watch it land on the wood. "Where did you write it?"

"I assume Giorgia told you." Mauro holds the unlit cigarette between his fingers.

"I read every line," I say. "I read every line of it, for her, and there was nothing like that in there. What trick did you use? Where did you write it?"

I see Giorgia bend over, though she's not here, the curve of her spine, the height from which I started falling when I realized—the *feeling, it's over, what I really feel.*

"There's no trick, Filippo."

"There must be. This … None of this is her."

"And what is it that should be her?" Mauro comes a step closer. "A miserable studio apartment, a job as a supermarket clerk? You?"

It's a design that extends back, the mapping has its origin in a place and time that I have no knowledge of, I'm sure of it: it was before me. I see through Mauro, his efforts, his help.

"It was your plan from the beginning."

He presses the toe of his shoe on the parquet, tugs his shirt down over his hip.

"No," he says. "I really tried to leave it to you. I told myself that you could do it, that maybe you were better than I thought. Instead you were a disappointment, Filippo. A predictable, bitter disappointment."

"You played us."

Out of my mouth, the accusation seems ridiculous; I hear myself speaking from the center of the stage: my performance is weak, the audience won't buy it.

"Played you? Me? No. There's only one thing I'm guilty of, and it's having given you time you didn't deserve." Mauro doesn't look at me, he's staring into the empty darkness of the audience section. "I should have realized it from the first draft. I offered you the chance to write about the person you supposedly love, and you came up with a shrinking violet, a lame array of clichés, soppy thoughts. A spineless jellyfish."

He comes closer still, his calm is studied, the boundaries of his character calculated.

"I had a moment of exasperation, but I decided to give you a second chance: I was curious." He makes a wide circle around my body. "You did not fail to meet my expectations. The second draft, Filippo ... Awful. I ask you to take over your exercise, and your response is a trite repertoire of images, a sickening characterization. Short skirts, bewitching looks, femme-fatale fantasies; and that ridiculous heroic air. A human being who doesn't hesitate, whom everyone likes. Dreadful."

"I trusted you," I finally manage to get out, when he's behind me where I can't see him.

"I trusted you too," Mauro says. "I stepped aside for you. I thought maybe you were what Giorgia really needed, someone undemanding, someone who didn't push her. Instead, here you are: it hasn't even been a year and you're already eager to trap her in your existence again, lock her away in a supermarket. Anything not to give up your version of reality, not to change the course of events. You like your life just as it is, rotting away, and you didn't think twice about dragging Giorgia down with you, you didn't stop to consider that she could have had something better."

"You have no right ..."

"And you? What right do you have?" Mauro is again in front of me, close enough to feel his measured breath on my face. "By what virtue, what noble spirit, do you exercise your power over Giorgia?

"You only want her so you can do whatever you want with her."

"It's the same reason you want her." Mauro's smile is unwavering, a sneer of lifeless triumph. "The difference between you and me is that I'm honest, and you pretend, you tell yourself the fairy tale of 'what's good for her.' Oh, what a laugh, hearing you constantly say that, and watching you deform her, fiddle with the doses: a little initiative here, two drops of submission there, and why not, while we're at it, let's let her believe that oral sex is her favorite pastime."

I reach out to grab him, but he sidesteps me; I trip and stagger. This isn't it. This is not how it ends.

"I love her."

"Filippo, for God's sake." Mauro puts the cigarette in his mouth again, this time looking for the lighter. "Your life was nothing but an attempt, you constructed a world, and Giorgia was part of it as a neutral, interchangeable element. It's not her you want back, but your dull days, your university memories, your sterile moaning."

We stand there looking at each other and the stage swallows us up. The truth no longer matters. Giorgia had turned to me, she recited it as in the most classic of dramas: "It's over between us." What? Why, Giorgia? What's gotten into you? What are you saying? Just now when everything has fallen back in place?

"What do you intend to do with her?"

Mauro blows a stream of white smoke towards the curtains, assesses me with his eyes.

"I have no plans."

"Your jester? A new script every season? A different character?"

He smiles again, he knows he's won the match.

"I'll do what you did with her," he says. "My jester. A new script every season. A different character."

I stand there watching the smoke drift away; in the smoke I see Mauro's face, then his eyes, and him, no longer there, moving away, rising over the ghosts in the audience, and he dissolves.

Applause. Take a bow. Curtain.

EPILOGUE

Filippo is reflected in the chrome surface of the coffee machine: red hair, light eyes, a scar on his left cheek-bone—eight years old, fell down the stairs, seven stitches; the scar has the shape of an Africa lying on its back.

The morning regulars have been gone for a good hour, and he goes on cleaning, polishing, wiping, even when it's no longer necessary. It's rare for anyone to show up at this time: the lunch break is far off, at the Polytechnic classes are in session. When he hears the sound of the bell that hangs over the door, Filippo thinks it must be someone looking for the bathroom; he leans over to slide the key within reach.

"Hey there, mon ami," the voice calls to him from across the counter.

Amelia smiles at him, her blonde hair tucked inside a beret, her hands in the pockets of her light jacket.

"Amelia," Filippo manages to say after a moment's hesitation.

"So you remember it, my name."

"What are you doing here?"

She looks around.

"I must have come to see you," she says. "I wouldn't mind a coffee while we're at it."

"Of course, sit down."

Filippo hides his confusion by grabbing a filter holder, then grinding the coffee. That way the ritual preliminary questions are easier: How are you? The university? The theater? With his head focused on choosing a cup, it's no trouble for Filippo to avoid what he wants to avoid and bury the subject in an unfeeling corner of his consciousness.

As Amelia sips the coffee, he watches her. Her neck is bare, a vivid trace in his memory. It's impossible that so much time and yet so little time has passed, and that she's there for real.

"And you, how are you?" she asks, when she's finished.

Filippo gives a pleasant account of nothing, insignificant events, bills, his mother's anxieties, and Amelia laughs, just as he expected.

"I don't live with Mauro anymore," she says.

Filippo knows that this is the real reason for her visit; he leans over the counter, crosses his arms.

"Why didn't you respond to my messages?" she asks.

He wipes a drop of water with the back of his hand. "I needed some time."

Amelia nods, and again reaches up to shift her hair to one side; when she finds it tucked in the beret, the gesture is suspended midway, and Filippo suddenly feels a strong sense of familiarity. It's like coming home, and finding a friendly face waiting for him. After that, they chat about neutral topics for a while.

"Hey ... I'm thinking about leaving the university, or

transferring to a state college. I don't want Mauro to pay for my studies anymore," Amelia says, getting up, when it's time to go. "I rented a room in the Loreto district, I have a job as a salesclerk."

"Where?"

"At the Carrefour on Via Spinoza, near the bank."

Filippo watches her seesaw back and forth—she's a little girl. In one of the adaptations of this play, he should make her think twice, persuade her to rush back to her brother, finish her studies; tell her that it was a stupid idea, the prelude to failure.

"So how about it? Shall we go out some night?"

She's just as he remembers her, there in front of him as well, like the first day he met her—fair and blonde, carefree. Filippo really would like to tell her: it's a dumb idea, Amelia, a bad idea.

"Sure. Saturday?"

She smiles, and Filippo notes a dimple on her chin, a detail he hadn't noticed before then.

"Saturday. Eight. 17 Via Pecchio."

When she leaves, Filippo watches her walk away, he watches her even after she's gone; then he reviews her crossing her legs at the table, the green dress under her jacket, the small knots of her folded fingers.

It's a new exercise.

ACKNOWLEDGMENTS

My thanks to Marco, Chiara, and Claire for believing in this project and in me, and for their indispensable, impeccable work. A thank you to Elisabetta Sgarbi for her confidence and fervor, and to Oliviero and Ilaria for their dedication and attention to the text. Without the fundamental contribution of these individuals, there would not have been a book, nor any acknowledgements to write.

My thanks to Dr. Federico Stifani for the professional contribution and the human generosity with which he conducted our encounters.

My gratitude to Francesca Asciolla, a fantastic and extremely competent woman. For reading, supporting, and putting up with this story since before it even existed and we were just two enthusiasts who had never met face-to-face. Committed to sharing more Proseccos together and fewer guided tours of monumental cemeteries.

A thank you to Massimiliano Racis, an invaluable beta reader and someone whose civility is from another time; to Alex de Meo, a fervent reader and tireless advisor; to Luigina for her support at less happy moments. My gratitude to Gabriella, whom I am fortunate to call a friend—I can never be grateful enough for the kindness she shows me.

My thanks to Michela for the sincere friendship we have shared and for her ability to be happy for me.

My thanks to my family—to Renata, Giovanni, Maria Rosa, Gabriella, Marco—to my mother, to my father, to Laura. Thank you for always ensuring me a place where I am free to be myself even at my worst, thank you for loving me no matter what, thank you for being my inspiration.

Thank you to those who first listened to the beginning and the end of this story, which is a small thing, whereas there have been other, bigger things that no one will ever be able to print.

And a thank you to Lucio for having been who he was. When we meet again, we'll be young together.

TRANSLATOR'S NOTE

Giorgia's emergency rhyme is my English version of *À la claire fontaine*, a French folk song. The vocal exercise on page 112 was developed by actor Vittorio Gassman. Lines quoted at various times in the novel (and at one point adapted in improvisation) are from William Shakespeare's *Twelfth Night*, and from *The Awakening of Spring: A Tragedy of Childhood* by Frank Wedekind, translated by Francis J. Ziegler.

ANNE MILANO APPEL has translated works by a number of leading Italian authors for a variety of publishers in the US and UK. Her most recent translations include works by the award-winning Antonio Scurati and Paolo Maurensig. Her awards include the Italian Prose in Translation Award, the John Florio Prize for Italian Translation, and the Northern California Book Award for Translation. Her website is: amilanoappel.com.

On the Design

As book design is an integral part of the reading experience, we would like to acknowledge the work of those who shaped the form in which the story is housed.

Tessa van der Waals (Netherlands) is responsible for the cover design, cover typography, and art direction of all World Editions books. She works in the internationally renowned tradition of Dutch Design. Her bright and powerful visual aesthetic maintains a harmony between image and typography and captures the unique atmosphere of each book. She works closely with internationally celebrated photographers, artists, and letter designers. Her work has frequently been awarded prizes for Best Dutch Book Design.

For the title, a brand-new and highly versatile font by Alejandro Paul was selected. It is called Magari, which is an Italian word meaning "maybe" or "If only!" Italian classics and typical mid-nineteenth-century German condensed serif typefaces inspired its aesthetic. It was selected by the cover designer because it evokes the theater. The theater curtain in the picture behind the boldly spaced letters reminds accomplished German photographer Martin Sigmund of a blank canvas or a plain white sheet of paper—a place where worlds are made.

The cover has been edited by lithographer Bert van der Horst of BFC Graphics (Netherlands).

Suzan Beijer (Netherlands) is responsible for the typography and careful interior book design of all World Editions titles.

The text on the inside covers and the press quotes are set in Circular, designed by Laurenz Brunner (Switzerland) and published by Swiss type foundry Lineto.

All World Editions books are set in the typeface Dolly, specifically designed for book typography. Dolly creates a warm page image perfect for an enjoyable reading experience. This typeface is designed by Underware, a European collective formed by Bas Jacobs (Netherlands), Akiem Helmling (Germany), and Sami Kortemäki (Finland). Underware are also the creators of the World Editions logo, which meets the design requirement that "a strong shape can always be drawn with a toe in the sand."